Moment in Time

A Circle-D Saga

Book 2

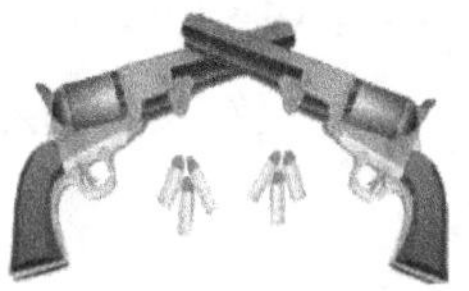

Nancy M. Wade

GARNAN Enterprises, LLC

Copyright

Moment in Time is a work of fiction. Names, characters, places, and incidents either are the product of the author's imagination based on some real historical events or are used fictitiously. Any resemblance to actual persons, living or dead, events or locales is entirely coincidental.

This book is protected under the copyright laws of the United States of America. Any reproduction or unauthorized use of the material or artwork contained herein is prohibited without the express written permission of Nancy M. Wade.

Published in the United States
GARNAN Enterprises, LLC of Ohio 2019 – First Edition
GARNAN Enterprises, LLC of Ohio 2023 – Second Edition
ISBN - E978-1737699842
ISBN – 978-1737699866

Cover art design by Efrain Cintron

Titles of Nancy M. Wade

<u>Circle - D Saga</u>

Book 1 - *Endless Circle*

Book 2 - *Moment in Time*

Book 3 – *Gun for Hire* (coming 2023)

Reflections: A Sentimental Journey

Frontier Heart

Courtship of Laura

<u>A Meadowood Mystery – Series</u>

Scarecrows and Corpses

Reunion with Death

Deadly Bones

Berry Little Murder

Acknowledgments

Thank you to both Alice Simms and Kathleen Miller-Clark for their time, support, reviews and suggestions.

Thank you to my great-nephew, Efrain Cintron, for his artistic drawing depicting the essence of the Moment in Time story.

A special thank you to my husband, Gary, for his support and encouragement during all of my writing efforts.

Table of Contents

Prologue
Wyoming 1930

Alexander Dunlap sat easy in the saddle, his eyes squinted against the glaring hot sun and dry Chinook winds blowing across his land. His land. He proudly surveyed the cattle grazing across the rolling acres of sparse bunch grass. He had worked hard, even as a young lad, to build this ranch; the same scrap of land his parents first claimed and settled back in 1884. His father, James, had been killed by a low-life, no-good gunslinger and his mother Maggie, worn down in her prime, died trying to hold onto this same piece of land in Deer Springs, WY. But nothing or no one would take this ranch away from him now. *"Times had been tough before, and he'll get through them again; at least he was better off than some of them sod-busters trying to plow dried up dirt. No sir, he'd sacrificed too much over the years to see it all wasted by some hard times and drought,"* thought Alexander.

Alexander's face turned toward the western sky, searching for signs of rain among the thick white clouds floating overhead. A face etched with wrinkles caused by too many years exposed to the harsh climate of the Wyoming range; too many years frowning over things he couldn't change and fights he couldn't win. Hair once jet black was now liberally sprinkled with strands of gray; its shaggy unkempt length poked out from beneath his worn Stetson. He dragged a faded kerchief from around his neck and mopped the sweat from forehead and neck as he kneed his gray mare into a slow gait across the pasture. He rode toward the sound of his sons' loud voices as they chased each other around his parent's old homestead cabin.

"I can too beat you," shouted ten-year-old Samuel.

"Aww, you're just a dumb kid," taunted his older brother. At the ripe old age of fourteen, Alex Dunlap Junior liked to lord over his younger sibling.

"Am not!" shouted Sam as he launched his wiry body at his brother's taller, lean frame. The two boys began wrestling and rolling in the dirt.

"Knock it off!" shouted their father, "or I'll knock it out of you with my belt. What the hell are you fighting over this time?"

The boys instantly broke apart; not wanting to feel the thick leather strap across their backsides again.

"Nothing," both boys replied simultaneously, looking at each other and giggled nervously.

"We were just fun'in'," explained Alex.

"You've got work to do. Stop wasting time," ordered Alexander. "Go round up those stray calves from the north pasture before they go missing. We've been losing more cows than what we should lately. I don't like it none. Take your useless brother along; show him what to do; maybe he can learn something."

Sam waited silently; head hung low, cheeks stained red. His father's barbs stung once more as he stole a peek between his brother and the domineering figure on horseback.

"Sure Pa. We'll bring 'em back. C'mon Sam," replied Alex.

The two boys ran over to the thin stand of birch trees where they had tied their horses. Sam climbed onto a large rock to help him get a leg up and reach the stirrups of his saddle, quickly mounting. The brothers galloped toward the northern boundaries of their ranch in search of the strays.

As soon as they had cleared the rise that separated pasture from the homestead and were out of sight, the boys slowed their horses to a trot.

Alex glanced over his shoulder then shook his head. "Whew, I thought we were gonna git it for sure. Didn't you?"

"Why's Pa so mean? You ever see him laugh, just once?" Sam's voice barely louder than a whisper.

"No, come to think of it. I dunno, maybe when you get his age, all your good times are gone. I'll have to chew on it some." Alex tried to assume a solemn and wise countenance but couldn't avoid a giggle escaping from his pursed lips.

"What's wrong with me?" cried Sam. "I can't do nothing right. Pa don't never look at me like he does you." A tear slid from his eye and he swiped it away angrily.

"Now you quit that. Don't like hearing that kind of talk. You do plenty of stuff good. Ain't nothing wrong with you. Why, nobody could fix that old steam tractor like you did! You're real good with your hands."

"Thanks, Alex, that's right kind of you to say. But I'm just a dumb kid. Pa's right."

"No, he ain't."

"Maybe someday, I can be just like you," Sam mumbled beneath his breath, but his big brother heard him anyway.

Alex reached across his saddle and clapped an arm about his younger brother's shoulder in a brief show of affection. They broke apart as he kicked his horse into a gallop. Both boys shouted and hooted in glee as they charged across the prairie.

PART I – ENGLAND 1943
Chapter 1

The troop ship plowed ahead; cutting through choppy gray waves of the frigid North Atlantic. Samuel Dunlap stood at the railing of the US Army Transport (USAT) George Washington, cupping a lit match to his cigarette, shielding the meager flame from sprays of water and gusts of wind. He sucked in the cold morning air, tasted the salt spray and felt the chill on his cheeks. It was a welcome change from the stuffy confines of the close quarters below.

They'd been at sea for twelve days now; boarding in the dark of night and then herded like cattle through narrow companionways and a maze of hatches. Close to four thousand men, each carried heavy duffel bags, bedrolls, and weapons; they now shared narrow aisles and cramped spaces, bedded down on swinging hammocks that hung three-tiered high. Bodies sprawled everywhere; guys caught up on reading or engaged in cards and dice games. Long lines waited for tasteless chow that was dumped onto a tin plate and men ate standing up in whatever empty space a person could claim. Their monotonous daily routine would end all too soon when their ship arrived in England.

Sam stared across the bleak ocean that stretched endlessly toward the horizon. Through the gray mist, he could just make out the shapes of the other transport ships and light cruisers in their convoy.

The vast space reminded him of the endless plains back home…the ranch and his father; the futility of trying to fill his brother's shoes and win his father's approval. He finally gave up and left; joined the military to make a man of himself, recalling his father's taunt as he hopped aboard the Army transport bus. Well, he made it through boot camp without killing himself, so maybe he'll have some chance of proving himself yet. Who knows?

Sam flicked his cigarette into the dark waters below, pounded the rail with his fist; irritated with the hold his old man's words still had on him, memories he couldn't shake. Why did he still let his slurs bother him?

His thoughts strayed to his brother Alex. He hadn't seen him in close to two years now. Alex had gotten out. Alex enlisted right after Pearl Harbor, putting his pilot crop dusting skills to good use now in the big flying fortresses with the Army Air Corps; leaving his younger brother behind. Without Alex acting as a cushion, Sam's life on the ranch had been pure hell. His father's wrath and constant criticism chipped away what thin layer of confidence he had, but he learned to hide his own anger and vowed one day it would be different.

Maybe, just maybe, he'd get lucky for once and be assigned to a base near his brother Alex; at least they'd be in the same country. He silently said a prayer for his brother's safety, wondering what he was doing and hoped he could find him despite the craziness of war.

Sam was nudged from his thoughts when a hand clamped down on his left shoulder; he turned to see his friend and bunkmate, Peter Shultz, come to stand alongside the starboard rail. Pete leaned over to watch the ship's wake and peered into the foggy sky.

"How many more days do ya think we'll be on this tub?" asked Pete.

"Not too many. I heard one of the swabbies say we should be in port by Tuesday."

"Good. I don't know how many more days I can take chowing down on them beans and salt pork. Man, what I wouldn't give for a good ole beef steak like we had back home. At least we had vittles a man could cut his teeth on," said Pete.

"Yeah, even when times were tough, we'd butcher one steer to see us through the winter. Nothing like a thick slab of beef sizzling over an open fire," agreed Sam. "Makes my mouth water just thinking about it."

Sam had met Peter Shultz at Maxwell Field in Montgomery, Alabama. Both men gravitated toward one another upon hearing a common language – Western cowhand. Pete's family ran a small spread in the panhandle of Oklahoma; some head of cattle and a few acres under the till. Until the drought of the thirties hit them hard; worse in April of 1936 when the land became covered in what was known as the "black blizzard". Years of plowing on dry, rain barren earth in America's heartland had created a dust bowl so bad, it caused topsoil to blow away with the prairie winds. A black cloud of dust filled the air and covered everything and everyone in its path. There were no crops, both animals and humans starved alike. Mortgages were unpaid and banks foreclosed; Pete's family lost their farm and their dreams. Pete joined the military when his ma and pa took the younger kids back east to live with kinfolk. Now he stood on the deck of a ship staring at more water than he'd ever seen in his lifetime.

"Think we'll see any action?" questioned Pete.

"Dunno. Guess it depends on where they send us."

"Sometimes I lay in my rack and think about the war. I'm scared, Sam. Scared I'll let my buddies down. Scared I might be a coward."

"Now you listen, you're no namby-pamby! You wouldn't be here if you were. Hell, I've been scared my whole life; we'd be a damn fool not to be. Ain't nobody I'd rather have by my side than you, Pete."

"We'll look out for each other, partner," Pete agreed as he shook Sam's hand.

"Count on it."

Suddenly horns blew and whistles sounded, seamen ran toward gunnery stations as a voice over the loudspeaker commanded, "Man your stations!"

Pete and Sam looked at each other and the commotion they found themselves in the middle of, then high tailed it to the below decks where they had been previously instructed to go.

"What's going on?" asked Sam, grabbing the arm of a seaman hurrying past them.

"German U-boat sighted. Captain's gotta defend the ship!" shouted the sailor above the blaring horns.

"Whoa, didn't plan on seeing action this soon," declared Sam as he and Pete joined their unit below.

"Hey, I don't swim too good," confided Pete.

"Don't you worry none, I'm not planning on getting wet today. You just keep those fingers crossed that these swabbies know what they're doin'."

They hunkered down, listening to the shouts and orders overhead and hardly dared to breathe, their fate in the hands of strangers. They heard distant rumbles of explosions and their transport ship rocked and rolled precariously as their convoy destroyers and cruisers laid a pattern of depth charges into the path of the submarine. Minutes dragged into hours before the all clear sounded.

Sam pulled a shaky hand through his short-cropped black hair and expelled his held breath. "See, what'd I tell you? We got a more important mission ahead of us; God didn't plan on drowning us before we get it done."

"Guess you're right. Still, I'll be damn glad when we leave this tub behind," said Pete. "I gotta go to the head."

Sam laughed out loud as his bunkmate went to change his britches.

Chapter 2

Controlled chaos ruled the docks at Liverpool, as arriving ships unloaded men and equipment by the thousands. American Longshore soldiers worked alongside the Brits in the ports of Liverpool and Southampton to organize both men and supplies.

Voices shouted and engines revved; the noise volume was ear-splitting. Trucks, buses and lorries lined up as men climbed on board. If it had four wheels, it was put into service to carry men away from the docks toward train stations where they would be further transported across the English Midlands. The men traveled across the English countryside to their assigned Army Air corps bases that dotted the once bucolic landscape.

Sam and Pete hoisted their duffel bags and climbed into the back of a lorry; crowding in along the flat bench seat, making room for more men. The driver ground his gears and put his foot down on the gas as the lorry lurched forward, bouncing along what appeared to be little more than a narrow lane to the nearby train station. Just when he had found a comfortable spot, it was time to bail out and find their designated rail car. Sam lined up with his unit then followed along into the crowded train car. Pete had claimed a seat and motioned Sam to squeeze in next to him.

"Sorry," Sam said to the private behind him that had eyed that same seat. He wasn't really sorry, but it seemed polite to say so.

"Thanks pal," he told Pete as they stood their duffels between their knees and tried to stretch out their legs in what little space there was between seats.

A blast of steam, a loud whistle, and a belch of black smoke announced the train's movement as it began its laborious journey. Steel tracks rumbled and groaned under the weight of forty odd cars coupled together clickity-clacking across the land. Sam and Pete joined a division of men in crowded cars, traveling to unknown bases and futures.

"Guess we can open these envelopes now," Sam remarked to Pete. Each man had been handed sealed orders as they boarded their railcar.

Pete ripped his envelope open and removed a typed letter and an attached bi-folded pamphlet. Pete scanned the written orders quickly then raised a questioning glance to Sam. "Duxford – 78th Fighter Group."

Sam finished reading his own orders and smiled broadly as he slapped Pete on the knee, "Duxford it is, same fighter group. What squadron?"

"Dunno, says I'll get a squadron assigned upon arrival. How about you?"

"My orders say I'm to report to the 82nd Fighter Squadron of the 78th Group. Sure hope we can get the same squadron," Sam replied.

"Would you look at this?" Pete said as he flipped open the folded brochure. He read the first page then turned it over to continue. "Looks like some kind of etiquette thing."

Sam read aloud from the Army literature, "*It is always impolite to criticize your host; it is militarily stupid to criticize your Allies.*" Sam unfolded the pamphlet and looked at the pictures included, and other cautions listed. "Guess we aren't supposed to act like big rich Americans with our Hershey chocolates and pockets of money when the Brits have been doing without for years now. They don't want us to embarrass our British hosts. Humph!"

"I dunno about you, but those pockets of money weren't requisitioned to a lowly private. My pockets are empty except for a few bucks," lamented Pete.

Sam laughed, "Yeah, well maybe you shouldn't have gambled on the ship so much. How many times did you lose to Jimmy Parks on dice?"

"Is it my fault those dice kept rolling snake eyes? Think he had them fixed somehow."

"So how far is it to this place Duxford? Am I gonna get some sleep or wind up being bounced off this train in the next hour?"

As Sam speculated his plight, a conductor made his way through the crowded compartment and heard the question. "Duxford and Essex are approximately three hundred and ninety-eight kilometers from Liverpool; you'll be onboard for a good four hours, gentlemen."

"Wow, that far, huh? Guess I'll make myself comfortable then," said Sam as he propped his booted feet on top of his duffel and lowered his cap to shade his closed eyes.

"Looks like a good idea, Pard. Shut eye it is."

Over three hours later, their train rumbled into the station near the town of Peterborough. The railcar rocked and jolted to a stop, knocking Pete off balance and causing Sam's propped feet to fall from his makeshift footstool.

"Where are we?" Sam asked the conductor as he peered out the window.

"Deenethorpe RAF base, outside Peterborough, sir."

"Yeah?" Sam studied his surroundings with interest. "I think that's where my brother's stationed. He's with the 401st Bomber Group at Deenethorpe," he informed Pete. "At least he was, according to his last letter home; been awhile though."

"How long has he been over here?" asked Pete.

"About two years now. Hope I get to see him."

Pete and Sam watched a group of men get off the train, then get into waiting trucks for their remaining journey.

The train lugged to a start again, slowly rolling to the next stop along the route. Sam studied the countryside sliding by, noting the green fields and hedgerows defining small plots of land. Certainly looked different from the vast acres of open land that Sam was used to back home. Loosely stacked stones created squares of walled-in farmland; a few cows and grazing sheep wandered the confined squares. Sam wondered what the significance was of the spots of pink or blue colors he saw on the sheep's wool.

They arrived at Northampton and more men left the train; in a few minutes the engine lurched forward and continued down the tracks. Cambridge station came into view as Pete and Sam gathered their belongings in readiness to depart. Their next destination the fighter group assigned to Duxford base.

"Well, here we go," Sam said as he and Pete hefted duffels to shoulders and stepped off their railcar then boarded the waiting lorry.

The American Eighth Air Force shared bases with the British Royal Air Force; they were crowded into an area of England that was only a forty by eighty-mile strip north of London. Their taxi and runways cut into once rich pastures and buildings were erected on farmland still needed to produce food for a hungry nation. Hospitals and mess halls or barracks were hidden under thick canopies of trees or tucked between grazing pastures in an attempt to not rape the land and disturb the bucolic farmland more than was necessary. Smells of grease and oil mixed with rural farm animal odors.

Metal Quonset huts served as barracks, heated by a single wood or coal burning stove. The barracks remained cold and damp from rain in winter with their daily ration of only one bucket of coal for heat; in summer the men sweltered and baked under the hot metal roofs. A dozen or more men shared these elite sleeping quarters.

Sam and Pete considered accommodations on base were little better than the Atlantic transport ship as they literally ran from one side of the compound to the other to visit latrines and communal showers or the mess hall that was located on the opposite side of base. The only upside was at least they had fresh air.

Their fighter squadrons provided escort to the big flying fortresses – the B-17 bombers – and it was the ground crew's job to keep those planes fit to fly. Sam and Pete were both mechanics on the P-47 Thunderbolts and P-38 Lightning fighter planes and the newer P-51 Mustangs that had just arrived. Both men soon fell into a routine that saw the beginning of their day start at three or four in the morning as they readied aircraft for that day's mission.

It was after sunrise on a Wednesday morning when Sam and Pete joined two other mechanics in the mess hall for breakfast. Their labors were done for now until the squadron returned from the day's sortie, then they would get to perform their magic of patching up aircraft filled with bullet holes and shrapnel. The aroma of chipped beef on toast, SOS as the men called it, greeted their nostrils as they joined the chow line and made their way to an empty table.

"Rumor has it, today's mission is gonna be a bad one. Heard some guys talking about this daylight bombing; makes our guys sitting ducks up there," Pete whispered to Sam.

"You shouldn't be talking about operations; somebody could overhear you. 'Sides, that's what the fighters are for, protect the fortresses from the Luftwaffe."

"I know, I know, but still… daylight bombing might be more accurate, but our losses are staggering. Half those guys don't come back," Pete argued.

"My brother's one of those guys, so stop talking about it. You hear?"

"Sorry, Sam, I forgot. You hear from Alex since we got here?"

"No. I'm waiting for our first weekend pass so I can get over to Deenethorpe."

They finished their meal in silence; Sam's thoughts filled with worry for his brother and the need to find him. For now, he had a job to do, and he'd have to bide his time.

Alex stumbled into his quarters and collapsed onto his narrow cot, exhausted from the day's mission and the de-briefing afterward. All he wanted now was sleep and warmth. Alex Dunlap was an old man of twenty-seven compared to the boys on his crew; the lines in his face and the thousand-yard stare that never left his eyes made him appear even older, much older. Facing death every day and knowing you must do it again, and again, took its toll.

Alex flew on the *Pretty Lady,* a B-17 bomber known as a flying fortress, in the greatest show of absolute devastating power against the common enemy – Nazi Germany. The air war was a slow brutal battle of attrition; men took to the skies at dawn to face annihilation from enemy fire or flak before dropping payloads of deadly bombs on their targets below.

Alex closed his eyes tightly, tried to blot out the image of his buddies' fortress exploding in flames right before him as anti-aircraft artillery on the ground made a direct hit. Shrapnel ripped through the shell of the heavy bomber; the ball turret gunner was torn away like a balloon suddenly let loose; the airman screaming as he plunged to his death. It was a sight Alex couldn't forget.

The Germans had chains of radar stations along the coastlines between Norway and northern France. It was the job of Alex's squadron to fly across that coastline knowing they would be strafed by fighters or buffeted by those deadly black clouds of flak blooming around them. The night flights they first made were safer for crews but less accurate in their bombing results. Targets were missed and cities filled with civilians were hit instead. The Brits didn't mind, it was payback for all the civilian life they had lost in the German blitz of English cities such as London and Coventry.

Now, a year later, with the use of the secret Norden bombsight, planes could fly at higher altitudes in the daylight and drop their payloads with a surgical accuracy on industrial targets, but daylight meant the enemy could also see them coming and going. They got two chances to shoot them down. The further and deeper the mission took them into Germany, the heavier the losses suffered by the bomber groups.

Alex lay on his bunk, his eyes stared at the ceiling but saw again the flames erupting and black smoke billowing from the ground far below as he dropped his ordinance. He would never know how many innocent people his bombs might have killed; he didn't want to know. He just followed orders and aimed his bombsight on whatever factory or steel mill he was told.

He shivered and clutched the thin wool blanket tighter; he still felt the cold from the arctic temperatures whistling through the plane. They bit into a man's skin, despite the alpaca-lined leather flying jackets and boots. Oxygen masks iced up and fingers ached from the cold, on the verge of frostbite in the higher altitudes. At least as bombardier, he had some level of heat in the Plexiglas nose of the cockpit; it was worse for the waist gunners mid-ship and radio operator who had no heat and suffered severely from the frigid temperatures.

Alex reached for the crumpled paper he had thrown to the floor last night, a letter from his brother Sam. He smoothed out the single sheet of paper and read it again. *"Stupid kid. What the hell is he thinking? Joining the Eighth - is he a fool? Why'd he want to be involved in this mess?"* Alex thought.

Chapter 3

Sam studied the broken propeller again, walked under it and fingered the shaft and blade. The plane had taken a round right through the center of the blade creating a starburst hole. If the shot had hit more to the left or right or even higher, it likely would have split the propeller and sheared it clear off and the fighter would have crashed. That pilot was one lucky son of a bitch.

Newly promoted Sergeant Dunlap moved among the planes, inspected damage and tagged which aircraft was a category A with only light damage or a category B with heavy damage that required hauling them into a hangar for serious repair. Sam and Pete had learned to work as a team; they played off of each other's strengths and as crew chiefs, they now had the reputation for the best aircraft maintenance in their squadron. Sam nodded to Pete as they tagged the last plane; each man added final remarks to their clipboard checklists.

"We've got a good routine. Feels like Pete and I've been working together forever, instead of a few months," Sam thought to himself as he turned toward his friend.

"Let's move that Mustang into the hangar and see what we can do about that propeller and shaft," Sam directed.

Pete spoke to a pair of mechanics nearby, "Hey Robbie, you and Jimmie finish up on those hydraulic lines on that Thunderbolt then give us a hand moving this Mustang."

"You got it, Sarge."

Sam and Pete each took hold of a wing tip while the two mechanics lifted the tail and pushed the dead plane, rolling it into the open hangar for repair.

"Thanks guys," Sam said.

"So, what do you think?" asked Pete.

"I think the propeller needs replacing and we don't have any spare parts, that's what I think."

"So, what d'ya want to do?"

"Not sure yet. Let me see what I can come up with. If we could just replace that one blade, the rest of the propeller would be okay. Hmmm," Sam said as he tapped on the metal and studied the damage again. He walked around the plane, scratching his head like he always did when he was deep in thought.

Suddenly, Sam snapped his fingers and smiled broadly. "Ever do any smithy work back home on the ranch, Pete?" he asked.

"Yeah, some. What d'ya have in mind?"

"I'm wondering if that farm outside base has a forge and anvil. They've got horses; they've got to shoe 'em, don't they? If we can use some of their smithy tools, we could try bending that metal and remake that one blade."

"You're a genius, Sam," exclaimed Pete.

"No, I'm not. Let's just see if it works first. Gotta run it by the Captain."

Alex sat with his crew members in the briefing room and waited with the other men of the bomber group. The table before them with the relief map and today's targets was covered with a large cloth; they would study its details, memorize terrain and locations soon enough. A haze of stale cigarette smoke swirled above their heads; men spoke softly to friends sitting nearby or murmured silent prayers in the pre-dawn darkness.

Alex had awakened at four, ate a quick breakfast then made his way in the pitch darkness to the briefing hut. His thoughts and concentration were on the mission ahead; he had an idea of where they would be sent next and prayed that he was wrong.

Chief of Staff Rogers entered the building, walking briskly up the center aisle.

"Ten-Hut!" he called.

Men jumped to their feet and stood at attention, saluting General Eaker as he strode to the front of the room. The general returned the salute, "At ease."

Chairs scraped lightly as men took their seats again, eyes focused on the chart displayed and prepared to learn the day's mission.

"Men, Operation Hydra provides support to the RAF as we take out the factories in Peenemunde that build Germany's new V-2 rockets. These pilotless rockets are terrorizing London and other British cities; they must be stopped. Colonel Rogers is passing out your maps and timetables now. Major Winter will provide your weather forecast; I'll turn the briefing over to him," the general concluded.

Alex read the flimsy, his information sheet that listed target names, route and timetable for the mission. He would need to study the map table along with the other bombardiers and locate his designated target position.

Major Winter pulled down an overhead screen as a projector flickered to life; a hazy map of northern Germany and the Baltic Sea appeared.

The major held a wooden pointer and tapped the map, "Your route will be to fly across the North Sea, toward Denmark and the northern coast of Germany then east toward the canals at Peenemunde on the Baltic Sea. You can expect overcast skies and cloud cover for most of the route, some mild crosswinds six MPH on takeoff."

Fifteen minutes later the briefing finished, men stood and prepared to leave. They would pick up their parachutes and emergency first aid kits then prepare to board their planes. Alex glanced around, noting the solemn faces before him on men who came from all walks of life – volunteers all; farmers, lawyers, teachers, shopkeepers, and miners. Brothers all, committed to this mad and glorious task before them. Sadly, Alex knew some of these faces he would never see again. Would today be his day?

The crew gathered around the *Pretty Lady*. Alex did a final check on the racks of the four-thousand-pound bomb payload, nodding to his crew chief that all looked okay. Cases of ammunition for the fifty caliber Browning machine guns were already on board. The crew chief had all engines running for instrument check then quickly shut down to conserve fuel until time to taxi out.

The *Pretty Lady* was piloted by a young history teacher named John Stone; a quiet man with an even, unflappable temperament. The Captain commanded respect from his men and in return, they received a sense of security; he'd get them home safely. She had nineteen missions stamped on her hull; just six more and their tour of duty would be complete. They could go home if they survived; every flight was a gamble with the odds against them.

Slowly, the flying fortresses lined up for take-off in two rows. The pilots pushed throttles forward and each heavy plane rushed to the end of the runway; lifting, clawing its way into the sky, first the left row then the right in turn – avoiding each other's prop wash. Within minutes the entire group was airborne and formed into their squadron flights as they turned and headed toward their destination.

In the early morning dawn light, the citizens of Essex and Northampton listened to the roar of engines overhead and felt the rumble of the mighty fortresses; their thatched roof homes shook, and windows rattled with the vibrations. A few people said a silent prayer for the young men flying into harm's way.

Chapter 4

Sam approached the Upton farmhouse, parking his jeep on the gravel drive near the barn. He had explained his idea to Captain Barnett and received the green light to speak with the local farmer. Now he had to see how agreeable their neighbor would be to lend his blacksmith tools.

Sam knocked tentatively on the kitchen door of the two-story clapboard house. He listened to sounds of movement in the house and stood patiently waiting until the screen door was cautiously pushed open by a middle-aged woman; she dried her hands on the apron tied about her waist and gave him a tentative smile.

"What can I do for you, young man? Are you from Duxford?" Mrs. Upton asked as she took in his uniform and insignia. "You one of them Yanks?"

"Yes, ma'am. Is your husband about? I wanted to know if he might have some smithy tools."

"You'll find him in the barn tending the animals," she said as she pointed to the rickety structure across the yard.

"Thank you, ma'am. Sorry to bother you."

"No bother, uh, Sergeant…?"

"Sergeant Dunlap, ma'am, of the 78th Fighter Group," Sam introduced himself.

"Well you go on down to the barn then, Sergeant Dunlap, just holler for Ben; he's in there."

Sam entered the barn; dust motes floated in the filtered sunlight seeping through cracks in the rough wooden walls. He stood for a minute, letting his eyes adjust to the shadowy interior.

"Mr. Upton? Can I speak with you, sir? Your wife said I'd find you here," called Sam.

"Who's there?"

"Sam Dunlap, sir, from Duxford base."

"C'mon in. I'll be with you in a second."

Sam looked around the dimly lit barn, his eyes lighting up at the sight of an anvil and forge in the back corner. Tools hung on nails between wall joists and rafters – scythes, shovels, pitchforks, sickles, hoes, all manners of farming implements - even an old plow and leather yoke with harness.

A sow made her presence known with a loud snort; her straw-filled pen occupied a corner of the barn. Barnyard smells filled Sam's nostrils. He noted half a dozen milk cows grazing on the sweet grasses of the fenced meadow. A rooster chased a trio of loudly squawking hens across the adjoining barnyard and into the coop.

Sam shuffled his feet in the dirt and loose straw as he waited on Mister Upton; a wave of homesickness washed over him as he surveyed the peaceful farm scene.

"What can I do for you?" asked Ben Upton as he approached the American. "You one of them fly boys?"

"Hello, Sgt. Dunlap, sir, from over at Duxford," Sam greeted as he extended his hand. "I'm a mechanic, crew chief assigned to the fighter squadrons."

The farmer wiped his hand on the seat of his overalls before shaking Sam's hand. "You can call me Ben, I don't rank a *Sir*, sergeant."

"I've got a broken propeller blade and was wondering if I could borrow your smithy tools and forge to fix it," Sam said as he got right to the point of his visit.

"You know what you're doing with those kinds of tools? Forge needs a hot fire; I don't have enough coal on hand to burn for that."

"Yessir, um Ben, I worked blacksmith chores back home on our ranch. Um, well, now that it's warmer weather, we don't need our ration of coal for the barracks; I figured I could use that."

"Well… you bring down that broken blade and I guess we'll see what we can do. You say it's from one of the planes?"

"Yessir, off a new Mustang fighter. I've got to get her fixed and don't have any spare parts. I'm hoping your forge will be the answer to my problem."

"Come around tomorrow; I'll lend you a hand."

"Thank you, Ben. Appreciate it."

Sam jumped into his Jeep and took off back to base to inform Captain Barnett of the good news. As soon as he parked, he sought out his commanding officer walking among several shot up planes in the open hangar.

"Captain," Sam called out.

"Well Dunlap, what did you find out?" asked the slightly overweight captain. He surveyed the damaged aircraft under his command; an unlit cigar stump clenched between his teeth as his hand shaded his eyes from the noon sun. He appeared to most as a brusque man of few words, but Sam had grown to admire and respect his commander's knowledge and mechanical ability and the two men admitted a grudging fondness for one another. Sam thought Barnett was really a kind, fatherly type at heart and fought hard to hide it; he'd do anything for the man.

"I found us a forge that we can use. With your permission, Sir, I'd like to have Pete Shultz help me take apart that Mustang prop. Between us, I think we can pound out that metal and rework the blade. I'll have to use a good ration of coal from base though."

"Take what you need. This plane's more valuable than a stove belly full of coal. When can you start?" asked the officer.

"Tomorrow, Sir. Mr. Upton told me he would lend a hand too, sir. He was very friendly."

"Good. That's good. You get that Mustang flying again, Dunlap, and I'll see that you and Shultz are granted a three-day pass."

"Thank you, Sir! You can count on us to get the job done."

The next morning, Pete and Sam loaded the damaged propeller blade from the Mustang into the back of the Jeep. They had both struggled with the propeller since dawn; using a blow torch to cut away the shattered blade from the shaft.

Ben Upton greeted them as they drove into the barnyard and parked near the barn entrance.

"Good morning, boys."

"Morning, Ben. How's the fire looking?" asked Sam. He had returned the previous evening with several bags of coal so the farmer could stoke up the fire in the forge and get it burning super hot by the time they arrived.

"Just about ready," answered Mr. Upton. "Come see for yourselves."

Pete, Sam and Ben entered the open barn, waves of heat radiated from the furnace in the rear of the building. Not wanting to become roast pork on the hoof, Maggie the sow had been removed to the cooler enclosed chicken pen.

Sam nodded in approval as he viewed the blazing coals. The men quickly began to work, the broken metal was thrust into the hot coals where it soon began to glow red. Ben pumped the forge bellows as Pete and Sam took turns hammering the torn metal edges over the anvil surface. Slowly the pliable steel flattened and welded together, forming a solid whole surface. The heated blade was plunged into a bucket of cold water, steam rose into the air surrounding the furnace. Sam held the blade with a pair of long tongs, then thrust it again into the fiery coals to heat once more.

The process was repeated three more times until the steel strengthened and conformed to the shape of a propeller blade. Satisfied with the results, Sam and Pete plunged the blade into the water to cool one last time. All three men were soaked in sweat from their toil and the confines of the sweltering barn, but happy with their labors.

Sam slapped Pete on the back, "Let's get some cool air." He dragged the back of his hand across his forehead, wiped away stinging sweat running into his eyes.

"You said it," Pete agreed.

As the men sat on the soft grass, their backs leaning against the wooden fence rails, they were greeted by Mrs. Upton balancing a tray of mugs filled with cool ale.

"Thought you could all use a cold drink," she said.

"Much obliged, ma'am," Pete and Sam both said as they raised their glasses to her in a salute.

Sam pulled out of the Jeep two remaining bags of coal and handed them to Ben Upton. "Thank you for the use of your forge. This is small payment, but maybe you can make use of this coal next winter."

"Thank you, we certainly will. Glad we could be of assistance to you Yanks and the war effort," Ben said as he shook hands with the men and bade farewell.

Once back on base, Sam and Pete spent the rest of the afternoon welding the new blade back onto the propeller shaft and assembling the unit onto the nose of the Mustang. They tested its balance and rotation by hand then decided to give it a final test.

"Climb into that cockpit, Pete, and start her up. I want to watch the rotation under power and make sure she won't wobble or shimmy."

"Got it," said Pete as he sat in the pilot seat and switched on the ignition.

"Take it slow, yeah that's it. Now give her some more power, okay back her down," directed Sam.

Captain Barnett and Lieutenant Anderson entered the hangar, following the sound of the revving motor. Both watched the proceedings as Sam and Pete put the Mustang to trial.

"Think we've got your bird ready to fly again, Lieutenant," said Sam as he smiled proudly.

Pete shut the engine off and climbed down from the fighter then joined Sam, admiring their work.

Anderson shook hands with the mechanics as he smiled and fondly patted the nose of his plane.

"You boys certainly live up to your reputation for the best maintenance in the group. Well done!" said Captain Barnett, "and I haven't forgotten my promise. You can pick up those weekend passes at my office."

"Thank you, Sir," both men said in unison and saluted smartly.

Chapter 5

Both Sam and Pete wore their dress uniforms as they waited on the station platform for the next train. Their shoes were shined; hair combed and slicked back. They were eager and ready to go to town.

"You sure you don't want to come to London with me? I'm going to visit every pub in town and maybe find me a sweet little English gal," Pete proclaimed.

"Well, just don't get yourself in trouble, partner. I'm on my way to Peterborough and Deenethorpe base to find my brother Alex. Maybe next time, huh?"

"No problem, Sam. I know you're anxious to meet up with your brother. Hope you find him."

The train whistled and blew off some steam as it entered the station. The placard in the window read southbound – London.

"Guess that's my train. Hey, be careful. See you back in camp Monday," waved Pete.

Sam stepped back into the station as the train slowly rolled away. He checked his watch then glanced at the large clock on the station wall.

"What time is the northbound train due?" asked Sam to the station master.

"Should be here in the next ten minutes, Yank."

"Thanks." Sam paced back and forth across the platform a second time and exhaled in relief as he heard the locomotive round the bend and slow to a halt in the station. He boarded as quickly as he could, found a seat then nervously watched out the window as the peaceful English countryside slid by on his way to Peterborough.

He was excited and worried at the same time. *"Why hadn't Alex answered his last letter? Was there something wrong? Was he injured?"* Sam tormented himself with his fears and thoughts. He tried to wait calmly as the train chugged along the tracks, but on the inside his emotions did flip-flops and his stomach felt like battery acid. Soon, soon, he'd be there soon and would see for himself.

An hour later, Sam hailed a taxi and asked to be driven to the front gate of Deenethorpe. The base sat on the outskirts of town and Sam found himself facing a security guard at the main gate.

He showed his identification and his liberty pass then explained that he was there to find his brother Alexander Dunlap with the 401st Bomber Group. The guard studied his paperwork, went into his guard shack and made a phone call, then came back out and handed Sam his papers.

"Okay, you'll find the 4-0-1 quarters a half kilometer down this main road, then take the right turn and should be about the second or third building. Watch it, you're close to the west runway down there."

"Got it, thanks," said Sam as he started walking on the shoulder of the perimeter road. Ammunition trucks and men in open lorries drove past him as he continued his trek. Twice he had to step off the road to keep from being run over as another vehicle hurried by.

Sam halted and stepped onto the berm again as a horn beeped loudly. He was surprised to see the Jeep come to a stop near him.

"Where you going, sergeant? Want a ride?" a young corporal asked.

"Yeah, okay. Know where the 401st is billeted?" asked Sam as he climbed into the passenger seat of the Jeep.

"Sure thing. Hop in," said the young soldier.

Alex lay on his bed, his forearm slung across his eyes, shielding them from the visions that swam before him. He couldn't sleep, afraid of the nightmares, but his exhausted body couldn't summon the energy to move either. A slight noise in the doorway made him turn his head toward the dim light and shadowy figure. *"Funny,"* he thought, *almost looks like Sam standing there."*

Sam let his eyes adjust to the darkened room, then spied his brother in the far corner of the narrow barracks. In a few long strides, he crossed the open space.

"Alex," called Sam, all the joy of seeing his brother echoing in his voice.

"Sam? Is that really you?" Alex rubbed his eyes and struggled to sit up.

"Hello Brother!" Sam wrapped his arms around Alex's shoulders in a bone-crushing bear hug. He'd never been happier to see someone more. "Thank God you're all right and in one piece."

"What the hell are you doing here?"

"I've got a three-day pass; first chance I've had to find you," Sam said.

"No, I mean, what the hell are you doing in England? You crazy?"

"What's wrong with you? Gonna hog this whole war to yourself?" Sam laughed. "I joined up as soon as I could."

"You always were a stupid kid. Why couldn't you just stay home and stay safe?" Alex reached for a crumpled pack of cigarettes laying on a makeshift table next to his cot. His hand shook as he lit the match then took a long drag on the tobacco.

Sam studied his brother's unshaven appearance; the sweat-stained and rumpled flight suit, the dark circles under his eyes. "You look like shit. When's the last time you slept?"

"I dunno; yesterday maybe. The *Pretty Lady* caught some flak; we've been grounded for a few days until she gets patched up."

"*Pretty Lady*, that your ship?" Sam asked.

"Yeah, best fortress in the squadron. We just need to keep her flying for a few more missions then we can go home."

"How many?" Sam asked, knowing the crews stamped their kills or missions on the fuselage. Each plane kept its own scorecard.

"Twenty," Alex answered quietly, coughing slightly as he tried to rouse himself and stand. He swayed, the room spun dizzily as Sam made a grab for him and helped him back onto the bed.

"I think you need some sleep. We can talk afterward, maybe grab something to eat or even a beer. How's that sound?"

"I can't; faces haunt me when I close my eyes," Alex whispered in a voice so low, Sam had to strain to hear.

"Go to sleep, brother. I'll sit here with you and keep your ghosts away. You're safe now, close your eyes, just sleep."

Sam massaged Alex's shoulders, touched his cheek and stroked his forehead; he recalled all the times their mother's magical touch had comforted them in just this way. Sam tried to infuse that same calm and sense of comfort now. Alex had always been the strong one, it was difficult to witness his breakdown now. Sam could only imagine the horrors his brother had seen and the dangers he faced each time he took off.

Sam took the chair next to Alex's bed, his feet propped up on the side of the cot, he dozed off for a few hours himself until the loud rumble of returning bombers woke him. He left Alex snoring loudly and ran outside to watch the squadron of heavy fortresses return to their base camp. A few planes limped back; damaged wings, a pattern of bullet holes sprayed across a fuselage. Sam stood and watched one plane circling above the field, waiting to land until his buddies were safely on the ground. Only one landing gear was visible and both starboard engines shot flames and smoke as the heavy fortress lined up with the runway close to the end of the row of barracks. It inched itself lower and lower, finally touching down, crabbed sideways with one wing tip plowed into the soft ground as the plane shuddered to a halt. Crew members jumped down from the open midship hatch. Sam could see the pilot pulling on his co-pilot who was slumped forward over the controls. Sam automatically ran toward the heavy plane.

Fire crews rushed to fight the flames shooting from the damaged engines; trying to keep the mighty fortress from exploding with its combined fuel of ammunition and gasoline. Sam reached up to the hatch under the cockpit, pulling open the hinged door wider.

"Hey, give me his legs. I've got him," yelled Sam over the noise of the raging fire and shouting crewmen.

The pilot struggled to carry and slide his unconscious friend toward the open portal. He managed to lay the co-pilot on his back and dangled his legs out the hatch then guided the rest of his body as someone on the ground caught the weight of his buddy. A minute later he dropped to the ground himself and hurried away from the burning plane. He saw his co-pilot being hoisted onto a stretcher and loaded into a waiting ambulance before he turned to thank the soldier standing off to one side.

"Don't know who you are buddy, but thanks for the help," the Major said as he extended his hand to Sam.

"No problem, Sir. Sergeant Samuel Dunlap of the 78th, sir."

"Well I must say, you're the most well-dressed ground crewman I've ever seen, Sam Dunlap." The major laughed as he pointed to Sam's dress uniform now soiled with wet soot and muddy stains.

"Yes Sir, guess I wasn't thinking about my uniform."

"So, what are you doing at Deenethorpe, Dunlap? Aren't you stationed over in Duxford?"

"Came to see my brother, Sir. He's with the 4-0-1."

"Find him?"

"Yes Sir, I did. I was in his quarters over there when I heard the commotion."

"Thanks again for your help. Not every man would run toward a burning airplane. I won't forget you or your deed, sergeant," the major stated as he climbed into a Jeep with other crew members and left.

Sam peered into Alex's open barrack door; he was still asleep. That's good. He needed to find the location of the latrine and see if he could clean up and inspect any damage done to his one and only dress uniform. He shook his head as he walked across the base to find what he needed.

"What was I thinking?" Sam berated himself. Shaking his head again, *"Guess I didn't think; I'll never learn,"* he told his inner self. So absorbed with his thoughts, he almost walked into the path of an oncoming car. He jumped to the side of the tarmac as a staff car waving a general's one-star flag from its front bumper honked loudly.

The car stopped in front of the operation's headquarters and Sam watched as a pretty gal in a WAC uniform jumped out from the driver's side and quickly opened the general's car door, snapping to attention with a brisk salute. Sam recognized Brigadier General Ira Eaker, the deputy commander of the Eighth Air Force, as he marched into the building. He'd been at Duxford once.

The WAC stood at ease next to the vehicle, she nodded and smiled at Sam.

"Sorry about that, sergeant. Didn't mean to frighten you off the roadway."

Sam moved closer to her, hoping to get a better look at the beauty with the silken voice. He politely tipped his hat to her, as he stared at the softly curling auburn hair escaping from her pert uniform cap. Hazel eyes, flecked with gold, crinkled at the corners as she smiled at him again and extended her hand in greeting.

"No harm done?" she asked.

"No ma'am. No harm done. I was just looking for the latrine so I could clean up, didn't pay any attention to the approaching car. My fault," Sam told her.

"It does appear that you've had a bit of a mishap, ah, Sergeant ..."

"Dunlap, ma'am. Sgt. Samuel Dunlap."

"Nice to meet you. I'm Subaltern Mary Barnes of His Majesty's Auxiliary Territorial Service."

"Oh, I thought you were a WAC; you know, American Women's Army Corp, but I should have known from your accent."

"Hmm, we try to lend assistance where we're needed. Right now, the general's regular driver has been hospitalized for appendicitis, so I've been assigned to fill in for her."

"Oh. Do you like driving for the General?"

"Doesn't matter what I like. I'm doing my duty, sergeant."

"Yeah, well, I guess I better be about mine. I've got to make myself presentable," Sam said as he decided on which building would likely be what he needed.

"Would you like some help?" Mary offered. "I keep a kit with me for just such emergencies."

"Thank you, that's kind of you to offer," Sam replied.

"Hmm, perhaps you ought to step into that building next door and slip off those trousers. I'll see what I can do to remove some of that mud."

Sam's face turned beet red as he glanced at her expression to see if she was serious. She was.

"Go on, I promise not to look. Just hand out those trousers and you can work on that jacket with this," Mary said, as she handed him a stiff bristled brush.

The knees of his trousers were damp and muddy from where he had knelt under the weight of the unconscious man. Entering the empty briefing room, Sam timidly slipped out of his pants and stood in his boxer shorts, tossing her the soiled pants. God, he hoped no one walked in on him; he didn't know how he'd explain his current predicament, standing around in his underwear. While he waited, he brushed his jacket as best he could, removing the soot smudges but not having much effect on the other stains. It would have to do.

"All right, sergeant, I've finished. I'll just hang your trousers on the doorknob, shall I?"

Sam grabbed his pants and pulled them on as quickly as he could. He raced outside to speak with Mary again before she drove off.

"Thank you, Mary. May I call you Mary? I'd really like to see you again. Do you get any days off?"

"Yes, Sam, you may call me Mary," she said softly, her smile reached her eyes and gave Sam all the encouragement he needed.

He smiled broadly as he told her, "I'm on a three-day pass from Duxford, here to see my brother, but he'd understand if I tell him I met a pretty gal."

She hesitated as she looked him up and down then made her decision. "Well, I'm not on duty Sunday," she replied then jotted down her telephone number and address on a scrap of paper.

"Is this nearby? I'll try to find it. Sunday would be great."

"Very good, sergeant. I need to get back to my station; General Eaker will be finished soon."

"Thank you again, Mary. You've been very kind. I'll look forward to Sunday." He tipped his cap to her again then turned to jog back to Alex's quarters, whistling an off-key tune as he ran.

Mary stood watching him as he ran off. She shook her head and sighed heavily. *"Oh my God, I hope I'm not making a mistake. He reminds me so much of Timmy,"* she thought as a tear trickled from her eye.

Alex was awake and changing his clothes as Sam entered the barracks. He looked much better; less haunted.

"Thought I dreamt you; where've you been?"

"I don't know where to begin. Hey, I've got a date for Sunday!" Sam exclaimed, wondering how he could be so lucky.

"Wow, little brother, you move pretty fast. Not the scared kid I remember; you've changed."

Chapter 6

Sam and Alex spent all day Saturday together; Alex showed Sam around base and introduced him to his fellow crew members of the *Pretty Lady*. Sam wanted to see the lady in question, so Alex led him into the hangar designated as repair shop.

"Here she is. That plexiglass nose is my office; where I sit when I'm dropping my payload," Alex explained as he pointed to the cockpit and nose of the huge plane.

"Man, these birds are huge; especially standing this close. Not like working on a fighter," Sam said as he walked under the wings of the mighty fortress. He ran his hand along the skin of the ship's belly, feeling the bullet holes gained on the last raid.

The crew chief and mechanics nodded to Alex and as they continued the repairs. Sam paused to watch their progress.

"Having problems with that horizontal stabilizer?" Sam asked the crew chief.

"Yeah, but we'll get her fixed. You can't keep these big birds down for long. I've seen 'em shot up worse than this and still manage to fly home," said crew chief Frank Miller.

"Good to know," said Sam as he and Alex left the hangar and headed toward a squat building serving as the officer's club on base. "You sure I can come in? After all, I'm only a lowly non-com."

"Cut it out. You'll be with me as my guest. Don't let me pull rank on you, brother." Alex laughed and jostled Sam as they entered the doorway.

They found an empty space at the bar and climbed onto a pair of wooden barstools; Sam knew his sergeant stripes were drawing frowns from a few of the seated officers nearby. He squirmed as he glanced over his shoulder and smiled slightly to a captain perched on a stool at the end of the bar.

"I feel like a fish out of water in here. Not exactly welcome," Sam whispered to Alex.

"Two beers, please," Alex told the bartender. "Here, have a drink and relax," he said as he slid a cold mug of frothy beer toward Sam.

Sam raised the glass to his lips just as a hand clamped down on his shoulder. He turned on his stool to face the intruder.

"Hello again, sergeant. I take it this is your missing brother?" he asked as he greeted Sam.

"Yes sir, my brother Alex Dunlap."

"Major Simpson, Lieutenant Alex Dunlap, sir, of the 401st," Alex saluted.

"At ease, Lieutenant. Your brother and I are old friends. He came to my rescue yesterday and lent me a helping hand."

"It was no problem, sir," stated Sam as he watched his brother eye him speculatively. Sam noted that the disapproving frowns had disappeared on the group of officers sitting nearby as they eavesdropped on their conversation.

"You boys enjoy your beer," the major said as he shook hands with Sam.

"Thank you, sir."

Alex and Sam both swiveled on their stools and turned their backs to the room of curious bystanders. The two brothers looked at each other in silent communication and then laughed out loud.

"Want to tell me what that was all about? How'd you suddenly become bosom buddies with the major?"

"It's a long story. His plane had a rough landing yesterday and all I did was help him get the co-pilot out of the cockpit. Dude was knocked out cold and the major had to push him out of the forward hatch. No big deal, all I did was catch him," Sam said in an abbreviated version of what happened.

"Yeah sure, that's all it was, huh? Couldn't have been that burned plane I saw next to the *Lady's* hangar, could it? I think you just made a friend for life; Major Simpson's a good guy, real straight shooter."

"Humph, he seemed pretty decent; as far as officers go, that is." Sam laughed and jabbed his brother in the arm.

"I'm proud of you Sam," Alex told him as they left the clubhouse; he draped his arm across Sam's shoulder in a quick hug like he did when they were young boys.

"Really? That means a lot to me, you know that, don't ya?"

Uncomfortable with his display of emotion, Alex pivoted on his heel and moved aside. "Yeah, well, don't let it go to your head!"

Sam cleared his throat, swallowing a lump of pent up feelings and swiped a tear that had appeared in the corner of his eye.

"Have you heard from Mother lately? Any news from home?" asked Alex as he scuffed his boot in a bit of loose dirt and stared into the setting sun.

"Got a letter about a week ago. She's okay; Pop is about the same, still mean as hell," answered Sam.

"Guess some things never change," remarked Alex.

"No, guess not. Pop was appointed as the local stock inspector, according to Mother. Bet that made old man Logan fit to be tied," Sam said with a short laugh.

"Well, maybe Pop will finally be able to stop some of our cattle from goin' missing," Alex said.

"Yeah, maybe." In an instant Sam was transported back to Wyoming; he could see his father standing over him with belt in hand. The cruel sneer and dark expression on his face as he swung that leather with all his might, inflicting as much pain as possible. It didn't matter how small the mistake or perceived crime; no excuses, no amount of talking would make him change his mind. Sam shivered in memory.

He quickly looked away, cleared his throat and sought to change the subject.

"Hey, why don't you come along tomorrow with me and Mary? We'd have more time together and I don't think Mary would mind. Heck, I only just met her. We can tour London or something."

"You want me to go along on your date? Are you nuts?" asked Alex in surprise.

"No, I mean yeah, I want you to come. Say you will. It'll be great."

"I will, only if this gal doesn't mind. How'd you leave it with her? Meeting her someplace or what?" Alex asked.

"She gave me her number and address; told me to ring her up first thing in the morning. We can agree on time and place then."

"All right then. Let's get some shut eye; you can bunk with me. Dan Walden's cot is empty; Dan won't be needing it anymore," Alex said as his eyes once more reflected a haunted vision.

In his mind, he saw the young navigator's quick smile and easy manner then felt the same despair wash over him as when he witnessed the destruction of the *Baby Doll* and its crew. His friends, bunkmates, gone in an instant with a fireball explosion and there was nothing he could do but watch from his glass perch in the nose of *Pretty Lady*.

Sam heard the pain in his brother's voice and saw the dark shadow cross his face when he spoke of the missing navigator. He wanted to ask about him but realized it was a painful memory better left alone.

Sam tried to change the somber mood, "Hey, race you back to the barracks. Bet I can beat you now that you're such an old man."

Alex gave himself a mental shake, "Think you can, kid? Go ahead and try. Ready, set, go!" exclaimed Alex as he broke into a sprint before Sam could react.

Sunday morning, Sam dialed the telephone number Mary had written; he waited nervously as the phone rang four times before a soft female voice answered.

"Hello? This is Mary Barnes."

"Mary? This is Sam Dunlap; we met the other day. You helped clean my uniform."

"Yes, Sam, I recall. How are you?"

"Fine, thanks. Are you still agreeable to meet me today? I was wondering if you would mind if my brother Alex joined us?" asked Sam.

"Your brother? Well, yes, I suppose that would be okay. Have you been to London since you arrived? Perhaps you would enjoy seeing some of the sights?"

"Yeah, sure, that would be okay, I guess. Where can I meet you or pick you up?"

"Find your way over to the village of Peterborough and wait for me at the rail station. Shall we say ten o'clock?" Mary suggested.

"Great, we'll meet you at the station then. Look forward to seeing you again, Mary," said Sam as he hung up the telephone and turned to Alex.

"All set. She said to meet her at the station; we'll go down to London for the day."

"Did she mind my tagging along?" asked Alex.

"No, she was okay with that. What do ya think? Want to spend the day playing tourist?"

"Sure, why not. Might be fun at that. I haven't done much since I've been here."

"Okay then, let's get going!" said Sam as he adjusted his cap, tipping it to one side in a rakish fashion.

Mary waited outside of the train station; she kept a watch for her American escorts as she wondered again for the tenth time whatever possessed her to agree to go out with someone she'd just met. She nervously tucked a strand of her luxurious auburn hair behind her ear where it had escaped from its neat rolled chignon. She wore a dark blue skirt with a yellow and blue floral blouse, its high neckline becoming but prim and proper; a lightweight blue sweater draped across her shoulders. Mary glanced at her wristwatch again.

"Hello, Mary!" waved Sam as he and Alex approached the lone woman waiting by the station doorway.

Mary studied the two handsome men; she was struck again by the similarity to her beloved Timmy. Alex stood an inch taller than Sam, but both men had lean builds and the same coloring in eyes and dark hair, obviously brothers. She closed her eyes for a second to banish the past memory and prepared to greet the approaching men.

"Hello. You must be Alex. I'm Mary Barnes," she said as she extended her hand to Alex then turned a radiant smile on Sam. "Nice to see you again, Sam."

"You're awfully pretty without your uniform. Uh, sorry, that didn't sound right. I meant you look very nice in civilian clothes," Sam stammered. He felt like a fool as he watched Mary accept his left-handed compliment and tried not to laugh behind her hand.

"Ah, well, thank you, sergeant; I mean, Sam," she said as she swallowed her giggle.

Alex shook his head as he watched his little brother get his big foot out of his mouth. It was apparent that Sam didn't have much experience with the gentler sex. Still, he had to admit, he knew how to pick the pretty ones. Mary was a looker; he couldn't help stealing more than a glance her way. Alex admired the gentle swing of her skirts and the allure of her womanly figure hidden beneath the conservative outfit.

Sam bought their tickets, and the three of them boarded the train ten minutes later. Sam and Mary sat together as Alex took the seat across from them. Alex liked the advantage of having the better view of Mary.

The English countryside slowly slid by as the train gained momentum heading south toward London. Great manor houses spread their stone wings across the hilltops, homes of the landed gentry, while the nearby village cottages dotted the surrounding land. Elizabethan and Jacobean brick structures, built centuries earlier, draped their roof edges with the graceful summery vines of lavender wisteria.

The three rode together, staring out the windows, then Mary tried to break the awkward silence between them.

"Ah, Alex, have you been in England long? How about you, Sam?" she asked politely.

Alex dragged his eyes from the passing scenery to the more pleasant face before him. "I've been here a little over two years now. I joined up right after Pearl."

"Are you a pilot?" asked Mary, noting the wings pinned to his jacket. She watched the play of emotions, brought on by her question, cross Sam's face. She was curious about the relationship between the brothers; she was certain she detected pride, or was it envy in Sam's eyes?

"No, ma'am. I'm a bombardier; didn't qualify as a pilot," Alex answered her, his face mirroring pain for a split-second.

"You never told me that," said Sam as he studied his brother's reaction.

"Yeah, well, there wasn't much to tell. I'm okay with what I do; I'm an important member of the crew," replied Alex, a bit more defensive than he meant.

"Never said you weren't," said Sam.

"Just drop it."

"Sorry, Mary. I don't know what you must be thinking of us," apologized Sam.

"I think I see two brothers who need some time together. How long has it been since you've seen each other?" she asked, guessing the truth.

"Couple of years," said Sam. "I joined up as soon as I could, hoping to join my brother. Spent six months here before I found him."

"And now you have. Wasn't it fortunate that you are both stationed so nearby?" commented Mary.

"I suppose so. So, Mary, how long have you been serving with the ATS?" Sam was equally curious to learn more about Mary.

"Well, I worked as a Land Army Girl for two years, then decided to join the ATS after my parents were both killed during the blitz in London."

"Sorry about your parents," Sam said softly.

"Thank you; the blitz destroyed a lot of families," Mary replied as she pretended to rummage through her purse, needing the time to get a firm hold on her own emotions.

"Did you say land army? What's that?" asked Sam.

"You know, we Brits have been fighting the Germans for several years now, while you Yanks are just getting started. What with all the men going into service, someone had to work the farms and keep food on the table. That's what the land girls are all about; women volunteer to leave their homes and go work the farms up north – plowing, tending crops, milking cows. It was hard work; I didn't do any actual milking, but I did do other chores; I have a whole new respect for farmers. I didn't really mind it though; I'm a country girl at heart. I grew up near Hastings."

Sam smiled broadly, respect and admiration growing for the petite woman beside him. "Bet you'd look cute milking those cows. You'd fit right in on the ranch!" exclaimed Sam.

"Ranch? Whose ranch?" confused, Mary glanced between the two men.

"Ours. We're from Wyoming. Our family owns a cattle ranch that our grandfather built back in the 1890s." Alex answered her.

Mary laughed, "Oh, a new place. Farms and estates here date back hundreds of years."

Humor restored, both men chuckled and agreed. "See what you mean. You Brits do have a few more years on us, at that."

"Here comes Victoria Station. We need to get off here," directed Mary as the train slowed to a stop.

Chapter 7

Compared to the peaceful countryside settings surrounding their air bases, London screamed chaos and bustling activity. Cars and buses raced down streets, and people hurried along the sidewalks. The entire city moved at a frantic pace; Sam and Alex each stared in wonder as if they had been sleepwalking before and now were suddenly awake.

"Where's everyone going?" asked Sam as they left the station and walked around barricades and piles of stone and rubble along the street.

"Better move along before we get run over," exclaimed Alex.

"We can walk from here if perhaps you would like to see Buckingham Palace?" suggested Mary as she pointed to the imposing five-story stone mansion filling their horizon.

"Swell, doesn't look too far," said Sam.

They began their journey with Mary acting as tour guide. "To your left are the Royal Mews; the King's stables."

"Mews, huh? That's a pretty fancy name for a barn. So that's where they keep their horses?" asked Alex.

"Yes, horses and carriages too. The royal coaches are magnificent. They're used by the royal family for special events now, but I imagine they were the main transport at the turn of the century," Mary explained.

"Wow, impressive," said Sam as they walked past the perimeter of the grounds and watched the stallions and mares being exercised in the fenced confine.

The trio continued making their way toward the square with its fountains and statuary celebrating Queen Victoria in front of the huge palace. Alex and Sam took up protective positions along each side of Mary, but Sam frowned as he saw Alex claim her hand as they walked. The three resembled the Wizard of Oz characters skipping down the yellow brick road.

"Look, see the flag above the palace?" asked Mary.

"Yeah, Union Jack flying proudly," remarked Alex.

"That signifies that King George Sixth and the royal family are not in residence today. If they were here, the Royal Standard would be evident, not the Union Jack," explained Mary.

"So where are they if they're not at home," wondered Sam.

"Hmm, likely they left the summer heat of the city and went to one of their other residences, perhaps Balmoral Castle in Scotland."

"Guess that's like FDR leaving the White House for Hyde Park, right?" commented Sam.

"Probably," said Mary.

"Hey, what's that place?" asked Alex as he pointed toward a sizeable military structure across the way.

"Oh, that's Wellington Barracks. Home of the Guard Divisions – royal regiments and grenadiers," said Mary proudly.

"You mean those guys who wear the funny looking hats and stand in front of the palace gate all day?"

Mary laughed, "Yes, those guys. Come on, if we hurry, we can just catch the changing of the guard. You don't want to miss that!"

They dashed across the square, around a pair of wooden barricades and came to a halt in front of the tall iron gates blocking the entrance to Buckingham Palace. A pair of solemn, silent guards stood at attention on each side of the gate; their bright red tunics with gold shoulder epaulets shined in the sunlight. Alex and Sam studied the guards frozen in place, tight chin straps holding their black fur beefeater hats in place. The brothers shared a moment of silent communication as they each glanced at each other and then away to keep from laughing.

Mary caught the unspoken exchange as she wagged a finger at each of them, "Have some respect, please."

"Sorry." Sam snorted a laugh then said, "Doesn't look like any kind of uniform I'd want to be seen in, let alone fight in."

"Well, of course not! These are ceremonial guards. It's an honor to be a Palace guard," she admonished him.

They watched the salute, rifles on shoulders, and the changing of guards' ceremony then moved on down the street.

"Where to next?" asked Alex.

"Let's take the bus straight away toward Westminster Bridge. You'll want to see the Thames and Big Ben," Mary said.

"Hey, here comes one of those double-decker buses. Can we hop on that?" asked Sam.

"Yes; just stand near the street and hold out your arm. The driver will stop."

The bus pulled over, and the three quickly climbed on board, taking seats as the conductor made his way down the aisle to collect fares. Sam grinned as he slid closer to Mary and left the opposite place open for Alex. Alex saw the move and raised an eyebrow, shot his brother a look, silently conceding Sam had won a point.

"Two shillings, mate," said the conductor.

Sam offered various coins in the palm of his hands. "Which one is a shilling?" he asked. "Take what you need to pay for the three of us."

The conductor nodded and plucked a few coins from Sam's hand. "That'll do. Have a good day."

"Thanks," said Sam as he leaned back in his seat and smiled at Mary.

"How far do we ride this?" asked Alex.

"Not too far. We can hop off before crossing the bridge and walk from there."

"Okay, lead the way."

As the bus drove them closer to the riverfront, the damage to the city became more evident. Once graceful Georgian architecture with ironwork railings and balconies now stood as skeletons with bombed-out roofs; others had sustained blasts that sliced through the brick and mortar, halving them like a knife going through butter. Empty shells where once families lived or citizens worked, now stood as grave witnesses to the horrors of war. Several structures had windows boarded up with sheets of plywood; others stood unscathed but bursting at the seams as multiple families now occupied space previously reserved for one. Sandbags were stacked high to create protective walls near subway entrances, now bomb shelters.

Alex quietly stared out the bus window at the wreckage and havoc; he knew his bombing had created similar scenes in many cities of Germany and throughout Europe. He turned in his seat; he didn't want to witness the reality that haunted his dreams.

"Geez, I had no idea London looked this bad. I mean, you hear stories but until you see it…wow. We had Pearl and all, but nothing like this," Sam said.

"You really are a dumb kid at times," Alex told Sam. "What d'ya think happens in war?" He shook his head morosely and turned away from his innocent brother.

"My family lived about two blocks from here," Mary said softly. "You, Americans, are lucky the war isn't being fought on your shores."

"Guess you're right," said Sam. "Gee, I'm sorry."

"No need to be. Come on now, this is supposed to be a holiday!" Mary scolded. "Stop looking so glum."

Through all the bombing and horrors that the Nazis had thrown at them, Londoners had held on; came through with even more resolve to not only survive but to defeat their enemy. People went about their business. Street vendors still hawked their wares on corners, enticing customers to shop their black market produce and goods.

Mary explained that rationing was stricter in England than in the United States as she pointed to the sellers; fresh fruits and vegetables were a luxury for civilians as troops received priority shipments of food. Local constables added to their duties the enforcement of ration books and were forced to arrest any black-market profiteers.

They rode past Kensington Gardens; clouds gathered overhead, blotting out their sunshine, and produced a light mist. So typical for a London summer.

"Even the royal flower beds now grow vegetables needed for the war effort. Cabbage and carrots have taken the place of roses and petunias," Mary explained. "I've got a tiny plot at home too."

The British government promoted a *Dig for Victory* campaign to encourage people to grow their own food, similar to the *Victory Gardens* back in the States. The royal family supported the effort with their own garden example.

Mary reached for the signal cord above her head and tugged lightly. "We need to hop off just ahead."

"Gotcha," said Sam as he rose and made his way toward the front of the bus to exit.

Security was tighter along the Thames and more evident with barbed wire strung along the riverfront blocking access to the Houses of Parliament in Westminster. The massive tower at the north end of Parliament housed the clock and bell that tourists called Big Ben. Sam and Alex each craned their necks to look upward at the impressive clock face atop the tower.

"Has it been hit by any of the bombing raids?" asked Alex as he pointed to the clock.

"Once. One of its clock faces on the east side has been blown out, but that's all," replied Mary.

"Guess the Luftwaffe's aim ain't so good if that's all they managed to do," Sam said with a laugh.

"Did you know? Big Ben's bell kept chiming right on through that raid too. I rather like that act of defiance," Mary told them proudly.

"Huh. No kidding!" exclaimed Sam.

"If we just make our way down this lane, you can see Westminster Abbey and then maybe stop in one of the pubs nearby," Mary suggested.

"Now you're talking," said Alex. "I'm dying of thirst; a pub sounds like a great idea."

"All right then, won't be but a few minutes from here."

The men spoke all the appropriate compliments about the historic church as Mary explained the significance of Westminster Abbey; its many kings and queens buried there or who had been married there. Mary saw the men's eyes glaze over and caught Sam yawning. It was obvious that both brothers were more interested in the promised pub than continuing to play tourist in the ancient cathedral.

"Ah, I see. Shall I stop playing tour guide and lead the way to the Red Lion?" asked Mary.

"If you please," said Sam as he grinned at her.

"Right. Straight away then. Just down this lane."

The Red Lion Pub sat on a brick-paved lane so narrow that only a cart and buggy could pass down it, definitely no room for a modern vehicle. The din of voices and glass mugs clinking heralded the thirsty travelers as they entered the establishment. The tavern was crowded with both locals and servicemen who roared in laughter or slung insults at each other, their voices rose and fell in waves. The Brits and Americans were both well represented; uniforms of various colors and insignia sat shoulder to shoulder at the bar.

Alex and Sam pushed through the crowd, guiding Mary to a small vacant table. They settled onto some hard, wooden chairs as a plump gentleman with a soiled white apron tied about his rotund belly approached their location.

"Need a menu or just drinks?" he asked.

"What do you think? Everybody hungry?" asked Alex.

"I could do with a bite," answered Mary as she cast a questioning look toward Sam.

"Yeah, sure. What's the special today?" Sam asked the barkeep.

"Well, we've got bangers and mash or shepherd's pie today, mate."

"Hmm, I'm not a big fan of lamb, so I guess bangers and mash it is," Sam ordered.

"Make that three," said Alex as he indicated both he and Mary would have the same. "Okay with you, Mary?"

"Yes, that's fine, thank you."

"What'll you have, ale or stout?" asked the waiter.

"Have any chilled lager?" asked Alex. "I can't get used to your warm beer."

"We try to keep a nice cold lager on hand for you Yanks, since you boys aren't man enough to drink a good strong stout, like our Guinness." The barkeep laughed at his own joke and slapped Sam on the back as he pushed his way back toward the bar counter and kitchen entrance.

"Yeah, well, just watch some Brit try and smoke one of our American cigarettes and cough his lungs out. Guess they just aren't man enough to take our strong tobacco," Alex defended his fellow

Americans in the room; his belligerent voice rising in volume with each word.

Mary glanced from one brother to the other then shook her head. Alex displayed a sudden antagonism that both surprised and dismayed her. However, Sam's silence puzzled her more.

Sam didn't add to his brother's argument and chose to watch quietly; his eyes reflected his disapproval. It wasn't his place to criticize his older brother and chastise him in front of strangers. He raised his eyes toward Mary and met her questioning stare before he nervously looked away. How could he explain to her that the man he knew before the war would never have acted like this?

Their drinks were served; Alex and Sam quickly lifted mugs to quell their thirsts while Mary sipped hers daintily.

Sam downed half his stein of the cool ale. He wiped his mouth with the back of his hand, "Man that was good."

"I needed that," agreed Alex. "Barkeep bring two more!" he called as he waved his empty mug in the air.

"Hey, slow down," warned Sam.

"Who are you to tell me how much to drink? I'll have ten more if it suits me," growled Alex.

"What the hell's gotten into you?" Sam stared at his brother. "I'm sorry Mary. I must apologize for our bad manners again."

Mary sat with her hands folded in her lap; she had no words for what had suddenly become an awkward situation.

"Perhaps this wasn't such a good idea," she directed her comment to Sam as she watched Alex elbow his way into the men crowded at the bar. "I think we should leave as soon as our meal is finished."

"I really am sorry, Mary. I don't know what's gotten into him. I feel terrible about this," Sam stammered.

Alex made his way back across the crowded pub; one arm draped across the shoulders of a fellow American soldier that he dragged toward their table.

"Hey, look who I found!" he exclaimed as he drew the soldier toward Sam and Mary.

"No, it can't be – Chris Hartman, you old so and so. What are you doing in England?" Sam jumped up and greeted his friend with a handshake and slap on the back.

"Same as you, fighting the damn war!" answered Hartman.

"If you aren't a sight for sore eyes. That an airborne patch I see on your sleeve?" asked Sam.

"You bet. Airborne all the way; I'm with the *Screaming Eagles* 101st. But hey, you guys going to introduce me to this pretty lady?"

"Sorry, Mary, this is Christopher Hartman – my best friend and neighbor back home in Wyoming. Chris, this is Mary Barnes. She's with the British ATS; drives generals around," Sam winked at Mary as he made the introductions. He watched Chris smile broadly at Mary and hold her hand a bit too long in what should have been a brief handshake.

"All right, enough of that. Go get your own girl," Sam admonished jokingly.

Alex finished the third stein of beer then slammed it down on the table. "So, tell me why anyone would want to jump out of a perfectly good airplane? You must be nuts or something."

"Maybe something like that. But man, look at you, flying those big birds!" Chris said as he punched Alex in the upper arm.

Platters of tantalizing hot food were placed before the three seated at the table. Steam rose above the sausage links and scoops of mashed potatoes.

"You want some?" asked Sam. "Smells pretty good. I'll share; let's get an empty plate."

"Thanks, but that's okay. I'll need to be going soon; I'm with some of my squad," Chris said. "Oh hey, forgot to tell you, it's like old home week. Guess who else is over here? Would you believe…?" he was interrupted by a voice calling his name.

"Yo, Hartman! Get your tail moving; we're leaving," shouted a tall sergeant in a similar uniform and insignia.

"Gotta go. Stay safe. See you both when this is over," Chris Hartman said as he shook hands and hurried out the pub door with a final wave goodbye.

"Funny running into Chris Hartman. Sure was good to see him again," Sam said and smiled. "Small world."

"Yeah, small world," Alex slurred as he picked up his fork and ate a piece of sliced sausage.

They ate in silence for several minutes; satisfying growling bellies and doing the food justice. Alex ordered another beer, causing Mary to dart a second questioning glance at Sam.

Sam raised his eyebrows and shook his head in answer to her silent question. He finished his plate and waved to the waiter for the bill, paying for his meal and Mary's.

"Hey brother, you're on your own for your meal and the beer. I've taken care of Mary and me. I don't have enough cash to cover your bar bill," Sam told Alex.

"Don't worry about it. I've got it."

"Good. Mary and I are leaving. We're going to hop on the next train north. You coming?"

"Not until I finish my beer. Think I'll stay," Alex said.

"You sure? Think you can get back to base okay?"

"I don't need you babysitting me. Go ahead, just go," Alex shouted above the noise of the pub crowd.

Mary and Sam slowly made their way to the door with one backward look at Alex draining his mug and reaching for another.

Another person sat observing the Dunlap brothers from a dark corner of the pub. His thin lips curled into a sneer as he watched the pair and hatched a plan of his own.

Chapter 8

As they boarded the northbound train to Peterborough, Sam kept looking over his shoulder, hoping to see Alex enter the train station.

"Do you think we should have left him there?" asked Mary, a worried frown upon her face.

"You heard him; he doesn't need anyone. I don't know what to say. He's changed, Mary." Sam dragged his fingers through his hair, then dropped his hand in despair.

"I'm sure it was just the drink; too much alcohol," Mary said as she laid a hand on Sam's arm to try and offer some comfort.

"There wasn't any need for him to act that way. He was fine earlier, then suddenly he turned into someone that I don't know and don't care to know."

They took their seats and watched silently as the station slipped from their sights while the locomotive gained speed and headed northward.

Sam glanced about the carload of people; everyone going home from a day in London. Some were probably workers, others out for a day shopping with parcels tucked under their arms. He leaned closer to Mary so he could speak more privately.

"Bet you're sorry you ever agreed to come out with the Dunlap boys. Some date, huh?" Sam asked in a low voice. "I'm really sorry we messed up your day."

"You did nothing of the kind. I enjoyed being with you, Samuel Dunlap. As for Alex, I'm not one to judge."

"Yeah well, he's my brother and I can tell you … he was acting like an ass. Never thought I'd say it, but he's become just like our old man."

"Is that a bad thing?" asked Mary.

"Sure is. My father is a mean spirited, bad-tempered man quick to accuse and slow to forgive. Looks like Alex is cut from the same cloth."

"Tell me about your home, the ranch," Mary said as she reached for Sam's hand to hold and direct his attention away from the darkening landscape rushing by and his even darker thoughts.

Sam turned to Mary and studied the petite girl next to him; tendrils of silky auburn hair had escaped their pins. So kind and gentle. Her hazel eyes reminded Sam of autumn forests changing colors from deep green to sparkling gold. He was mesmerized as he stared intensely into those pools. He dared to touch the smooth, creamy skin gracing her cheeks; his lean fingers brushed a curl behind her ear as he raised her chin to press a light kiss upon her rosy lips.

Mary closed her eyes, his tender kiss a whisper clinging to her mouth. The moment was so sweet and unexpected. "Sam, um, I…"

"Sorry Mary, I shouldn't have done that."

"No, it's just…I mean, that is, I didn't mind," Mary said softly, stumbling over her words as she tried to sort out the myriad of emotions rushing through her head. Unwanted visions of Timmy suddenly invaded her thoughts, and she guiltily pulled her hand away.

Sam watched her face as she spoke. His mind had latched onto a spark of hope with her words until he saw a flicker of sadness cross her eyes as she turned from him. Her actions confused him; he thought she welcomed his kiss. Was he wrong?

"Sam, I like you very much. But I don't really know you yet and would like to take time to do so. Do you understand?"

"Of course. I didn't mean to make any fast moves on you. Sorry. I just got caught up in the moment; you're so pretty, Mary, you make me forget myself."

Mary blushed at his compliment. She could see in his eyes that he spoke from the heart. It wasn't some line a soldier laid on a local gal.

"Now it's my turn to apologize. I liked your kiss, I did, but I lost my fiancée in the war and I'm not quite over it. Someday, I'll tell you more. I just can't say more now," Mary told him quietly as she squeezed his hand and watched for his reaction.

"Boy, am I dumb. It figures that a good-looking gal like you would have a boyfriend or someone special. I guess I overstepped," Sam said as he bent forward, arms resting on knees, head hung low. If he could fall into a deep hole at that moment, it would be the only thing that would save him.

"Sam, please don't beat yourself up. You couldn't possibly know; it's been two years since Timmy was killed in action. I just have to learn to cope and move on with my life. Some days I think I'm actually doing that, and then without warning, a word or look will bring him rushing back into my mind."

"Do you want me to leave? I can sit somewhere else," Sam asked, his expression as forlorn as the gray misty skies outside.

"No, I don't want you to leave unless you want to."

"All right. I'll ride with you as far as the Cambridge station. I need to get back to base; my leave ends at midnight. Will you be okay going on to Peterborough by yourself?"

"Of course. It's only one stop further up the line. I'll be fine," Mary said as her eyes darted about the train car noting how many people were present. She was reassured when she recognized two elderly ladies from her village and thought they were likely riding to Peterborough. "I see some of my neighbors on board; we'll all be hopping off at the same station. I shan't be alone."

"Are you sure? I hate leaving you like this, but it will save me a couple hours if I can get off at my own stop. I'm not much of a gentleman; can't even escort my lady home to her door."

"I understand, really, I do." She clutched his arm, a twinkle in her eyes, "Sam, in two weeks, I'm working at the USO dance being held at Stanton Hall in Huntingdon. Do you think you could come?" Mary asked.

"How could a guy turn down an invitation from such a sweet gal? If I can get away, I'd love to come. What date is the dance?" His mood turned right side up again.

"July second, a Friday night. I think the USO wants to make it a bit of a celebration for your Independence Day." Mary laughed as she admitted, "Naturally, we don't celebrate that date in England."

"Ah, yeah, I can see where you wouldn't," Sam agreed and laughed along with her.

"You never did tell me about your home," Mary reminded Sam.

"Well, that might have to wait until our next meeting, looks like we're rolling into Cambridge station. Gosh, I hate to leave you Mary," Sam said as he moved into the aisle.

Mary raised her head to look up at him as he made ready to leave. Sam seized the moment to lean down and press another light kiss to her moist lips.

"Next time, we'll spend the day together by ourselves," he promised.

"I'll look forward to it," she told him with a big smile and sparkling eyes.

London fog, thick as pea soup, shrouded the crowded King's Crossing train station as Alex waited on the train platform. He stood among people ready to board the last northbound train of the evening. He felt himself being jostled and pushed about in the throng and twice caught himself from stumbling. He wasn't so drunk as not to be able to stand upright. What the hell?

The train approached the station, blowing steam from its whistle with a single toot and began to slow. Alex now teetered precariously near the platform edge overlooking the rails as he felt a hand on the center of his back.

"Hey, watch it buddy!" Alex yelled. He twisted to see who was behind him when he was suddenly grabbed by a pair of strong arms and hauled away from the dangerous edge.

"Come on, Mack. Let's see some ID," demanded a Military Policeman as he dragged Alex through the crowd and back into the station building.

The locomotive had come to a stop and passengers boarded, grumbling and tired, eager to get home. A man slipped into the rear door of the train car, found an empty row of seats then watched the MP take Dunlap into custody. He missed this time, but there'd be another.

Alex stumbled into a chair and dug out his wallet with his Army identification. He pulled out his dog tags for the MP to verify name, rank, and serial number.

"Good thing I came along when I did Lieutenant, or you'd be plastered all over that track now. You trying to commit suicide or something? Looked like you were ready to jump."

"Are you crazy? I wasn't planning on jumping in front of a damn train. I was pushed. Didn't you see the guy behind me?" Alex demanded.

"No, I didn't see anybody but you ready to step off that edge. It's a wonder you can even stand at all. You smell like a brewery. Think you better sleep it off tonight in the brig," the military policeman told him as he climbed into a waiting Jeep.

Alex was placed in the rear seat with a second MP next to him as they sped off to the American headquarters outside London and the Army stockade. A fierce headache throbbed behind his eyes, and with every pothole the Jeep hit, Alex thought his head would explode. *"God, he couldn't be more miserable,"* he thought as his hands pressed against his temples in a futile attempt to hold his head together.

In the morning, Alex knew he'd have to call his commander, Major Simpson, to get bailed out. His stupid actions were going to put him in real trouble with Simpson. If he were lucky, he'd get grounded. If they really wanted to punish him, they'd make him fly again.

Either way, it didn't look good.

Chapter 9

Two days later and two nights spent in the stockade, Alex stood at attention in front of Major Simpson's desk for twenty minutes, his knees threatening to lock, as the major studied the papers before him. He waited to hear his punishment for the drunk and disorderly charges that were written up by the military police at HQ.   No one believed him when he swore that he hadn't planned on jumping in front of that train but was actually pushed from behind.

"Do you have anything to say for yourself, Dunlap?" demanded the major. Simpson leaned back in his chair and frowned at the young lieutenant before him.

"Sir, I admit I had too much to drink, but I wasn't overly drunk. I was trying to get back to base by taking the train. I was pushed from behind, maybe it was too crowded or an accident, but I swear I did not intend suicide. Those MP's wouldn't listen to me."

"It would seem you did more than talk."

"Uh, well, I might have punched one of them when they tried to shove me into a cell," Alex said as he shifted his weight from foot to foot and cast his eyes downward.

"Well, Dunlap, I have no choice but to charge you with 'actions unbecoming an officer.' The MP has agreed not to press charges, or you'd be facing an assault offense too. We are at war, lieutenant, take the fight to the enemy, not our own servicemen." The major rose and paced his narrow office before turning to face Alex again.

Alex remained at rigid attention, his eyes now forward, his breath held as he waited to hear his fate.

"I'm busting your rank down to Second Lieutenant, Dunlap, and you'll be written up, but I'm not grounding you. We need every crew member, especially bombardiers; the war mission is too critical to lose even one. I'm putting you back on flight status tomorrow."

"Yessir, thank you, sir." Alex saluted smartly.

"And you better stay sober, young man," cautioned Major Simpson as he returned the salute. "Dismissed."

Sam and Pete waited with members of their ground crew as multiple squadrons from the 78th Fighter Group returned to base following the morning's mission. Sam held a hand above his eyes to shield them from the glaring sun as he counted the planes coming in for landing.

"There's Anderson, here comes Cameron; come on boys. Just two more and my squadron's all back," stated Pete as he watched the fighters land.

"Five, six, here comes seven," Sam counted as he stared at the sky. "Uh oh, we got one smoking. That doesn't look good," Sam commented as he watched a Thunderbolt dip its wings and bounce landing gear once then twice on the hard tarmac before it slammed into the ground, nose down.

"Come on boys, let's give the fire crews a hand!" yelled Pete and Sam as they sprinted toward the wrecked aircraft.

The pilot tried frantically to get out of his plane; the plastic canopy locked and wouldn't open as flames began to ignite. The pilot screamed as smoke filled his cockpit.

Sam reached the plane first, a large wrench in hand, with one thought – break that damn cover and help that man out. He climbed onto the slanted wing, reached the cockpit and motioned to the pilot as he used the heavy wrench to hammer the lock with all his strength. Sam could feel the heat from the flames; smoke filled his nostrils, stung his eyes, and blurred his vision. He hit the canopy several times before the plastic cracked and the lock gave way. The trapped pilot and Sam both pushed on the broken canopy, freeing it.

Blasts of water from the fire hoses drenched Sam and the injured pilot as they staggered away from the burning plane. Medics ran up to them and led them toward a waiting ambulance.

"Take care of him. I don't need that," Sam told the medic who was trying to force Sam onto a gurney.

"Sergeant, let me do my job. Your hands are badly burned. You're coming with me," the medical corpsman commanded as he pushed Sam into the ambulance.

Sam looked down at his hands, surprised to see the blackened and red skin. "All right, all right. Somebody let my crew know where the hell I am," Sam yelled back to the men gathered about the wrecked plane.

Two hours later, Captain Barnett approached Sam half reclining on a narrow cot in the hospital ward. His hands were bandaged past his wrists, and he sported a few cuts and minor burns on his face and neck.

"How do you feel, sergeant?" asked the captain as he slowly sat on the edge of the bed.

"I'm okay, sir, just a bit groggy from some stuff they gave me for pain. I'll get back to work," Sam said as he tried to rise and fell back again. His voice sounded strange to his own ears, distant as if coming from a tunnel.

The captain chuckled as he pressed a hand on Sam's shoulder and guided his head back onto the pillow. "Think you better stay here for just a while longer, Sgt. Dunlap. That's an order."

A doctor read the clipboard attached to the foot of Sam's bed, noted the time then checked on Sam's vitals as he examined his patient who had finally succumbed to sleep.

"How bad is it?" asked Captain Barnett.

"Oh, he'll be okay in a week or two. He's got some bad burns on his hands, mostly second degree, but there are a few spots of third-degree burns we're concerned with. He's under morphine right now for the pain; I doubt he'll recall your visit come morning."

"Take good care of him, doctor. He's one of my best crew chiefs and we need him." The captain patted Sam's shoulder affectionately. "He's special, this one, like a son to me. I want him to have the best care."

"You can count on it, sir," answered Dr. Cooper.

"How's that young pilot that Sam pulled to safety?" asked the captain.

"He'll make it. He's in our burn unit. We'll be shipping him stateside on the next Red Cross hospital ship. He's lucky to be alive."

"I'm glad he'll have a future, and his life wasn't wasted on some tarmac. Thank God Sam got to him when he did," exclaimed Captain Barnett. "That boy deserves a medal; they both do, and I'll see to it."

The captain shook the doctor's hand and left the hospital ward, heading to the hangars to hear more details of the crash and to check on the rest of his men and the status of his fighters.

Sam walked into the repair hangar, noted which aircraft were being worked on and which members of his ground crew were around. His hands were still heavily bandaged, but after three days in sickbay, he couldn't take just lying about anymore.

"Hey Sarge! How ya doing?" greeted Joe Carter, one of the ground crew in the 82nd squadron.

"Not too bad, Joey. What's the deal here?" asked Sam.

"Got a broken wheel strut on this one. Cameron's bird needs some engine tuning, running rough and pistons been misfiring. Nothing major."

"Okay, good. You get Mike Burnside to do the weld and have Sergeant Shultz check it when he's finished. You okay with handling Cameron's engine?"

"Yeah, sure, no problem."

He spoke to a few of the other crew members as he inspected some of the work being done and made suggestions on a few others.

"Uh-huh, thought I'd find you here," said Pete as he wiped greasy hands on a towel hanging from his belt and walked toward his friend.

"Yeah well, where else would I be?" Sam asked as he watched everyone busy, going about the business of keeping these aircraft fit to fly.

"Doctor say it's okay for you to be here?"

"There's nothing wrong with me but some burns on my hands. My mind still works, you know. Just 'cause I can't hold a socket wrench doesn't mean I can't direct someone else."

"Okay, I hear you. What do you need from me?"

"Check up on the weld Burnside is putting on the wheel strut, would you? Make sure it's solid and will hold. That's all, I guess. My team knows what they're doin', and it doesn't look like we've got any major repairs right now."

"No problem. Now why don't you get out of here? Didn't I hear Captain Barnett tell you to take a few days leave?"

"Damn, everyone wants to get rid of me," Sam joked. "You're worse than a mother hen."

Sam headed back to the barracks, changed into some clean khakis then walked over to the canteen where the sole telephone booth stood.

He slid a coin into the slot and listened as it dropped; a dial tone hummed a few seconds later, allowing him to dial the number Mary had given him. He waited anxiously as the phone rang on the other end of the line. She was likely on duty. What chance would he have of finding her home? The line rang five, six times; Sam took the phone away from his ear and was about to hang up when he heard a familiar voice.

"Hello? Hello?" Mary asked breathlessly.

"Mary? That you? It's Sam," he said as he smiled into the mouthpiece of the phone, happy to hear her voice.

"Oh Sam. I thought I heard the bell; I was just coming in," Mary explained. "How are you?"

"I was wondering if you had any free time. Can I come up to see you?"

"That would be lovely. I'm off duty today, back on tomorrow though. I've been out trying to buy what bits and bobs I could find."

"I can hop a train now and be there in an hour or so. What d'ya say?" Sam pressed the receiver tightly against his ear, willing her to say the words he wanted to hear.

"Aren't you on duty?" Mary inquired. "Can you just take off now?"

"I'm on leave a few days," Sam said. "I'll explain when I see you."

"Well, all right. Come ahead. I'll fix us a lovely tea."

"Right. I'm going to try and catch the next train."

Sam hung up and ran a half jog to the base entrance. He spied a couple of guys climbing into an idling Jeep and called out to them.

"Hey, can you give me a lift into town to the train station? I need to catch the next train north."

"Sure, hop in Sarge. What's the hurry? You got a pretty gal waiting at the other end of the line?" The corporal laughed as he put the Jeep in gear, and they rumbled away.

"How'd you know?"

Chapter 10

Sam knocked on the faded blue door of number twelve Midsomer Way. Waiting with arms behind his back, he grinned from ear to ear at first sight of Mary's shining face as she opened the portal wide.

"Hello Mary! I made it."

"Obviously," she laughed. "Come in, please. I'll just put the kettle on, and we can have tea."

Sam followed Mary into the small but cozy flat. His eyes scanned the sparse furnishings, taking in the crocheted doilies adorning the arms of the single stuffed chair. A hurricane lamp set on a small table next to a worn settee; two odd glass candlesticks with partially burned tapers adorned a scarred mahogany sideboard. A vase of daisies attempted to brighten the tiny space.

Mary stepped into the room and caught Sam's perusal of her battered furnishings. "It isn't much, I know. But…oh my God, Sam! You're hurt. What happened to your hands?"

Sam had forgotten his bandages as he raised his hand to her. "Oh these. It's nothing; some burns. I'll be fine. Don't worry about them."

"Come sit down. Are you in any pain?" Mary asked, tenderly. She motioned Sam to join her on the short settee. Worry lines wrinkled her brow and tears moistened her eyes as she looked at his poor hands and wrapped her arms about his shoulders.

Sam engulfed her in his strong arms, returning her welcoming hug as he held his injured hands away from her body. Would she be repulsed by his touch?

The tea kettle whistled and drew Mary's attention. She pulled away to enter the kitchen, removed the pot from the electric hot plate, and poured the boiling water into a porcelain teapot to steep the scoop of black tea leaves. She placed the floral-patterned teapot on a tray, found two cups without chips, and added a plate of scones with jam.

Mary placed the tray on the living room sideboard then poured cups of tea for herself and Sam. She glanced at his hands then looked away, catching her lower lip between her teeth.

"Can you manage?" she asked as she held the steaming cup before him.

"Yeah, I'll make do. Promise not to spill it."

"Are you sure you're okay? Tell me what happened? Why didn't you call me sooner?"

"It's only been a few days; really, it isn't serious. We had one of our planes crash land, and I helped the pilot escape the cockpit. There was a fire, that's how I got burnt. Doctor says the bandage can come off in another week."

"You were very brave," Mary told him as she pressed her palm gently against his cheek.

Sam turned his head away, breaking the contact. "No, I'm not brave. If I were brave, I'd be fighting Germans on the front lines, not playing it safe in a repair hangar."

"What you do is important," Mary argued. "You're doing your part. Would the war end sooner if you were being shot at? How would that help?"

"You're a woman, you don't understand," Sam said in a harsh voice. "I feel like a coward."

"Now you listen to me, Samuel Dunlap. You are no coward. Do you think that pilot would be alive today if you had been in a foxhole somewhere?"

"Somebody would have done the same."

Mary held his face with both of her hands and stared intently into his eyes. "You don't know that. That pilot is alive because of you. Only you were brave enough to risk flames and certain danger. That is not the act of a coward. I won't listen to that kind of talk."

"I think you see more in me than what's there."

"And I think you need to stop seeing yourself through someone else's eyes. Be your own man, Sam, not what your brother or even your father thinks you are."

"You don't know my family," Sam said as he paced the confines of the narrow room.

"Then tell me about them," Mary demanded.

"I don't know where to begin. Alex and me, we grew up on a cattle ranch in the high plains of Wyoming. My grandparents set out from St. Louis in covered wagons back in the 1890s on the Oregon Trail. They broke down and never got to Oregon, but they did file a claim on a piece of land in Wyoming and struggled to build a home and raise some cattle. My father used to tell us stories when we were kids; about the gunfights and wild times back then. Never had much and worked damn hard for what we do have."

"Sounds like you hail from good pioneer stock. I've read stories of your American West," commented Mary as she listened to Sam's story.

"I think they were from Scotland originally, my grandparents. My grandmother's maiden name was Dougherty. I don't know anything about her folks or even what part of Scotland they came from. Maybe someday I'll try to find out."

"And what about your own father and mother? You said Alex acts like your father. Why is that?" prompted Mary.

"For as long as I can remember, Alex was always the favored son that could do no wrong, and I could do no right. My old man was strict and took a strap to me more times than I care to recall, especially when he drank; didn't matter what the occasion was. Alex used to try to shield me; he took the blame a lot of times. I probably could not have survived my childhood without him. He's the oldest son, so he'll inherit the ranch when the time comes."

"What will you do? Will you go back home to live on the ranch too or live somewhere else?"

"I dunno. Ranching is all I know, that and being a grease monkey. 'Suppose I could open my own repair garage and make a living. Haven't really thought about it."

"What about your mother, Sam? You haven't spoken about her. What's she like?" asked Mary.

"My mother, Katie Canavan, married my father in what you would say was an arranged marriage. Their parents had pledged them both as children. She's a quiet woman; I don't think I ever heard her argue with my father. Whatever he says is law, and if she feels differently, I've never heard her express an opinion. My mother leads a lonely life; I think her children were everything to her. Now that we're grown and are out of the house, I honestly don't know what her life must be like. Funny, now that I'm away from there, I can see that more clearly."

"We don't often really know our parents," Mary spoke softly as she stared at the framed photograph of two people smiling at the camera.

She reached for the picture and pointed to the pair. "These are my parents, Edith and Robert Barnes. They married young, very much in love, had a big church wedding and I came along less than a year later. They were consumed with each other; always together, not letting other people get close. Sometimes I even felt like an intruder and yet, I miss them terribly."

"I'm sorry. You said they were killed in the blitz? How did you … that is, uh, were you there too?"

"No, I was working as a land girl then up on a farm in Nottingham. They were alone in the townhouse in London when the house suffered a direct hit. I was told later that they had died together," Mary told Sam as she placed the photograph back on the table and wiped the tears silently sliding down her cheek.

Sam cleaned her face with the back of his gauze wrapped hand. "I would have liked to have met them. They produced a wonderful daughter." He gave her a tender smile. "No more tears."

Mary returned his smile and nodded shakily.

Hampered by the thick bandage, Sam tried to drag his fingers through his hair, as was his habit but was stopped by Mary's gentle hand as she stroked his forehead and drew his hand downward. Their eyes met as he brushed a kiss across her fingertips. Neither moved; the only sound in the room, the ticking of a clock, and the soft breath shared by two. Sam leaned toward Mary and claimed her lips in a kiss that blossomed from sweet to demanding.

Mary caressed Sam's cheek, her hand dropping to his shoulder as she surrendered herself into his embrace. They clung to each other as two people swept away in a storm of passion.

Sam was the first to come up for air. His eyes searched Mary's. Did she experience the same strong pull as he did?

"Mary?" Sam started, unable to express himself in words. In awe, he touched her hair; his bandaged hand caressed the length of her arm.

Mary tried to calm her breathing; her heart still raced in her chest. She laid a tremulous hand upon his broad chest.

"I know. I can't explain it; I was attracted to you the first time I saw you with mud splattered all over your uniform. What is it between us?" she wondered.

"I want you Mary, but not like this," he said as he lifted his wrapped hands. "When I make love to you, I want to be able to touch you and feel your silky skin. I need to make you mine," Sam whispered.

His lips moved across her cheek, pressed butterfly kisses against her neck then returned to claim her lips once more. He was intoxicated with the scent and taste of her.

Mary blushed at his passionate words and promise of more to come. With both hands, she pushed lightly on his shoulders, held him away as she floated back to earth and tried to calm her spinning world.

"We must slow down; it's too soon. I don't seem able to think straight when I'm around you," Mary admitted.

"I care for you like I've never cared for anyone before. I've confided in you, things I've never told anyone before. I can't begin to tell you how important you are to me, Mary. I realize we haven't known each other very long, but sometimes that's all it takes."

Sam pulled Mary into his arms again, cuddled her to him against his chest, guided her head to rest upon his shoulder. He picked up her hand and studied the fragile bones, the smooth skin, and carefully trimmed nails – so feminine and dainty. He kissed her palm lightly and heard her sigh softly. They held each other for a time, reluctant to let go, but knowing they must.

Finally, Sam roused himself and stood, pulling Mary to her feet. "I've got to go back to base and you've got duty tomorrow. It will seem like an eternity, but I'll see you again next week at the USO."

"You're coming?" Mary asked.

"Yeah, if you're going to be there. I expect you to save all your dances for me. I promise not to step all over your toes, although I'm not a very good dancer."

"All right, Sam Dunlap, I promise all my dances to you." Mary's smile lit up her entire face as she stood on tiptoes to kiss him goodbye. Her eyes twinkled as she admitted, "I'm glad you came today."

"You have no idea how special this day has been for me. Thank you," Sam told her as he slowly opened the door and waved goodbye.

The ground crews were kept busy as the fighters scrambled every day to escort the heavy bombers on another mission. Sam and Pete worked throughout the long nighttime hours with every available crew member to patch up, repair, and refuel aircraft so they'd be ready for the next dawn sortie. The long hours and lack of sleep were taking their toll as tempers flared, and men grumbled, fistfights breaking out over minor things.

"Keep your grubby hands off my toolbox, Makenzie; I'm missing my socket wrench. Where is it?" demanded Robbie.

"You're crazy, I don't have your damn tools," shouted James Makenzie. A shoving match ensued as accusations were hurled and each man threw a punch.

Pete and Sam had to rush in and separate the two men before they each got into more trouble than they needed.

"Cool off. Robbie! Is that your damn wrench lying under that cowling cover?" asked Pete as he pushed his mechanic toward the corner.

"Back off, Makenzie. Go take a coffee break. If you guys can't work together, I'll see that one of you gets transferred. That what you want?" ordered Sam.

"No Sarge. We're a team; just don't like being accused of thieving."

"All right. I understand; we're all on edge," Sam said. "Go get some food or some shut-eye."

Robbie and Jimmy walked away together; Sam saw them shake hands and head toward the mess hall.

Sam tried not to think about the fact that every mission the fighters flew meant his brother Alex could be flying as well in the big fortresses. He hadn't spoken to him since they parted in London.

Rained poured down in buckets for three days straight, and Friday was no exception. Meadows, roads and landing strips became muddy bogs. A four-wheel-drive Jeep was the only vehicle able to cut through the muck. Aircraft remained parked on runways and inside hangars.

Flight crews were thrilled to enjoy the downtime; bad weather meant no flying missions. The USO dance became a welcome diversion for the men stationed at Duxford, and Debden RAF as well as Deenethorpe airbases. Groups of men crowded into Stanton Hall at Huntingdon, filling the school's large gymnasium. USO donut dollies manned a booth in one corner of the room; the women handed out warm donuts, cups of coffee, and a friendly welcome to every serviceman. A long table was placed along another wall and held two large punch bowls with cups.

The hall was festooned in red, white, and blue crepe paper and since the colors represented both England and America, all were happy. A pair of flags, the Union Jack and the Stars and Stripes, stood at attention.

Local girls from surrounding areas rode horse-drawn wagons through the heavy rain to arrive at the dance. Their dresses may have been dampened but not their spirits. Everyone chatted animated, excited for the dance and a bit of romance in the arms of a handsome soldier.

Four local musicians crowded onto a makeshift stage erected along one wall. The men, too old for active duty, performed civil defense duties but still enjoyed a toe-tapping rhythm. A small set of drums sat behind and to the side of an old piano with one gentleman playing double bass, and another musician performed double duty on a saxophone and clarinet. Dulcet melodies filled the air as the combo played a popular tune from Benny Goodman. A few dancers took to the floor then more joined them, quickly filling the space, gliding and stepping to the big band music.

Sam and Pete arrived with the men from their squadrons and joined the line formed at the hall entrance. Sam brushed off raindrops clinging to his jacket and for the third time in the past hour, inspected his uniform to ensure it was still neat and clean. He had taken pains to scrub off the previous stains and restore his uniform's proper appearance for the big dance.

A string of ten tickets was being sold for one dollar, a dime a dance, with the proceeds being donated to the Red Cross to help the war effort. Men eagerly bought a fist full of tickets and hurried over to the line of ladies seated along the dance floor. Matrons and young girls alike giggled and blushed as their hands were claimed for a spin around the floor by a dashing soldier.

Sam walked about the room searching for Mary, afraid he might have missed her, or she had been claimed by another soldier. He exhaled his relief when he spotted her serving coffee alongside one of the donut dollies in the corner. He made a beeline to her in four long strides.

"May I have a cup, please?" he asked. His hand caressed hers as he reached across the countertop.

"Oh Sam! I've so glad you made it. I've been watching for you all afternoon," admitted Mary.

"Aha, you have, have you? Well, here I am, how about joining me?" Sam invited her as he held his cup of coffee up and pointed to a pair of empty chairs.

"Miriam, can you take over for me for a few minutes, please?" Mary asked one of the women wearing a Red Cross uniform.

"Of course, go ahead, Mary."

"Thank you. I'll be back to relieve you later."

Sam and Mary took their seats, the coffee was forgotten as they sat holding hands, enjoying the nearness of each other. Sam tried to read Mary's thoughts as he became lost in the depth of her hazel eyes. Mary silently studied Sam - his expression so serious.

"It feels like a month since I've held you," Sam whispered to her as he squeezed her hand.

"The week has been extraordinarily long," agreed Mary. "Maybe we can try a few steps on the dance floor?"

"Like I said, I'm not the best dancer, but at least I'll get to hold you in my arms."

Mary placed her hand along his shoulder as Sam drew her to him and they moved as one across the dance floor to the sweet strains of Glenn Miller's *Moonlight Serenade*. The elderly musicians did their best to play the popular song and were treated to a round of applause from their appreciative audience.

Sam felt a tap on his shoulder, someone wanting to cut in, and turned to find his brother Alex.

"May I?" Alex asked as he reached for Mary's hand and twirled her into his arms, smoothly gliding her into the next dance number. Alex wore his trim officer's dress uniform, the rakish hat with leather brim; he portrayed a dashing sight, so polished and sure of himself. Several female eyes admired him as he took command of the dance floor.

Sam stood alone on the floor as he watched his brother steal Mary away from him. Dancers stepped around him; embarrassed, he made his way back to their empty seats along the wall.

Alex danced with suave confidence; he spun and dipped Mary, eliciting a gasp and squeal of surprise from her. Sam seethed as he stared at the pair. His girl. His brother. He could kill him.

What chance does he have? Of course, Mary would be impressed by Alex; he's an officer, not an enlisted man. He dances like Fred Astaire, not somebody with two left feet. He always could do everything better. How's a guy supposed to compete with someone like that?

Mary and Alex finished their dance as the combo took a ten-minute break. Sam's glum face greeted Mary as she found him among a gathering of people near the punch table.

"Sorry, Sam. I couldn't resist dancing with the prettiest girl here. Mary moves like a dream," Alex commented as he grinned widely and kissed Mary on her cheek.

Mary glanced between San and Alex. She could see the anger building in Sam's eyes.

"Have fun?" Sam gritted. He threw them both an angry look.

Sam glared at Alex while Alex grinned, pleased with himself.

Mary shook her head, appalled. Was he blaming her? "Excuse me, I have to go powder my nose," Mary said quietly as she turned and left the two men standing nose to nose.

Sam watched her trim back and the flick of her auburn hair as she strode away before turning to his brother. "Just what the hell kind of game are you playing?"

"No game. I just decided that I'd like to get to know Mary better."

"You leave her alone," Sam demanded.

"Why? I don't see a ring on her finger. Hey, they got any beer in this place or just this damn fruit juice?" Alex asked as he looked around at the food tables.

"What's the matter, didn't you get your fill of beer in London? So, what happened to your bars? You get busted in rank?" Sam suddenly inquired, noticing the change in Alex's uniform insignia.

"None of your business, brother," Alex sneered.

"Fine. Be that way, just stay the hell away from Mary. She's too good for the likes of you. I used to think I could never measure up to you, but I see I was wrong."

"Well, well. Look who's grown a pair. Army just might make a man of you yet!"

"Go to hell!" Sam growled as he stormed off.

Mary greeted a few of the local village women as she left the restroom. She stopped as she scanned the hall searching for Sam, noting he and Alex were no longer together.

Alex spotted Mary alone and quickly strode to her side.

"How about one more dance, Mary? Sam went outside for some air."

"All right. I suppose so," she agreed reluctantly. She glanced about before accepting her dance partner's hand.

Alex expertly maneuvered her again onto the dance floor, keeping step with the fast-paced music, twirling her in a circle then back into his waiting arms.

As the music slowed, Alex continued to hold Mary in his arms, gliding across the dance floor in smooth practiced steps. He pulled her closer as he whispered in her ear. "Mary, Mary spend the night with me. Let me love you as I yearn to do. I've been a dead man walking, and now for the first time in a long time, I feel alive again because of you."

"I can't Alex. You mustn't say things like that. I'm sorry, but you have the wrong idea about me. I'm not that kind of girl."

"Is it Sam?"

"Yes, um… I promised, that is, we have an understanding," cried Mary as she pulled out of his embrace and rushed outside.

Sam stood in the shelter of the roof's narrow overhang; raindrops pattered on the ground, a burning cigarette hung between his fingers, his thoughts on the woman inside. He looked up in surprise as Mary dashed out the entrance, saw him, and ran straight toward him.

He tossed the butt to the ground, it sizzled on the wet pavement, then held his arms open to Mary. She clung to him as his strong arms enfolded her slender body.

"I thought you'd still be with Alex. I thought you preferred him. What's wrong? Did something happen? Why are you so upset?" Sam demanded worriedly.

She shook her head no but continued to press her head to his shoulder, her arms wrapped around his broad shoulders.

"Stop talking like a fool; I don't want Alex. Just hold me," she murmured.

Sam caressed her smooth cheek, surprised to find it wet with tears, and tilted her face upward to press a kiss upon her lips. Mary sighed and returned the kiss; their embrace tightened.

"I love you, Mary," Sam whispered to her.

"Thought I'd find you two out here," Alex slurred as he walked toward them. He held a silver flask in his hand, raised it to toast the couple then drained its contents.

"Where'd you get the booze?" Sam asked as he watched Alex stumble and try to drink the last drop.

"Amazing what a few bucks can buy when you find the right people. Not that tea party slop they're serving in there."

"You're drunk! You disgust me," Sam said as he pushed Alex aside and tried to guide Mary back toward the doorway.

"Don't leave," Alex cried as he pulled on Mary's arm.

"Leave me be!" Mary tried to get away from him by pulling her arm free and firmly shoved him.

Sam saw red as Alex man-handled Mary. He pulled his arm back and let go with a strong punch aimed at his brother's jaw. His knuckles made contact, and both men yelled in pain. Alex fell to his knees in the rain; Sam pulled back a hand that stung with the abuse of newly healed skin. He stood cradling his damaged hand and stared at the man he once idolized.

"You stay away from Mary. I won't tell you again!"

With one last glance at Alex still sitting in a puddle, Sam pulled Mary against his side as he escorted her into the hall, protecting her from curious onlookers.

His knuckles were scraped and started to bleed.

"We better put some ice on that hand," Mary said as she pressed a napkin against the back of his hand.

"I'll be okay. I shouldn't have left you alone with Alex, and now I've embarrassed you in front of your friends. I'm really sorry."

"Will you please let me administer some first aid on that hand? I don't care what other people think; I'm just sorry to be the one to come between two brothers."

"You didn't; we've been growing apart for years, I just didn't realize how much until now," Sam admitted quietly. Regret and sorrow were reflected in his eyes.

Mary gently placed her hand on his arm. She could see the pain this estrangement caused; two brothers fighting over one woman — her. She didn't like to be the cause. She had to think of some way to mend the rift between Sam and Alex.

"Sam, could you escort me home? I don't want to stay at the dance." Mary picked up her purse from behind the USO table and said her farewells to the other volunteers.

"Yeah, sure, if we can get a taxi or some kind of ride," Sam said.

Mary borrowed a telephone inside the hall and found the number for a local cab company. They had to wait twenty minutes before the car was able to make it to the hall but were grateful for the ride from Huntingdon back to Petersborough.

Mary cuddled against Sam's shoulder during the slow journey. His arm automatically held her to him in a protective manner, but silence enveloped them as each mulled their own thoughts.

Dark, rainy, and dreary – the night reflected the mood of both Sam and Mary as they entered her small flat. Mary secured the blackout curtains then turned on the single lamp in her tiny living room. She turned to Sam, placed a hand upon his chest as she studied his solemn expression.

"I feel terrible about your row with Alex. You have to make things right again; you can't leave bad feelings and harsh words remain between you," Mary said.

"I know. You're right. I lost my temper when I saw him grab you, I'll wait until we both cool down then I'll speak with Alex. I'll make it right."

"Good. I couldn't forgive myself if something happened. You and Alex, you're family; that's what matters. Don't take that for granted; it can be lost in an instant," Mary said as she thought of her parents and loved ones gone.

"I promise I'll go see him. It's just that, well, I was scared Mary. Scared you'd want him and not me. He's an officer and all; I'm nothing," Sam said, dragging his fingers through his hair. He turned his back to her and spoke so low that Mary had to strain to hear.

Mary pulled on Sam's shoulder, forcing him to turn around and face her. "You are **not nothing**. How can you keep talking like that? Didn't we already discuss this? You are twice the man your brother Alex is. Now I won't hear any more of that."

Sam smiled as he watched the heat color her face as her temper flared.

"Guess old habits are hard to break. You're good for me, Mary," he said as he enfolded Mary in a warm embrace.

Sam gently touched her silky hair, rubbing the soft strands between his fingers. He inhaled the faint rose fragrance clinging to her as he spread feathery kisses across her cheek and down her neck only to pause before claiming her lips with his. His mouth slanted across hers, demanding and yet promising more as he felt her return the kiss with a passion of her own. He held her tightly against him; their breaths coming in fast gasps as each struggled to control their emotions.

"Oh Sam… Sam," Mary sighed.

Sam buried his face in her hair as he groaned and dropped his arms. "You must know how much I want you. I love you Mary. With every fiber of my being, I want to stay the night, but I won't. I won't press you. When the time comes, I don't want you to have any doubts; no regrets. I won't compete with a ghost."

Mary ran her hand along his strong jaw, his whisker stubble scratchy against her fingertips. She shook her head and smiled regretfully as a single tear slid down her face.

"I care for you Sam, so much so that it overwhelms me. Just give me a bit more time. Your patience is all I ask," she said.

Sam kissed her once more. "Goodnight, Mary."

Chapter 11

The War dragged on. American bombing attempts had been limited to striking at cities along the German frontier, but on July 24th,1943, the Allies began bombing deeper into Germany reaching Hamburg. The Eighth Air Force and its heavy bombers, with its escort of fighters began to make an impact on Germany's advancing momentum.

Britain's Bomber Command believed a saturation bombing of major German cities was the best way to cripple the Third Reich. However, the American commanders of the Eighth Air Force demanded only precision attacks against selected industrial targets such as oil production facilities or aircraft and ball-bearing plants, not devastating innocent civilian populations. The debate continued at Allied Headquarters as the best use of bomber strength in fighting the war and defeating Germany's air power.

The buildup of more bombing missions was not without consequence. Losses were staggering and morale plummeted as more and more aircrew were killed or captured by the Germans. The Luftwaffe started deliberately targeting particular bombing groups in an effort to eradicate each plane and crew. One group, the 100thBG, earned the ominous nickname of the "Bloody One-Hundred" because of so many casualties, almost ninety percent of its group.

In August, HQ decided to bomb the Ploesti oil fields in Romania. The new Mustang fighters, with their more substantial fuel reserves and longer range, were now deployed to escort the heavy bombers and take the fight to the Luftwaffe. Still, if casualties among the aircrews continued to climb, the air mission itself could be in jeopardy.

A joint meeting had been called for the command fighter and bomber groups; General Eaker would be announcing his new position and the passing of the baton of the Eighth Air Force to Major General Jimmy Doolittle. The meeting was being held at Deenethorpe base. Sam and Pete traveled with their squadrons and members of the 78th Fighter Group from Duxford. Sam hoped he'd find an opportunity to seek out Alex and try to mend fences like he had promised Mary.

Sam listened as the new general explained his policies and mission goals. He tried to keep his attention on the front of the room but surreptitiously searched the large hall for his brother Alex. He was surprised when he spied Mary sitting quietly in a back row along with other female drivers and attendants.

As soon as they were dismissed, Sam joined the mass of men exiting the conference; he was in search of Mary now but still sought his brother too. Spotting the line of parked vehicles alongside the building, Sam headed toward what he hoped would be General Eaker's car and his driver.

Crowds of men finally thinned out as Sam approached Mary. She stood at ease, wearing her smart ATS uniform, waiting on the general. She smiled broadly as he neared.

"Hello!" Mary greeted happily.

"Hello yourself," said Sam as he motioned her closer to the back of the car and out of sight of the doorway. He pulled her into his arms and claimed a quick kiss before their actions were witnessed. "I was looking for Alex, but I'll take your company any day!"

"I've got to go. Here comes General Eaker," Mary whispered as she hurried back to her post.

Mary held the door for the general then hopped into the driver's seat of the sedan. She turned the key to start the engine and heard a grinding noise instead of the hum of a motor.

"I'm sorry, sir. There seems to be some kind of problem," Mary told the general.

General Eaker opened his car door and stepped out. "Call motor pool; see if you can get another vehicle."

Sam witnessed the dilemma and hurried forward. "I'll have a look at her, sir." He saluted smartly then introduced himself. "Sergeant Dunlap, crew chief with the 78th Fighter Group, sir. I can try and see what the problem is if you don't mind waiting a few minutes."

"Fine. Go ahead, sergeant. Miss Barnes, please find me when we're ready to leave. I'll wait inside."

"Yessir. I will, sir," Mary answered.

Sam winked at Mary as he stripped off his jacket and opened the trunk to remove the car jack. Mary had initially parked the car off the side of the single-lane roadway, so Sam didn't worry about blocking any traffic as he worked on the vehicle.

He jacked up the vehicle then flagged down some of his ground crew who had piled into a Jeep heading back to base.

"Hey, Makenzie! You got your toolbox with you in that thing?" yelled Sam.

"Yep, sure do. I keep my eye on my tools."

"How about letting me borrow it, so's I can fix the general's car? Need socket wrenches and I dunno what else yet. I'll see to it that you get it back," Sam promised.

"Yeah, sure, Sarge. Seeing as how it's for the general's car and I trust you to take care of my stuff, unlike some people I could name," he smirked.

"Great. See you guys back on base later," Sam said as he hoisted the metal toolbox out of the rear of the Jeep.

They waved and drove off as Sam tried cranking the motor over again to listen to its sound.

"All right; let me see what's going on," Sam said as he placed the toolbox next to the front wheel and laid on his back to wriggle underneath the car, disappearing except for his long legs sticking out. He checked the fuel line then the oil pan as he spotted a leak; oil dripped slowly from a loose fitting. Maybe, if he could just tighten that nut…

"Mary, can you hand me that socket wrench and a five-eighth size sprocket?" he called out.

Mary searched through the box, found what she hoped was the wrench and correct socket then handed the tool to Sam's outstretched hand from under the car.

The general poked his head out of the doorway to see what was happening; Mary saw him and walked over to him to brief him on the repairs.

Sam squirmed about in the tight space, trying to adjust his angle and reach the problem. The socket didn't fit; he'd need a different size. He turned his head to try and see Mary's feet but didn't see her standing nearby. As he turned his head to the left, he saw a pair of combat boots and called out.

"Hey, buddy, can you hand me a half-inch sprocket? If you can look inside that toolbox, you should see one."

In the next instant, the jack was knocked out of position and the car slid off, trapping Sam beneath.

"Help! Somebody, help!" shouted Sam.

Mary and General Eaker both heard the frantic call and ran toward the disabled car.

"Oh my God, Sam! Are you all right? Can you move at all?" cried Mary.

"Jack up this damn car and get it the hell off of me!" yelled Sam. The drive train of the heavy vehicle was sitting a hair's breadth from his chest; he couldn't turn his head at all.

The general replaced the jack at the rear axle and quickly pumped the handle himself to raise the car. As soon as there was a space of daylight, Sam slid out from under the vehicle. He was panting heavily and covered in oil but otherwise was unharmed.

"Did you see the guy that was here?" he asked angrily as he searched the area. "If I get my hands on that jerk, I'll make him sorry."

"What do you mean? It wasn't an accident?" asked Mary. "I didn't see anyone else around."

"Thank God the ground was soft from all that rain we've had; I was lying in a little gully or that damn car would have crushed my chest."

"Sergeant, are you sure you saw someone by the car? Another soldier?" the general inquired.

"Yessir. I don't know who, but I saw a pair of combat boots standing next to me. I asked him to pass me a socket, and the next thing I knew, I was kissing the undercarriage."

"Serious accusations, but without proof, I can't act on it. I'd say you've made an enemy; better be on your guard from now on," the general advised.

"I plan to, sir. Sorry about your car, you've got an oil leak and cracked oil pan. Think the engine has run dry and seized. You better get another car from the motor pool, sir. This one's going to need some serious work."

"I see. Well, thank you for trying, sergeant. Better go get cleaned up. Certain you're okay?"

"Yessir, I'm okay. Thank you, sir."

Sam turned to Mary, "I'll catch up with you later."

He gathered up the few tools and closed up the box as he wondered who wanted him dead. Because that's what he would have been – squashed like a bug. Could it have been Alex? Would his own brother wish him dead? Dark thoughts swirled through his mind.

Chapter 12

October leaves were turning colors, reminding Sam of back home, and the weather had finally turned dry and cooler. Much better than the constant rains England usually experienced. Sam wiped his greasy hands on a rag and surveyed his work again before closing up the engine cowling.

"Give it a try, Robbie," ordered Sam.

The propeller began to rotate then gained momentum as the blades spun at high speed, blending the image of separate blades into one. Throttles were backed off; the aircraft vibrated and shuddered as the propeller came to rest, and the engine shut down.

"Think it's still out of balance, Sarge," commented Robbie.

"Think you're right," agreed Sam. "Go back over all the fittings on that propeller, tighten anything you can."

"Right."

Sam walked across the tarmac to their barracks. He'd been hard at work for the last fifteen hours. He was beat, and not being very effective any longer, and he knew it. He planned on getting some much-needed shut-eye, at least a couple of hours before their squadrons of fighters returned from the day's mission. Then it would start all over again.

A few of the mechanics in the barracks were in various stages of undress, or like Sam, trying to sleep. The outside temperature, at long last, equaled the Quonset hut inside temperature, finally making it comfortable to sleep without a stove burning to fight away the bitter cold or the sun beating down on metal huts so hot that you sweat to death.

A young private knocked on the barrack's door as he called out, "Mail call!"

A few of the men, who still had enough energy to move, greeted the courier and retrieved their welcome mail from home along with a few care packages.

Pete dragged his weary body over to Sam's cot and tossed a couple of letters onto his chest before he collapsed onto his own rack. He laid his head down and was out like a light in two minutes, clutching his unopened mail as he snored away.

Four hours later, the noise of aircraft engines circling overhead and landing nearby penetrated Sam's sleep drugged mind. He pried his eyes open and took stock of his surroundings as he sat up and rubbed his hand over a two-day growth of beard. No time to shower and shave now. As he started to stand, two envelopes fell to the floor. He bent and picked up the creased mail envelopes with the red, white, and blue stripes along the border and an airmail stamp affixed to the upper corner. He smiled as he recognized his mother's handwriting on the address; the other he didn't know but saw it had the same Wyoming postmark. They'll have to wait; he'd read them later. His men and those aircraft needed him now.

It had been a rough mission. Several fighters had to be tagged category "B" with heavy damage; the squadron lost three good pilots to crashes, and a few more were taken to hospital with injuries. The Luftwaffe was throwing everything at them; flak so dense you could walk across it, and fighters swarmed the big fortresses from all directions. Our fighters dove and swooped among the Germans, guns blazing, as they tried to protect the heavy bombers. How much more of this could they take? Staggering losses were adding up in both the bomber groups and the fighter groups.

"Okay everybody, take a break and get some chow. I need you at your best, and you can't do that on two hours of sleep and no food. Go get some of both but be back here by nineteen hundred hours. Got it? Be prepared to work the rest of the night to get these birds ready to fly," Sam ordered his men.

He grabbed a plate of food in the chow hall, not even tasting it, and couldn't name what he had just eaten. Sam had one thought in mind – a hot shower and an hour or more of sleep.

As he grabbed his gear and tossed a clean pair of socks on his bed, the motion knocked the thin envelopes onto the floor. He stooped and picked up the mail, glanced at it again, and promised himself he'd read his letters once he cleaned up.

Steam filled his nostrils as hot water poured over his head and massaged sore shoulders; Sam tried to scrub away the tiredness along with the dirt. He flexed his muscles, tried to work out the kinks, and stretched his arms above his head. A quick shave removed the heavy growth; he chuckled to himself as he thought of Mary; she'd never have recognized him if she had seen him earlier. She probably wouldn't have wanted to be within ten feet of him either from the way he had smelled.

"Ah, better. Finally feel human again," Sam said out loud to no one in particular within the latrine.

Sam carried his soiled clothes back to the barracks and stuffed them into a canvas bag under his bed. Maybe tomorrow he'd get a few minutes to run them over to the base laundry. For now, they would just contribute to the aroma of the many sweat-drenched men and unwashed clothes that filled the barracks and created the foul atmosphere they'd all grown accustomed to.

Sam sat on the edge of his bed and tore open the flap from his mother's letter. It was brief, only two paragraphs long. He skimmed it then began to read it a second time; his mind tried to absorb the words on the paper and what was unspoken between the lines.

"Dear Samuel," the letter began, *"Your father has had an accident. The doctor says he is paralyzed.*

I don't know how I can keep the ranch running. One of the neighbors has offered to help. I'm trying to reach Alex, he'll know what to do," signed, *Your loving Mother.*

Sam quickly ripped open the second envelope and unfolded the single sheet of paper. War Department censures had taken their black pens to a few sentences plus a word here or there within the letter; mustn't upset the servicemen with bad news from home or of the war they were smack in the middle of. Sam shook his head in annoyance at the useless and futile policy.

Sam's eyes scanned the shaky handwriting, then began to read it carefully as he deciphered the unfamiliar script. The letter was written by Chris Hartman's father from Cedar Hill ranch.

He unconsciously dragged his fingers through his wet hair, staring at the words in disbelief and then anger as he crumpled the paper in his fist.

"Sam," Daniel Hartman wrote, *"Christopher mentioned running into you boys while in London. I'm glad you had a chance to be together.*

I'm sorry, but I have some bad news for you. Your father was shot. It was no accident. Looks like he's paralyzed and won't likely walk again. I promise you; I'll do what I can to look into this; I have an idea of who might be behind it. Probably can't prove it.

Don't worry about your ma. Cedar Hill will do what we can to keep your ranch running; one of my wranglers will help out at Circle-D. It's the least we can do with you boys both being in the war," signed, *Daniel Hartman.*

Sam dragged trembling fingers through his hair then pounded his fist against the tabletop, angry and frustrated. Here he sits, thousands of miles and half a world away, fighting for what? He can't even protect his own family. Alex… he had to talk to Alex.

Sam ran out of the barracks toward the enlisted club and the telephone booth outside. He fumbled with a handful of coins and punched in the number for the 4-0-1 group office.

Sam listened to a minute of static squawk on the line before a voice spoke.

"Four oh one, Corporal Thomas," answered the clerk.

"This is Sergeant Sam Dunlap; I need to get a message to my brother Lieutenant Alex Dunlap. He's a bombardier on the *Pretty Lady*, thirty-second squadron. It's important; he needs to call me."

"Give me a second. What d'ya say the name was again, Mack?"

"Dunlap, Alexander. With the crew of the Pretty Lady," Sam spoke through gritted teeth, impatient with the clerk who wrote the information down.

"Okay. I'll get it to him. No promises on how soon. Dunno if he's on base."

"Thanks. Just get that message to him ASAP."

It was two long days before Sam was summoned to his squadron commander's office.

"Dunlap," the staff clerk shuffled through some papers on his desktop, "I had a call from Deenethorpe. You trying to get hold of your brother or something?"

"Yeah. We've had a family emergency. I need to talk to him."

"Well, I've got a phone number jotted down, it's here someplace, aha here it is. You're supposed to call this number at eighteen hundred today; says he'll be waiting."

The clerk handed Sam a torn piece of paper with a telephone number scribbled in a smudged pencil. Sam checked his watch; he had three hours to wait before he could call. He thanked the clerk and made his way back to the hangars and his ground crew.

Time still dragged on even though Sam had stayed busy servicing aircraft, overseeing refueling and loading ammunition. He anxiously checked his watch for the third time, and as soon as it was close to six o'clock, he prepared to dash back to the only telephone booth on base.

"Gotta make a call, Pete. Save me a seat in chow hall, will ya?"

"Sure thing, Sam. See you there," Pete replied, puzzled but not wanting to intrude on private matters.

Sam sprinted to the enlisted club and the available payphone. He hastily dropped in enough coins and dialed the number.

The call connected, and after two rings, Sam heard Alex answer.

"Sam? This better be good. What the hell's so important that some clerk had to track me down?" Alex demanded. "I've had messages left for me all over base."

"Did you get a letter from Mother?" Sam asked quickly, breaking into his brother's tirade.

"No. What's happened?"

"It's Pop. Mom wrote me that he's paralyzed and then I got a letter from Chris Hartman's father and he told me the old man had been shot. Hartman's are sending one of their cowhands to work at the Circle-D to help out."

"Holy shit. So now what?" Alex swore, his surprise coming through the line.

"Mother said she would try to reach you, and you're supposed to know what to do about all this," said Sam.

"Now what the hell am I going to be able to do from halfway around the world? Is she crazy? I really don't give a damn about that ranch and a bunch of flea-bitten cows," raged Alex.

"You don't mean that. You lived and breathed that ranch from the time you were little. You were the one who taught me how to work the cattle and the importance of the land. I can't believe you can turn your back on our heritage," Sam argued.

"Well, I am. I've got enough problems just trying to stay alive. Daniel Hartman is a decent man; he'll stand by Circle-D and see that the folks don't get run off the place. I don't see where we can do anything more."

"Guess not. Still… how's Mother going to care for an invalid and run a cattle ranch? Who's going to do the planting that's needed or herd those cows? One man can't do all that," Sam worried.

"Like I said, what are we expected to do about it? There's a war going on and we're smack dab in the middle of it. Listen, I'm sorry to hear about the old man; I really am, and I'd like to know what happened, but we'll just have to wait until this damn war ends."

"All right. I just wanted you to know. Hey, Alex…" Sam hesitated, nervous, before he continued, "I'm sorry about some of the stuff I said at that dance. I lost my temper, that's all," Sam apologized, his voice low as he spoke into the telephone receiver propped under his chin.

"Me too. I was drunk and acted like an ass. It was my fault. I'm sorry. You doin' okay?" Alex asked quietly, memories of him and Sam as boys floated before him.

"Yeah, I'm okay. You're the one I worry about. Be careful out there; don't take any chances, you know?"

"Sure, no problem. *Pretty Lady* has one more mission to fly, and we've got a ticket home. My war will be over. I'll look in on Pop when I get back," Alex promised.

"All right. Take it easy. I'll be seeing you," Sam said as he hung up the phone.

Chapter 13

Men silently shuffled into the briefing room. The black, pre-dawn morning hour reflected the somber mood of the flight crews as they awaited their fates. The rumor mill had preceded the weary men and only waited now to learn if the target they all dreaded was their next mission.

Chief of Staff Rogers entered the building. He strode slowly up the center aisle, not making eye contact with the pilots and crews he passed.

"Ten-Hut!" he called.

General Doolittle followed Rogers to the front of the long building. He paused as men took their seats, and all eyes turned toward him.

Throughout the summer and into the autumn of 1943, the air war had ramped up its intensity. Targets that directly affected the German war effort became high priorities. Ball-bearing plants, steel mills, shipyards, and munitions were in the crosshairs of the Eighth Air Force bomber groups.

In an attempt to continue the pressure on German forces, missions were flown almost daily but to the detriment and fatigue of the American flight crews.

Men watched and listened as the general named the designated target for today as the shipyard in dreaded Bremen, known as "Flak City," by the aircrew members because of the thick flak surrounding it.

A low murmur and grumbling grew and spread among the men as their fears were realized. Glaring images of the city of Bremen with circled targets were projected on the screen before them. The black and white pictures represented death, and an ominous, foreboding shrouded aircrews as they stared ahead, some with tears in their eyes, others visibly shaking. They didn't have time or the luxury for griping or disagreeing with the mission of the day.

There was too much to do to allow personal fears and worries to invade your mind. Weather forecasts, routes, fuel, and squadron formation details had to be absorbed if you wanted to survive.

Crews donned flight suits, then piled into Jeeps to carry them out to the airfields and their waiting fortresses to perform pre-flight checks and duties.

Engines roared; propellers wind milled as the ground shook under the mighty machines. Surrounding homes trembled with the vibrations and a rumbling noise filled the air.

Alex took one last look around at the familiar faces of his ground crew; he made a jaunty two-finger salute and waved goodbye to them as he hoisted himself up into the huge bird. He was scared, more than ever, and prayed no one had seen him lose his breakfast behind a parked fuel truck. He couldn't let his team down. He had to overcome his fears; men counted on him, the same as he relied on them.

"Please, God, don't let me let them down," Alex prayed as he strapped into his seat and prepared for take-off.

The *Pretty Lady* climbed and slipped into her combat box formation, a tight vee, as Captain Stone followed his flight squadron commander and maintained radio silence.

Squadrons of Mustang fighters formed up ahead and alongside the big fortresses. Their escort provided a modicum sense of security and confidence.

Alex smiled at the nose gunner and pointed to the planes flying ahead at their eleven o'clock position.

The gunner nodded and returned a thumb's up sign. He turned to continue his search of the skies for any possible enemy fighters hiding behind a fluffy cloud.

Ten minutes from the target, *Pretty Lady* lost an engine and began to fall behind from its formation and the protection of the Mustangs. She started losing altitude.

Swarms of Luftwaffe fighters came out of the clouds and began strafing the wounded fortress. All of the waist gunners fired away, while both the nose and belly gunner kept up a rapid barrage against the Luftwaffe threat.

Captain Stone spoke through his headphones, "Bombardier, drop your payload on my command."

Alex tried to jettison his payload of bombs, but the bomb bay door jammed.

"Bombardier to pilot, we've got a problem. Doors are jammed."

Suddenly, pilot John Stone put the heavy B-17 into a dive to escape the horde of fighters. As soon as he leveled out, Alex straddled the bomb bay doors, kicking at the latch until he was able to manually crank the doors open. He chose a target below and let loose his payload.

Pretty Lady turned hard to starboard to avoid the explosion percussions while trying to climb and gain more altitude to head back toward the North Sea and south to the English Channel.

Suddenly a burst of flak took out a second and third engine, and Stone feathered them back. Captain Stone nodded to his co-pilot, his eyes said it all as they grimly stared ahead.

Pretty Lady limped toward the Channel and home base, skimming treetops, then just above sea level. The tall northern coastal cliffs were ahead of them; their reduced power too weak to carry them above.

If they could just gain enough power to climb…

The Boeing B-17 "Flying Fortress," the primary heavy bomber of the Eighth Air Force, was famous for bringing crews home, even when three of its four engines failed, but not today.

Five miles from the safety of the English coast, the *Pretty Lady* crashed into the cold dark waters of the North Sea.

Sam had just completed patching a string of bullet holes in the wing of one of their Thunderbolt fighters when he heard his name being called.

"Yo, Dunlap! Hightail it over to the CO's office," shouted the duty officer of the day.

"Now what did I do?" asked Sam as he wiped his hands and stuffed his shirttail into his pants.

Sam entered Captain Barnett's office located east of the control tower and the far end of the taxi ramps. He was surprised to recognize Major Simpson seated in a corner side chair.

Sam saluted both men and stood at attention as he addressed his commander. "You wanted to see me, sir?"

"I believe you know Major Simpson?" inquired Barnett.

"Yessir, good to see you again, Major," Sam replied as he glanced between the two men. A cold hand suddenly clutched his heart, and a sick feeling grew in his belly.

"There's no easy way to say this, sergeant, but I thought you'd rather hear it from me than an impersonal letter. Your brother, Lieutenant Alexander Dunlap, was killed in action two days ago," Major Simpson informed him solemnly.

Sam blinked to hide threatening tears and swallowed a lump in his throat before he tried to speak. "Are you sure, sir? I mean, no chance of mistaken identity?"

"I'm sorry. *Pretty Lady* went down in the North Sea. The British Navy helped recover part of the wrecked aircraft and remains of all ten crew members. The nose piece with the aircraft's name was found too. We were able to make a positive identification on all the men," the Major explained.

"I'm granting you a twenty-four-hour pass, Sam. Take some time off; you've earned it. The War Department will be sending out their formal notification by telegram to your parents," said Captain Barnett.

"You have my deepest condolences, sergeant," Major Simpson said as he shook Sam's hand.

"Thank you, sir," Sam replied and saluted both men again as he turned to leave.

Sam walked slowly back to his work area; his eyes glazed over unseeing, his mind numb. First news of his father and now Alex. It was too much. He stood alone, staring at the ground as his hands clenched and unclenched into fists at his side.

Pete looked up from his work and saw his friend's face. He recognized that shocked expression.

"Hey, Sarge…" Robbie started as he moved toward Sam and was abruptly halted.

Pete held up a hand to the mechanic, stopping him. "Not now, Robbie. See me later."

"What's the matter with…" Robbie shut his mouth as Pete glared at him. He walked off, sulking.

Pete approached his friend and put an arm around his shoulder. He led him into a shadowy corner of the hangar and waited for Sam to speak.

"It's Alex. He's gone. Crashed two days ago," Sam said, his voice a hoarse whisper.

"Sorry, Sam. What can I do? You know I'm here for you, buddy," Pete offered his best friend a shoulder to cry on or an ear to listen.

"Think I just need to be alone for a while. Thanks, Pete."

"You got it," Pete said as he patted Sam's shoulder and left him with his solitary memories.

Chapter 14

There was little hope that the war would end soon for the boys to be home by Christmas. The approaching holiday was just another dismal date on the calendar.

Dwight Eisenhower was named supreme commander of Allied Expeditionary Forces on December twenty-fourth. Just a month earlier, the Western Allied heads of state - Roosevelt, Churchill, and Stalin - secretly met together for the first time in a place called the Teheran Conference. Plans were made for invasions and offenses, as the prolonged war would battle into the next year or perhaps longer.

Sam waited his turn in the long line formed outside the base telephone booth. Men were trying to reach loved ones back home, a quick two-minute holiday greeting allowed on Christmas Eve.

Finally, he got his chance to step into the red phone box and with a heavy pocketful of change, started making the overseas call. The operator took the number, and he deposited the required amount of money as he waited to hear his mother's voice.

"Hello?" Katie Dunlap answered. The phone line crackled with static, and she tried again to listen to the voice calling her on the other end of the line. "Hello, who is it?"

"Mother! It's Samuel, calling from England. How are you?"

"Oh, Samuel, it's you."

"Merry Christmas, Mother. How's Pop doing?"

"About the same. We're both about the same."

"I'll write you real soon. I promise," Sam said, dismayed by the melancholy tone of her voice. "I gotta go now; they're waiting to use the phone. I love you."

"Goodbye," his mother said as she clicked off the connection.

Sam quickly deposited a few more coins into the telephone and dialed Mary's home. Some of the guys were knocking on the door, complaining that he was taking too much time, hogging the phone.

He turned his back to them as he pressed the receiver to his ear and strained to hear the voice he craved.

"Hello? This is Mary."

"Merry Christmas, Mary. It's Sam."

"Merry Christmas! Where are you? I've got an automobile to use; I'll come get you," she said excitedly.

"I'm still on base at Duxford. Can you drive down?"

"Of course! Meet me by the front gate in an hour. I can't wait to see you."

"Come on, buddy; you had your turn!" yelled someone outside.

"Hey, I gotta hang up. See you in an hour," Sam said, smiling for the first time in months.

He hung up the phone and opened the door of the booth, stepping out as another soldier hurried to squeeze into the narrow space.

Sam rushed back to his barracks, splashed on a bit of aftershave, and put on a fresh uniform. He rummaged through his footlocker, impatiently tossing aside folded underwear and socks until his hand touched the package he sought lying at the bottom. A bright red bow adorned the gaily wrapped Christmas gift. Sam carefully lifted the compact square box and held it in his palm; he planned on surprising Mary on Christmas day. He smiled as he recalled the lady at the jewelry store fussing about and offering to wrap the box for him to present it to his special lady.

He dropped it into his jacket pocket, tucked his holiday care package under his arm, and pulled on a pair of gloves as he walked toward the main gate to wait on Mary. He couldn't believe his good luck, being able to spend the holiday with the girl he loved.

Temperatures dropped, and crystal snowflakes began to fall as the wintry afternoon sun started turning to dusk. Sam rechecked his watch then grinned broadly as an older model MG roadster slowly pulled to a stop.

The roadster's once dark green paint was now faded and scratched and sported more than a few visible dents; the torn edges of its convertible rag top flapped in the wind.

Mary rolled down the window of the two-seater sports car and leaned out, "Hello! Isn't she a beauty? Hop in!"

Sam tossed his package into the rear as he climbed into the left side passenger seat and gave Mary a peck on the cheek. She gunned the engine and made a U-turn in the narrow roadway.

"Where did you find this car?" asked Sam, laughing as they sped away; Mary shifting gears smoothly.

"My uncle used to drive in road rallies before the war, back in 1935. This was his car. My aunt loaned it to me last week; poor thing has been hidden away in a barn and covered in straw… the car, not my aunt," clarified Mary with a chuckle.

"Where's your uncle now?" asked Sam.

"He was killed in Dunkirk."

"Oh, uh, sorry."

Cold air whistled through the torn top, chilling the car's occupants. The loud noise from the motor prevented normal conversation, limiting it to an occasional shout and hand signals. Mary handled the sports car with ease as she zipped down the narrow country roads and around the hairpin turns.

"Bloody hell!" she exclaimed. Mary steered around a hidden curve, then suddenly depressed the clutch to the floor and stood on the brakes to come to a screeching stop within a foot of colliding with a small herd of sheep crossing the roadway.

"That was close," Sam said as they waited for the shepherd to move the animals out of their path.

"Hmm, it was, wasn't it?" replied Mary, a bit shook. "By the way, what's in the little package in the boot?"

"Huh? Oh, that, got a Christmas box from back home; thought I'd bring it along. Bound to be something good to eat inside; no sense leaving it behind."

"Jolly good. Here we go," Mary said as she put the car in gear and proceeded down the lane again.

They arrived at Mary's flat without further incident and before the snow began to accumulate measurably. She parked in front of the brick building and hurried to unlock the door as Sam followed her into the cozy warm apartment.

A festive yule log, decorated with sprigs of holly and fresh-cut evergreen boughs, sat in the center of the sideboard flanked by a pair of candles. The clean pine scent filled the room. Mary pulled all the curtains closed, still abiding by blackout regulations, before she lit the candles.

"I made the yule log in hopes I'd see you for Christmas. Couldn't put up a tree, but at least we have this bit of holiday cheer," Mary explained.

"Looks very nice and smells good too," Sam said as he took off his overcoat and hung it on the hook by the door. He secretly patted his jacket pocket, ensuring the small bulge was still there.

"I used my ration coupons for ingredients and cooked a plum pudding as a special treat," said Mary.

"Let's see what's inside my Christmas box. I might be able to contribute something to our meal."

Sam pulled out a penknife from his pants pocket and slit open the cardboard box. He and Mary both stared in wonder at the delicious and varied contents – a can of Spam, two Hershey chocolate bars, a bag of hard candy, a sack of walnuts, box of raisins, two pair of wool socks, a carton of cigarettes, small can of coffee, a bar of soap and container of shaving cream. Sam picked up and shook a small tin, decorated with a smiling Santa on top; the contents rattled noisily. When he pried off the lid and peeked inside, he saw the remains of broken oatmeal cookies reduced to crumbs but still edible.

"My goodness, a virtual feast! Is this from your mother?" asked Mary, looking at all the goodies.

Sam found the enclosed card and read the short greeting. "No, it's from our friends, the Hartman family. Remember meeting Chris in London? His mother made up gift boxes for both of us."

"Wasn't that sweet of her," Mary said as she hugged Sam and smiled. "You'll have to send her a thankyou note."

"Hmm, right, I will," Sam said as his thoughts strayed to his parents and the grief he had heard in his mother's voice over the phone. The loss of Alex still hanging like a black cloud over them all.

Mary saw the troubled expression on Sam's face. She reached for his hand as she spoke.

"I'm truly sorry about Alex. I heard about the crash. So many men were lost in just one mission. I was on base that day with the General, waiting for the return of the command. It was terrible."

"I had just talked to him on the phone about a week earlier. We kinda settled our differences."

"I'm so glad you did. Brothers shouldn't part in anger," Mary said quietly.

Sam's haunted eyes turned to Mary. "At Duxford, we knew it was a bad one. We lost several fighters too. I waited and waited to hear from Alex; it took two days before my commander gave me the news," whispered Sam.

"I heard the general say there were close to three hundred men lost from the group on that mission; some shot down and captured, more crashed and killed. Even the town's citizens have mourned the heavy loss of the airmen," Mary said.

He could only nod as he listened to her describe the black Friday when his brother died.

She reached for Sam and they held each other. Sam mourned the death of his brother; Mary relived the loss of her own family and loved ones. Sam's shoulders trembled as he gave way to his grief and allowed pent up tears to fall.

"How are you holding up?" Mary finally asked.

"Me? I'm okay. Just going about my work every day while some other guy fights and dies for his country," Sam growled.

Mary placed her hands on her hips, a stern expression on her face, looked him square in the eye, and lectured the man in front of her. Sam hung his head low with fists clenched as he listened to her angry words.

"Now see here, Samuel Dunlap, I'll hear no more talk like that. You are doing your duty and serving your country the best way you can. We've discussed this before. Are you going to spoil my lovely Christmas celebration with that black scowl on your face?"

"No. I'm sorry. Guess I was just feeling guilty, you know?" Sam admitted.

"I understand, believe me, I do. Don't you think that I question every day why my parents were killed, yet I was spared? Why me and not them? But we must go on living; it's up to us, the living, to continue fighting to make this a better world. If we give up, their sacrifice will be for nothing."

"You're right. I'm sorry. Gosh, I sound like a selfish bastard," cried Sam.

"No, you are not. You're a good man and you care about others. I know you loved your brother and that you're still hurting. He will always be with you in your heart."

"Thank you, Mary. How'd you get so wise?" Sam smiled then pulled her into an embrace again, kissing her softly.

She returned his smile as she gently touched his cheek, then threaded her fingers through his hair.

"Now, what about helping me prepare this supper?"

"Lead the way," he said as he followed her into the tiny kitchen carrying his box of goodies. He removed the key from the bottom of the can of Spam then cranked it along the edge to open the tin. The meat plopped out and into the waiting frying pan.

"Should I slice it or what?" Sam asked. The ham began to sizzle in the hot pan, a delicious aroma rose from the stove.

"Yes, of course. We can't eat it in one big block. I saved some potatoes from my garden before they went to seed. I'll peel two and boil them up, plus I think there might be a few carrots left too. Vegetables are in short supply; afraid this is the best I can do," said Mary.

"Sounds fine to me." Sam sliced through the block of ham and arranged it around the frying pan. "What else can I do to help?"

"You can scrape the carrots clean and cut them up while I fix the potatoes. They won't take much time to cook, and we'll have a perfectly lovely meal, plus my special plum pudding."

"Don't think I've ever eaten plum pudding. What's it like?" asked Sam.

"Oh, you'll see! It's a holiday favorite in England."

"If you made it, then I look forward to eating it," Sam said.

"How about turning on the wireless? Maybe the BBC has some nice Christmas music to put us in a festive mood," Mary suggested.

"You got it," said Sam.

With holiday carols playing in the background, Mary and Sam prepared their meal then set the table using mismatched china that Mary had salvaged from her parent's destroyed home. The flickering candles illuminated the room in a soft glow; a wintry fresh pine scent filled the air.

Sam closed his eyes; memories of past Christmases, roaring fires, and happier times drifted through his mind. A person could almost forget there was a war being fought.

"Shilling for your thoughts," Mary said.

"Hmm, nothing special really, just enjoying the moment; being here with you for Christmas. This is really nice."

"I'm so happy we could be together," Mary told Sam as she kissed him on the cheek. "Sit down, please. Let's eat before it gets cold."

Appetites sated, Sam and Mary relaxed on the living room settee, enjoying the music and evening solitude. They sat with hands clasped; Sam propped his feet up on the coffee table, and Mary laid her head on his shoulder. They cuddled close as Bing Crosby sang *White Christmas* on the radio, and Mary hummed along with the melody.

"You have a nice voice," Sam said. "I could sit like this for hours; it's so peaceful."

"Can you stay the night?" Mary asked, waiting to see what his reaction would be to her brazen invitation. She had summoned all her courage to say those words.

"What are you saying, Mary?" Sam asked as he dropped his feet, sat upright, and turned to face her.

"Do I have to spell it out?" Mary blushed as she lowered her eyes. She caressed his cheek, her hand dropping to his shoulder.

Sam gathered her into his arms and hugged her as he kissed her forehead, both cheeks, her neck then claimed her waiting lips.

"Let's go upstairs," Mary said as she stood and extended her hand to Sam.

He smiled, their eyes locked in mutual communication; he blew out the candles and followed the alluring swing of her hips as she climbed the staircase.

Mary pushed open her bedroom door; faded pink floral wallpaper adorned the walls. A single dresser rested against one wall with the welcoming down-filled double bed claiming the bulk of the space in the tiny room. She lit a short candle sitting on the dresser.

Sam framed Mary's face, his fingers traced the bridge of her nose, the line of her upper lip. His eyes probed hers as he asked, "Are you sure?"

She nodded yes as she stood on tiptoes to wrap her arms around his shoulders and draw his head toward her. Her lips met Sam's more demanding lips as his mouth claimed hers. The kiss was gentle yet searching, questioning, inviting more.

Mary stepped back, breaking free of the embrace to turn her back to Sam. She lifted her thick hair up off her neck as she offered the frock's zipper enclosure to him.

"Would you mind?" she asked, glancing back over her shoulder.

Sam readily complied with the lady's wishes as he slid the zipper tab down the length of her slender back, where it ended past her waist. His hands slid the parted garment off her shoulders as it dipped and rested against her bosom before dropping to the floor in a puddle at her feet.

Mary stepped out of the dress and slipped off her shoes, standing before Sam in nylon stockings and petticoat. Her nimble fingers began unbuttoning his shirt as she smiled enticingly.

Sam's mind raced as he viewed the woman before him. He quickly unbuckled his belt and kicked off his own shoes, his trousers next. The edge of the mattress pressed against the back of his knees as he gathered Mary into his arms, and slowly lowered her to its downy surface.

Both of their hands moved to anxiously remove remaining clothing as their bodies strained against their ignited passion. Sam's hands caressed Mary's slender back, marveling at the silky texture of her skin. Her arms pulled him closer. She moaned lightly, her right hand caressed the back of Sam's head, her fingers slid through the hair at the nape of his neck.

His lips left her mouth to kiss a trail across her cheek to her ear, where he nibbled lightly; his desire grew as he yearned to taste and touch every inch of her. Mary's faint perfume aroused him as his lips continued their journey back to her waiting lips as she offered her moist mouth up to his. His hand caressed her arm and slid down to find a ripe breast; his thumb drew circles around her nipple until the engorged bud rose to meet his hand.

His whiskers tickled her bare shoulder and breast. A chilled draft of air made her nipple stand taller as Sam's head lowered and took it into his mouth, suckling the rosy bud, sending ripples of pleasure through Mary's body.

Sam lowered himself above her waiting thighs. He probed gently then thrust suddenly. He rocked in and out, withdrawing then entering again, feeling Mary arch her hips and match his rhythm as their bodies came together. Their souls blended as one.

Later, they lay in the aftermath of their lovemaking; embers of their burning passion warmed their bodies and entwined their hearts. Neither person wanted the moment to end. Both fought the surrender to sleep as they watched the glimmer of dawn peek behind the shade of the room's single window.

"I love you so much, Mary," Sam spoke in the solitude of the dusky room, his arms holding Mary cradled against his chest.

"I think I love you too," Mary whispered. "It frightens me."

"Marry me, Mary," Sam asked as he held her tightly.

"Sam, oh Sam. I…" Mary spoke softly, a hot tear fell onto his bare chest.

"What's wrong? Don't you want to? Aren't I good enough?" Sam asked angrily as he sat up on the edge of the bed. He tried to see her face, read her expression in the darkness.

"No, no… you've got it wrong. It's just…"

"What? You tell me. After what we just did, why can't you answer me," Sam demanded. He grabbed his clothes from the pile on the floor and started dressing.

"What are you doing? Where are you going?" Mary asked as she saw him stand and finish buttoning his shirt, stuffing the ends into his pants; his actions felt like a door slamming in her face.

"I'm walking down to the station. I'll hop the train back to base," Sam growled.

"Please, Sam. Don't go like this. You don't understand," Mary pleaded.

"I told you I love you, Mary. I've asked you to be my wife. If you can't give me an answer, then what am I supposed to think? Is it Timmy? Do you still love him?"

"No, Sam. It's… I don't know. I'm not making any sense. I'm frightened. The war…" Mary began to cry, tears rolling down her cheek as she reached for Sam's hand. She sat on her knees in the middle of the bed, the sheet twisted about her waist. Her long auburn hair draped about her bare shoulders as she shook her head from side to side, searching for words to convey the tangle of emotions churning inside her; to explain thoughts and fears that she couldn't explain to herself.

Sam saw the pain in her eyes. "I'm not Timmy or even Alex. I won't abandon you. I can't guarantee that I won't get hit by a truck tomorrow or have a bomb fall on me from out of the sky. I want to marry you, Mary. All I ask is that you think about it."

Sam reached into his pocket and withdrew the gaily wrapped box. He placed the gift on her dresser as he opened the bedroom door.

"Merry Christmas, Mary," he said softly, then turned and closed the door behind him.

Chapter 15

January brought a bone-chilling cold and more rain to the English countryside, adding to the misery and bleak outlook of the men stationed there. Rumors were running rampant about plans for an invasion of Europe; when was anyone's guess. Air and ground crews alike wondered if they would be staying in Great Britain or relocating to positions in Europe as Allied forces advanced. The uncertainty was nerve-wracking.

Just when Sam thought things couldn't get any worse, he was told to report to the commander's office again.

"Now what?" thought Sam as he saluted his captain and stood at attention in the narrow space.

"A telegram arrived for you, Sergeant Dunlap," Captain Barnett said formally. He held out the yellow Western Union envelope.

Sam reluctantly took the telegram, turned it over, and slit the seal with his fingernail. The single sheet of yellow paper glared at him as he read the brief, clipped message. He raised his eyes to his commander and read the dispassionate words.

"Katie Dunlap stroke. Stop. Mother dead. Stop. Awaiting instructions on care of father. Stop. Signed Daniel Hartman."

"Hartman is our neighbor; his ranch is about ten miles away from our boundaries," Sam explained to the Captain. He stared again at the somber news and tried to summon a spark of emotion, some level of grief over the death of his own mother. He couldn't.

His feelings were locked away in a protective shell ever since Christmas.

"What did he mean about the care of your father?" asked Captain Barnett.

"Early in October, my father was shot in the back and is now completely paralyzed. He's bedridden. I don't know what's going to happen to the family ranch; there's no one left to run the place."

"Would you be able to run it, if you were there?" asked Barnett.

"Yeah, I guess so. But that's not the question, because I'm not there. I'm here and my brother's dead, and now my ma. Nobody left," said Sam. He shook his head and stared out the window.

"There have been instances when the Army has granted a hardship separation; an early discharge under special circumstances. Would you like me to see what I can do?" asked the captain.

Sam studied his commander, an inkling of hope building in his chest. "Even with the war?"

"Your brother had earned his right to go home, considering the length of his service and the number of missions he had flown. You've earned recommendations with your own life-saving actions and personal wounds. I think it is fair to say your family has done enough and earned the right to go home. I'll try to argue the point for you if it will help."

"Yes sir, I'd appreciate that, sir. I think our friends can care for my father for a while longer if they knew I would be returning home," Sam said.

"Don't get your hopes up and don't say anything to your men yet. I'll let you know," the captain warned.

"Yes, sir."

Sam left the operations building and started walking back towards the repair bays when he spotted Mary leaving the motor pool garage.

He hurried over to her, startling her as he grabbed her arm and pulled her into the shadowy garage building. He ignored the surprised stares of several mechanics and two other drivers.

Mary started to protest at being manhandled so.

"Just what do you think you're doing, Sam Dunlap? Unhand me right now," she demanded.

"Not until you listen to what I have to say," shouted Sam, then lowered his voice as he sought a private spot for them. "It's important. Please, Mary."

Mary studied his expression, noting the shadows under his eyes and the addition of worry lines across his forehead on so young a man. She waited for him to speak as she leaned against a garage door and shrunk deeper into the shadows seeking privacy from prying eyes.

Sam released his hold on Mary's arm and stood before her, shuffling his feet from side to side now, uncertain where to begin. He swallowed and looked her in the eye as he started to speak in a lower, hushed voice.

"I just got a telegram; my mom's dead. Barnett thinks I may be able to get a hardship discharge so I can go home," Sam explained.

"Oh, my goodness! What happened to your mother?" asked Mary, the full import of his words not registering with her.

"Telegram only said she had a stroke. Me, I think she died of a broken heart after losing Alex on top of Pop's injury. I guess she couldn't take it."

Mary rested her hand on Sam's shoulder. She wanted to offer her comfort and sympathy but could tell he was having none of that at the moment. Suddenly his words sunk in as her eyes widened, and her mouth formed a silent "O".

"Did you say you're getting discharged and will be leaving England?" Mary asked, anxiously.

"Yes, that's exactly what I said. Don't know for sure if that's going to happen.   But Mary, when I leave, I want you with me. I can't leave England without you. I love you and so I'm asking you again to be my wife."

"Sam, you must know how I feel about you. I've regretted our last conversation every day. Marriage is a big step; I want to be certain. You asked me to think about your proposal then, and I have."

"So, what did you decide?" Sam asked softly as he rubbed tendrils of her hair between his fingers. He noticed the bright emerald chips sparkling in her ears, his Christmas gift to her. She never looked prettier. He whispered sweet nothings in her ear as his hand slipped inside her topcoat to pull her closer to his body.

"Um, uh, you know I can't think straight when you do that," she breathed as she stood on tiptoes again to press her mouth against his. Her surrender was complete as she sighed, "Yes."

Sam dragged his lips from hers as he asked, "Did you just say yes? You'll marry me?"

"Yes, I'll marry you. I love you with all my heart, Samuel Dunlap." Mary laughed and wrapped her arms around his shoulders in a joyous embrace.

Sam returned her embrace and claimed her lips in a thoroughly passionate kiss that only ended when they realized they had drawn a crowd applauding, complete with catcalls and cheers.

Mary turned beet red as she hid her embarrassed face behind Sam's back. Sam attempted to break up their audience by waving them away as if they were a herd of cattle.

"Go on, get back to work. You've seen enough," Sam directed.

The soldiers grumbled and shuffled away as Sam and Mary walked out of the empty garage, holding hands and smiling broadly.

"So, now what?" Mary asked.

"Well, first, I wait to learn if my discharge is approved. Then, we've got tons of paperwork to file for application to be allowed to get married. We need approval from my commanding officer. You'd be considered a war bride."

"I see you've already looked into the requirements. Were you that confident I'd say yes?"

"Let's just say I was hopeful."

"Should I do anything now to prepare?" Mary asked.

"I dunno. Just be prepared to pack your belongings and limit yourself to one steamer trunk, that's all. You'll have to sort your stuff and decide what's important to you and what you can bear to part with. When I find out what kind of forms we'll need and what kind of questions they ask, I'll let you know. Guess it wouldn't hurt to have your birth certificate and stuff like that ready."

"All right, Sam. I'll do all of that, then I suppose we just have to wait until you know what's happening."

"Give me a kiss goodbye; I gotta get back to work before they just simply decide to court-martial me."

Almost two months later, on March 16th, Sam and Mary recited their vows before the base chaplain at Duxford. Sam looked dashing in his newly dry-cleaned dress uniform while Mary wore a white linen suit with an emerald green silk blouse that matched her earrings; the radiant bride held a bouquet of yellow tulips. Flashbulbs went off as someone snapped a photograph.

Major Simpson, Captain Barnett, Peter Shultz, Mary's friend Miriam Cooper, and her aunt comprised the entire wedding party. The Major offered to give Mary away while Pete and Miriam acted as best man and matron of honor.

Simpson and Barnett had pulled every string, even enlisted the approval of General Eaker, and called in every favor due them to help Sam get his discharge and allow him to marry his British war bride. The Major secured passage home for them on a hospital ship due to leave Southampton for New York in two days. The newlyweds would have to assist the hospital staff on board by working in the wards or kitchens, but at least they would have immediate free passage to sail to the States.

"Major Simpson, Captain Barnett – I'll never forget your kindness. It's been a privilege and an honor serving under your command, sir," Sam said as he saluted smartly.

Both officers returned Sam's salute then shook his hand in hearty congratulations. Everyone raised a mug of ale to toast the happy couple and bid them farewell.

Mary kissed each man on their cheek. "Thank you so much. You're all very dear men."

"Harrumph, uh well, you're very welcome, Mrs. Dunlap," said Captain Barnett, clearly embarrassed by the affectionate display.

"We've got to leave to catch the train down to Southampton," Sam announced to the small group. "Pete, when this is all over if you want a job, you've got one. Come look me up in Wyoming. You'll always have a place with me," Sam offered his friend, as they clasped each other in a farewell hug.

"I'll do that. Take care, you two!" Pete said.

As the bride and groom left the chapel, they were greeted by the ground crew of the 82nd squadron forming an arch of long-handled wrenches. Sam and Mary laughed gaily as they ducked and ran under the unique arch, receiving the well-wishes and congratulations of the squad.

PART 2 – WYOMING 1944
Chapter 16

The train conductor lowered the large steamer trunk onto the dusty station platform as Sam pressed a two-dollar tip into his hand and thanked him for his help. The exhausting journey cross country from New York took a grueling six days, sleeping upright in seats hard as a rock with little or no cushions. Now finally, they had arrived in Laramie, Wyoming.

Mary lifted her face to the warmth of the morning sunshine pouring down from the wide blue skies overhead. A light wind blew a fine layer of dust that quickly coated her trunk and shoe tops. Laramie appeared bigger than the villages she was accustomed to but nowhere near the size of London. She studied the women walking down a nearby sidewalk; noted their clothing style and the large western hats worn by many. Her own conservative fashion was in marked contrast; she knew the locals would quickly identify her as an outsider.

Sam and Mary each lifted an end of the steamer trunk and carried it to the street side of the rail platform. Light traffic traveled down the few streets in town. Sam scanned the approaching vehicles for any sign of someone from the Circle-D or even Cedar Hill.

He had wired Daniel Hartman from New York that he and his bride would be arriving in Laramie and had asked the neighbor for his help in securing transportation from the city up to Deer Springs. Now that they were this close, he was anxious to get home.

Mary perched atop the large trunk as she shaded her eyes with her hand and glanced about. She laid her small carpetbag at her feet.

"Is the weather always this delightful?" she asked.

"Hmm, what? No, this is just April springtime. Our summers are hot, dry, and dusty; our winters are fierce, cold, and snowy. No, madam, enjoy these mild temperatures while you can, they won't last," Sam explained.

"Oh," Mary replied, feeling overwhelmed as she realized her life had changed drastically and she would have much to learn about living in this vast open land.

A dark blue Ford pickup truck rumbled toward the train station, pulling to a halt in front of the platform. An attractive, older gentleman with salt and pepper black hair stepped down from the truck cab. He wore western boots, denim jeans, and a blue cotton shirt tucked neatly into his waistband. A black Stetson hat shaded his eyes as he spied the waiting couple.

Sam moved forward to greet him and clasp the extended hand in friendship.

"Mister Hartman, how are you, sir? Thanks for coming," Sam said, as he turned to Mary. "I'd like to introduce my wife, Mary."

"Hello," Mary greeted shyly.

"Nice to meet you, Mary. Imagine you two are tuckered out from your long trip. Let's get you loaded up and headed home," Dan Hartman said.

"Sounds like a good idea," agreed Sam.

The two men easily hoisted the steamer trunk into the bed of the pickup truck then tossed in the small carpetbag. Mary slid onto the wide bench seat, sandwiched between Sam and Daniel Hartman. A pleasant breeze blew in from the open truck windows as they drove through town.

The light wind loosened strands of her carefully tucked hair from its chignon as Mary studied the many storefronts flanking the main street and the two-story clapboard sided houses, so different from the brick or stone cottages of English hamlets.

"How far is Deer Springs from here? Does the town look like this?" Mary asked.

"Ha! Laramie is a thriving metropolitan city compared to Deer Springs," exclaimed Sam. "No, Deer Springs is just a small one-horse town, half-way between Laramie and Cheyenne. Probably only came to be from all the settlers breaking down on the Oregon Trail with no other place to go."

"We're a western cattleman's town, Mary, but I don't think we're as bad as what young Sam here is describing," said Dan Hartman. "You'll be surprised to see some of the new businesses growing in town; we've got ourselves a diner called *The Eatery*, and old Ben Murphy opened up a drug store, even Morgan's mercantile has expanded."

Mary stole a glance at each man, letting their comments and opinions sink in, as she wondered about this place, she would be calling home. She recalled bits of an earlier conversation with Sam when he had shared stories of his childhood, unhappy stories that perhaps colored his opinion.

As they drove northward, the outskirts of Laramie faded from view, and wide-open prairies filled the horizon. A sea of spring green grasses swayed their tasseled heads, undulating across the land like waves upon a beach. A wooden bridge rumbled under the truck's tires as they crossed the Lodgepole River; a deep torrent cascaded down the riverbed.

"Looks like the drought ended," Sam remarked as he noted the river depth and surrounding green fields.

"Yes, thank God. We had a wet winter and enough spring rains so far; I think it will be a good year," remarked Hartman.

"Oh my!" exclaimed Mary as she admired the range of mountains rising in the distance. "The tallest peaks I've ever seen were in the Scottish Highlands, but they can't compare to these."

Sam chuckled at her wide-eyed wonder. "Ma'am, welcome to the American West and the Rocky Mountains. That range ahead is called the Big Horn; we're near the edge of the Medicine Bow. Land here is rugged, wild; some places in the Medicine Bow have never even been touched by man, well maybe by Indians but definitely not any white man.

Daniel Hartman pointed out the road sign proclaiming Deer Springs then turned onto the county route. Within a few minutes, they entered the town of Deer Springs with its one main road that divided the center of town into a handful of short side streets. They drove past a post office, the new drug store, and two banks; a painted wooden sign hung in front of the jail and sheriff's office. Buildings were constructed in the western style with rough stucco exteriors and exposed wood beams. Hitching posts stood alongside the curb lane in front of storefronts and offices, parking for both horses and cars.

Hartman beeped his horn as he drove past *The Eatery* and waved in greeting to the woman busily washing the restaurant windows. He continued back out of town and past the local cemetery, north toward his own ranch.

"Maureen told me to insist that I bring you back for a mid-day meal. She won't take no for an answer," Dan told the couple.

"Maureen? Is that your wife?" asked Mary.

"Yes. I think she's got some foodstuffs set aside for you too. You won't find much at the house, Sam."

Sam nodded. He hadn't given any thought to the state of affairs at the Circle-D. He had no idea what the house looked like if it was clean or even had a roof overhead.

"Are things pretty bad? Maybe you better give me an idea of what's been happening," said Sam.

"Let's talk after supper. We'll be at Cedar Hill in a few minutes, and I can bring in Frank Costello; he's the one who really knows what's what. Frank has been lending a hand over at your place," explained Hartman.

"Okay, you're right. I probably should speak with Frank first before we head over there," said Sam.

They entered the driveway and stopped in front of the sprawling stone and cedar log ranch house.

"Place looks good. See you got it finished," Sam remarked then turned to Mary. "The Hartman's were just building this house a year before I left for the Army."

Mary hurried to brush off her dusty clothes and tuck her hair in place in an attempt to make herself presentable before meeting this new neighbor.

The noise of their truck door slamming shut resounded in the vast land. A moment later, the front door was thrown wide by a slim, middle-aged woman; her smile lit her face. Dark blonde hair was pulled back from her face, accentuating the bright blue eyes that sparkled in friendly warmth as she greeted her guests.

"Hello! Welcome home Sam. Come in, come in," she said.

Mary and Sam entered the Hartman home; Maureen hugged them both as introductions were made all around then led them into the spacious living space. Tantalizing smells wafted from the kitchen doorway; Sam's mouth began to water at the thought of a decent meal. He glanced over at Mary and saw that she was showing signs of being hungry too.

"It's awfully nice of you to treat us to supper, Missus Hartman. I have to admit, it's been a while since Mary and I have had a good meal," Sam said.

"Come sit down, please call me Maureen," she invited. "What can I get you to drink? Mary, would you like a cup of tea or do you drink coffee?"

"Tea would be lovely, but coffee is okay too. Whatever you have is just fine. Can I help you in the kitchen?" Mary asked, politely.

"Everything's almost ready, dear. You just go sit and make yourself comfortable. I just can't imagine how far you've traveled; my goodness, all the way from England," Maureen exclaimed.

Sam and Mary entered the large dining room filled with a long farm-house table and benches, two armchairs were positioned at each end of the table and above, hung a wagon wheel light fixture, unlike anything Mary had ever seen before. The room opened on one side to an expansive great room with a floor to ceiling stone fireplace. Broad cedar beams crisscrossed the tall, twenty-foot high ceilings. Sunlight streamed in through a wide picture window on the far wall; displays of dark red Indian paintbrush bloomed in the flower garden bordering the home's foundation.

"Your home is amazing," Mary said as she admired the log home. "You could put three of our English cottages into this one room," Mary exclaimed.

"We like our wide-open spaces in the West and our homes reflect it," Daniel Hartman chuckled.

"We've got some good beef steaks on the grill and all the fix'uns," declared Maureen as she placed bowls of steaming vegetables and mashed potatoes onto the table. "Don't be shy now, dig in. Dan, go bring in that platter of meat."

Mary and Sam exchanged looks of wonder at the quantity of food spread before them. After the rationing in England and the mess hall meals of Spam or powdered eggs, this was a feast fit for a king.

"I haven't had a steak like this since I shipped out," Sam said.

"Do you grow your own vegetables?" Mary asked. "I had a small victory garden back home, but with the war on, it's been a few years since I've enjoyed so many vegetables at once."

"We have our rationing here in the States too, but when you live on a farm or a ranch, you just grow your own. We might be short on gasoline and fabrics, even sugar is still rationed, but thankfully it doesn't keep us from eating well," Maureen explained.

Mary's eyes grew as big as saucers when the sizzling, juicy beef steaks were carried in from the grill. A thick slab of beef was laid on her plate, her mouth watered as she cut into the flavorful, succulent meat.

"Oh my, I've never tasted anything quite like this. It's delicious!" Mary exclaimed as she chewed with enthusiasm.

Sam laughed and dug into his own plate of food.

"Thank you both for this special welcome home. I appreciate it more than I can say. I know we won't be getting it at the Circle-D," said Sam.

Chapter 17

Frank Costello climbed behind the wheel of the old Chevy pickup as Mary and Sam thanked the Hartman's again and gave each a hug before departing for the Circle-D. After finishing their meal, Sam and Dan Hartman had sat discussing the problems at Circle-D and the condition of Sam's father. Now Sam was on his way home to see things for himself.

"Thanks for all that you've done, Frank. I hope I can count on you to stay on for a while and still lend me a hand," Sam said as he watched for Frank's response. "Surprised Pop still has this old truck; used to take a lot of work to keep it running."

Frank nodded to Sam as he put the truck into gear and started down the drive. Frank Costello had grown up in the neighboring county, only a few years older than Sam, he was a tall man with a lean build, not too many pounds to spare on his frame. His skin was permanently tanned with tiny crow's feet around his eyes from squinting in fierce summer sunshine or cold, harsh winds. Frank's dark hair grew longish in the back around his neck and peeked out from beneath his cowboy hat.

"How'd you miss not getting drafted, Frank," Sam asked. "Seems like most of the young men from these parts got called up or enlisted."

"Well, I wanted to serve but didn't pass my physical. Got a 4-F rating because of a skull fracture I got as a kid. Tried breaking a mustang horse one time, got kicked in the head when I fell off," Frank explained.

"Guess the Army's loss is my gain then," Sam remarked as they neared the western pastures of the Circle-D. "I'll sure be glad to get out of this uniform once we're home."

Frank slowed the truck and pointed as they rode near the perimeter fence line.

"Been keeping the cattle up in the northeast pastures and away from this area 'cause I don't have the time or manpower to fix that fence," Frank said.

"Well, now that I'm home, we'll see what we can do about re-stringing that fence wire and putting up some new posts. Grass is gonna run out soon on those other fields if we don't move the cattle over here. Guess I'll have to make this one of my priorities," Sam said as he surveyed the line of broken fence wire.

"Funny thing is…your Pa just strung that wire about a year ago; before his accident. Don't see any reason why that fencing should be down unless someone wanted it down," Frank said.

"Guess that's one of the things I'll have to have a look at too," Sam said quietly as he looked at the damage. "Keep going, let's see what the house looks like."

Fifteen more minutes of driving found them arriving in front of a two-story log home; several yards away stood a red-painted wooden barn and stable located near an abandoned, one-room sod hut.

"See that old sod building? That was my grandparent's original homestead. Can you imagine living in that?" Sam told Mary as he pointed out the dilapidated structure. "My parents built the big house when they got married. My Pop told us once, he had to promise my mother a new house before she'd agree to marry him thirty years ago."

A pair of tall, century-old elms stood as sentinels next to the log structure and spread their branches above the rooftop to form a shady canopy. The big leafy trees kept the house cool inside during hot summers and protected the home from raging snowstorms and heavy winter winds.

Mary gazed at the tall trees above the pitched rooftop, noted a pair of dormer windows cut into the high roof. The shingled roofline extended low in the front of the house to overhang an open porch. Narrow boards laid end to end covered the porch flooring, enclosed only by a rough railing. Two short steps led up to the front portal.

"It's not as pretty, or as big as the Hartman place, but it's home. I hope you can be happy here, Mary," Sam said. He gave her a half-smile, hesitantly. His own memories of the place were mixed and uncertain.

"It'll be our home; I'm happy just as long as we're together, wherever you want to be," Mary pledged to Sam as she wrapped her arms around him and kissed him. She watched his eyes and grim expression as he looked about the vacant yard and back to the blank windows of the log house.

"Okay, let's get this over with," he said, swallowing and taking a deep breath.

Sam placed a hand on the doorknob then turned to Mary and scooped her up into his arms. "I believe it is customary for the bride to be carried over the threshold," he told her as Mary laughed and clasped her hands behind his head.

They entered the shadowy front room; heavy cloth curtains were drawn closed across the two rectangular windows. Sam stepped inside and carefully lowered Mary to her feet as he tried to peer into the darkness.

"Wait here. Don't move," Sam cautioned.

The wooden planked floor needed swept, dirt and dried leaves were strewn about; most of the furniture wore a thick layer of dust. A pile of cold, black ashes lay in the hearth. Corners of the room sported cobwebs near the ceiling and who knew what occupants. Sam slowly moved about, gauging the condition of the place he had just brought his bride into.

The kitchen was no better - stale heels of bread and dried crusty food stuck to dirty dishes; half-empty coffee cups sat on the kitchen table; dregs of coffee grounds were spilled in the sink. Sam shook his head, disgusted.

"Not too cheery, is it?" asked Sam as he returned to the entrance, the only light coming in from the open doorway.

"Nothing a bucket of soap and water won't cure," Mary said, trying to be optimistic.

Frank came up the steps carrying three sacks of foodstuffs that Maureen had insisted on sharing with Mary. He hesitated and glanced back and forth between Mary and Sam.

"Where d'ya want these?" Frank asked.

"For the time being, put them on the table in the kitchen until we can find a clean place for them," Sam directed. He dragged his fingers through his hair and looked about the room again when a weak voice called out.

"Who's there? Who is it?" demanded a man's voice coming from the back of the house.

Sam looked at Mary, touched her cheek, then dropped his hand as he walked toward the short hallway and rear bedroom.

The house had been built with only two bedrooms upstairs and one bedroom on the ground floor in the rear of the house. A narrow staircase climbed to the second floor off the side of the short hallway, dividing the kitchen from the living room.

Sam entered the shadowy bedroom and approached the supine figure lying still on the bed.

"It's me, Pop, Samuel. I've come home."

"Humph," coughed Alexander Dunlap. A snarl curled his mouth, spittle on his lips as he sneered, "What are you doing here? War over?"

"No Pop, the war's not over yet. I came home to look after you and the ranch."

"I don't want you here. Why couldn't it have been you? Wish you had been killed and not Alex!" shouted the older Dunlap with his last bit of energy before he sunk back into the mattress.

A gasp caught the attention of both men as Mary stood in the doorway, having overheard the cruel comment of her father-in-law. She stood staring at the withered man in the bed, aghast at the cruelty it took to make such a statement. Her heart went out to her husband as she began to comprehend his anguished childhood.

"Who's that with you?" demanded Alexander.

Sam glanced at Mary as he answered, "That's my wife, Mary. I got married over in England."

"Well, I don't want her in here. Get out, I say! Out!"

"We're staying, old man, whether you like it or not. This is my home, my heritage, and by God, I'm claiming it," Sam shouted in reply, then turned and marched out of the dismal room, grabbing Mary by the elbow and propelling her back into the living room and out the front door.

Sam stood outside breathing heavily

Chapter 18

Rachel Yoder knocked timidly on the panel of the open door. Her long chestnut hair was pinned demurely into a tight bun at the crown, a soft cotton cap rested atop her head. Her plain brown dress hung to mid-calf in length, the bodice fitted snuggly and only adorned by a calico apron tied about the waist. She glanced about nervously, recalling the humiliation she experienced during her last visit here.

"Go on, you can go in," said Frank as he approached the house.

"Are thee sure?" asked Rachel.

"Hello in the house," he called out as he stepped into the living room.

Mary stepped out of the kitchen, wiping her hands on a bib apron that covered the front of her clothing. Her smile widened as she recognized Frank and took in the timid young woman at his side.

"Hello, you must be Rachel. I'm Mary. Thank you so much for coming to help. I'm so glad you came."

Rachel returned her smile and spoke quietly, "Friend Costello explained that thee just arrived from England. I can see that thou hath been busy already."

Mary nodded, "We cleaned the kitchen yesterday so I could put away our food and cook supper. Today we need to clean the big room and wash clothes. Can you help with that?"

Rachel's eyes darted to the back of the house, fearful, she listened to the sounds and cursing voices. She took a step backward as she heard Alexander Dunlap bellow in anger; his loud voice and words clearly heard.

"Dammit, I said leave me alone!"

"And I said you need a bath, and that's what you're going to get," Sam countered.

Sam had a large bucket of warm water and a bar of lye soap and intended to give his father a sponge bath from head to toe as he sat upon a bare wooden chair. Any water dripped onto the floor would be used later to mop it.

"I wouldn't be surprised if you have lice or any number of critters crawling on your filthy skin. Next, I'm going to strip that bed of yours and air it out. You can sit in that stuffed chair for a while; do you good to be upright for a change," Sam commanded.

"Since when did you get so damned bossy?" demanded his father.

"You should have seen the squadron of men under my command in England. I was a sergeant plus crew chief and kept my team in line," Sam boasted.

"Yeah? Think you're going to keep your old man in line now?" asked Alexander Dunlap.

"If I have to. I hope you'll learn I'm only thinking of your own good."

"Humph! Give me that rag; I can wash my own privates," Alexander growled.

"Fine, then do it," Sam said as he soaped up the rag and handed it to his father. He watched his progress before taking the bucket and pouring water over his chest and legs.

Sam lifted his father, wrapped Alexander's arms about his own neck and shoulders as he stood the man on his feet. He supported and balanced his father's weight while he wrapped him in a towel and dried his back and buttocks. Sam slowly lowered him into the dry upholstered chair to finish drying his legs, arms, and chest. He slipped a long nightshirt over his father's head then pulled up a pair of long johns. He had shaved him earlier at the onset of the bath and now studied the man before him; he resembled more the father he recalled.

"Well, you sure smell and look a lot better. How do you feel? Okay? You tired?" Sam asked.

Alexander rubbed a hand across his smooth jaw and grumbled under his breath, not wanting to admit he'd begun to feel like a dirty animal. Grudgingly, he mumbled, "Thank you."

Sam pretended he hadn't heard, knowing the amount of pride the old man must have swallowed to speak those words. He quickly removed the soiled clothes and bed linens then came back to lift the mattress and carry it outside. He hung the mattress across two strong ropes of clotheslines to let it air and dry; it was the best he could do. A large wooden barrel outside, near the kitchen door, was filled with soapy water to receive the dirty sheets and clothing where they would soak before being wrung out and hung to dry.

Sam entered the kitchen to find Mary and to meet Rachel.

"Hello. Sorry about the commotion, but he's all settled down now," said Sam.

"Good. I was just explaining to Rachel that I need her help with washing the clothes and putting the big room in order," Mary said as she smiled at Rachel, trying to reassure her that she would not be a nursemaid to the elder Dunlap. "I'll take care of feeding your father and making up his bed once everything is clean."

Wary, Rachel looked between Sam and Mary then nodded in agreement. "It would pleasure me to help thee."

"Thank you. If you can begin with the laundry, I will start washing down furniture in the big room," said Mary.

The two women rolled up their sleeves, a look of determination on each face, as they tackled the mammoth tasks before them. Mary swept the flooring and pulled down the dusty curtains, adding them to the wash barrel. She washed down the mantle, and all the table surfaces, dusted off the chair cushions, then took a wet rag to the filmy windowpanes.

Sam strung two more clotheslines between the house and one of the giant elms to hold the extra wash. Soon the sound of laundry flapping in the wind filled the yard. Sheets, towels, clothing, curtains – they were all washed and pinned to the line to dry in the fresh air and sunshine.

By noontime, Mary and Rachel stopped to fix food to feed the men and themselves. The women sat on the open porch sipping glasses of refreshing lemonade and enjoyed the cool breeze after their hard labor.

"I could not have completed so much laundry without your aid," Mary said as she smiled and patted Rachel on the arm. "You are truly a godsend."

"It is my duty to help thy neighbor," Rachel smiled shyly as she finished her drink.

"Oh, Rachel... I pray I can make Sam a good ranch wife. Everything is so strange to me; this wild land, homes so far apart. Our nearest neighbor is the Hartman ranch, and that's miles away. England was never like this," Mary confided, wringing a dish towel into a tight rope as she spoke.

"Thou will do fine. Your husband loves thee; he will help thee find thou way. Look at what thee has accomplished so far," Rachel reassured Mary.

"Thank you. You're very kind. You rest some more while I take some lunch to my father-in-law," Mary said.

Rachel nodded as Mary got up and went back into the house.

Carrying a glass of the lemonade and a cheese sandwich, Mary slowly entered the quiet bedroom. She set the tray on the side table and paused as she listened to the soft snores coming from the napping man. Mary carefully draped a light quilt across his chest and legs then tiptoed out of the room.

"Shall we go explore the barn? Sam told me there are chickens and a pair of milk cows. I haven't the foggiest idea about how to milk a cow. Do you?" Mary asked.

Rachel laughed softly, "I can teach thee."

Mary and Rachel walked across the yard into the shadows of the large barn. They immediately felt cooler inside the tall open structure. Straw was strewn across the dirt floor; the tall lofts above were filled with bales of hay, various tools hung on wall hooks, and several chickens skittered across the space in front of them. Two cows were tied in stalls along the right, they bawled loudly as they neared. A galvanized bucket hung on a nail next to one stall. A short three-legged stool leaned against one wall.

Rachel approached the cow, confident and natural in her manner. She patted the animal on its side and spoke softly to it. Mary looked on in wonder.

"She needs to be milked. See her udders, how full? Come, I will teach thee," Rachel said, pulling the stool over and adjusting her skirt to sit next to the animal.

Mary cautiously edged closer and squatted down to watch as Rachel grasped the cow's udder and pulled, squeezing to shoot milk into the pail.

"Oh my," said Mary. "I worked on a farm in England, but I didn't have to do the milking. I know about feeding chickens and gathering eggs; I even had my own vegetable garden, but cows… well, I guess I can give it a try."

Rachel and Mary exchanged places as Rachel placed Mary's hand on the cow's udders and demonstrated how she should squeeze to force the milk. It took her a few attempts, but finally, Mary proudly produced a steady stream. When she finished with the first cow, Mary moved on to the next one, positioning her stool and bucket and went to work.

Rachel began to rake the straw about, turning it over to freshen it then scattered a handful of corn onto the barnyard to feed the chickens. The coop was attached to the opposite wall of the barn; the hens' nests lined up in a row. Mary and Rachel filled their apron pockets with the brown eggs then returned to the house with their bucket of milk filled to the brim.

156

Rachel and Mary strained the raw milk, then poured the liquid into glass jars and placed them into the refrigerator. They put some of the milk with its heavy cream into the butter churner, added a small amount of salt, and then took turns working the handle up and down until Rachel proclaimed the butter was ready to scoop into a mold or roll into balls and wrap for the refrigerator.

Mary sighed as she looked around her clean home; fresh eggs, milk, and butter in the kitchen, the fruits of her productive labor would feed her family. Satisfied with her accomplishments, she exclaimed, "Wait until I show Sam what we did today."

Sam and Frank saddled up and rode the perimeter fence, inspecting the cut wire and making repairs where they could. Other stretches would require new barb wire. Dan Hartman was right. The spring rains had produced plentiful green grasses in the meadows; the cattle filled their bellies on the rich grass and grazed contentedly.

Frank pointed to the new calves following closely behind their mothers as they rode among the herd. Sam nodded as he tried to do a rough head count on the number of cows in the north pasture.

"Did Pop sell any cattle over the past year? If this is all of our herd, doesn't look as big as it should. We had more cattle than this when I left for the Army."

"I know he sold about twenty head, but that's about all. He was complaining about rustlers; swore he was losing cattle any time they grazed in the far north fields. Didn't have anyone to stay with the herd out there," Frank explained.

"Hmm, well, I can see we've lost some cattle. A blind man could count these cows and come up short," declared Sam. "We're going to need to get our brand on those new calves as soon as we can. I want to make sure they're marked as ours."

"Okay, Sam. If we fix that fence line on the western meadow, we can move 'em over and do the branding," Frank said.

"Need to make that fence our priority tomorrow," Sam said as they headed their mounts back toward the ranch house.

The men dismounted near the barn, allowing both horses to freely roam in the adjacent corral. The horses whinnied and drank thirstily from their water trough, then gobbled the fresh hay and clover in the feed tray.

"Guess we better see to the other animals in the barn," said Sam as he entered and approached the cows in their stalls. They were chewing their cud contentedly. "Huh, looks like they've been milked. Wonder who did that?"

"Chickens have been fed too, and all the eggs have been collected," remarked Frank, as he closed the door on the chicken coop after encouraging the hens to run inside.

"Well, well. I need to check on the old man and see how the girls are getting along."

"I'd say they've done a fair day's work from that yard full of laundry drying on the line," Frank said. He grinned as he opened the kitchen door and sought out Rachel.

Both Mary and Rachel sat enjoying a cup of tea at the kitchen table as the men entered the house. The rich aroma of bread baking in the oven teased the senses. Frank and Sam were amazed at the difference in the house; everything was organized and in its place with windows that sparkled in fresh, clean-smelling rooms.

"Am I in the right house?" asked Sam with a chuckle as he bent to press a kiss upon Mary's cheek.

"Welcome home," Mary greeted Sam, a smile spread across her face from ear to ear. "What do you think?"

"Madam, I think you have performed a miracle."

"It was Rachel; I couldn't have finished half of this without her. Wait until I tell you what else we did today!" exclaimed Mary.

"Only takes one look around to see you've been busy," said Sam.

"I learned how to milk a cow," said Mary proudly. "Rachel showed me, and then we even made butter."

Rachel nodded and smiled shyly; her hands folded in her lap. Pride was a sin, but she couldn't help feeling a great sense of pleasure.

"My farm wife!" declared Sam as he kissed her soundly. "I'm real proud of you, Babe."

Frank spoke up and addressed Rachel, "Thank you for all your hard work today. I'll drive you home whenever you're ready."

Mary clasped Rachel's hand in friendship. "I don't know how I would have managed without you. I've learned so much from you too. Can you come back tomorrow?"

"Yes," Rachel replied as she smiled and looked between Frank and the young couple. "It has been a good day."

"Has the old man been a problem?" asked Sam as he quietly pointed to the back room.

"No, he's been fine. I took him in a tray for lunch, but he was asleep. We need to bring in his mattress and set his bedding to right.

He'll be wanting to stretch out after being propped in that chair all afternoon," said Mary. She watched as Sam silently walked down the hallway toward his father's bedroom, not wanting to wake him if he was still asleep.

He found his father awake and just finishing a glass of lemonade. Alexander turned at the sound of Samuel entering the room.

"How are you, Pop?" asked Sam. "Need to use the commode? We're going to bring in your clean bedding and get you squared away pretty soon."

Alexander grunted as Sam lifted him and placed him on the commode chair then discreetly turned his back. Sam carried the empty tray back to the kitchen then went outside to heft the feather bed off the line and bring it back inside. Sam turned screws on the bed frame to tighten the ropes more taut then tossed the mattress onto the rope bed.

"Pop, I'm going into town tomorrow and see about getting you a wheelchair. There's no reason why you can't get around the house better or even get some fresh air on the porch. Don't like seeing you shut into this room," Sam said.

"I don't want folks in town pitying me," stated Alexander.

"Well hell, everyone in town knows about the accident and that you can't walk," Sam said.

"Wasn't any damn accident. I got ambushed and shot in the back. Wish it had killed me."

"I want you to tell me everything you can remember about that day. When you're up to it, we'll sit and talk; you can tell me about what's been happening on the ranch, too," said Sam.

"A lot of good it'll do," argued the elder.

"I can't fix what I don't know about," stated Sam emphatically.

"I don't know 'bout sitting in a wheelchair on display, looking like a cripple," grumbled Alexander.

Sam gave his own grunt as he studied his father. "Well, you are a cripple, and the wheelchair will let you get around; do more for yourself. I didn't bring my wife home to be a nurse for your sorry ass. You can start doin' for yourself."

"We'll see," murmured Alexander Dunlap as Sam spread his bedcovers onto the clean mattress and lifted him from the chair onto the soft bed.

"That's right, we'll see who wins this argument. Somehow, I favor myself," Sam told his father as he made him comfortable then left the room.

"Is he all right?" Mary asked, concerned, as Sam returned to the kitchen.

"Yeah, he's fine. Stubborn as ever, but he's coming around. It would kill him to admit that in the last twenty-four hours, he's been better cared for and fed than in a long time," Sam said.

"Um, I tried getting him out of that room, but he wouldn't let me," Frank defended himself.

"Oh, I don't blame you, Frank. I can well imagine he bullied you into letting him lay in that pile of filth, too proud for his own good. Well, that ends. I'm going to find him a wheelchair. He'll use it if I have to lock him out of the house to force him to learn to be mobile," Sam declared.

"Oh, you wouldn't!" Mary cried, shocked at her husband's lack of compassion.

"He's got to learn he is only as much a cripple as he wants to be. I know he lost the use of his legs, but he's still got two arms and hands; he's still got a brain. I won't see him wither away."

Mary saw the determination in her husband's eyes and knew his father had met his match. It would be a war of wills, and she had no doubt that Sam's will was forged in steel.

Mary laughed, "I can see my peace and quiet is likely to be short-lived. Rachel, you may want to wait a few days before coming back. There are sure to be words tossed about that will shock your tender ears."

"As thee wishes," replied Rachel softly.

Chapter 19

The road between the Circle-D ranch and Deer Springs twisted and turned across a valley and between two low mountain ranges; it was partially paved with blacktop but mostly dirt and gravel with a hundred potholes and ruts. For the second time, Sam swerved sharply to avoid hitting a deep hole in the roadway.

"Oh!" Mary yelled as she clutched for the door handle and hung on to keep from sliding across the Chevy truck's bench seat and collide into Sam.

"Sorry 'bout that," said Sam. "Tried to miss breaking an axle in some of those deep holes."

"I'm okay."

"Just hang on, we're almost there," said Sam.

They lumbered into Deer Spring's business district, all four blocks of it, and pulled up near the Morgan General Store. Sam parked the truck then hopped down quickly to lend a hand to Mary.

"I want to ask in here about a chair for Pop," Sam said.

"Fine. I'll just browse about, shall I? We do need a few things for the house," Mary said as she entered the general store and paused to scan the wide variety of goods. "Oh my, they do appear to stock everything."

"Go ahead, have fun. I'm going to speak with the clerk."

Mary nodded as she walked between the rows of clothing, fingering the marvelous fabrics, and admiring the American styles. She had not seen this much merchandise for sale since before the war. It was mind-boggling; as if there was no war going on at all. Her eyes grew even wider as she rushed over to the grocery aisles, delighted with the array of fruits and vegetables readily available, unheard of in England.

Sam left Mary to shop and approached the clerk behind the front counter.

"Mornin'. Is Mister Morgan around?" Sam asked.

"Yes sir, he's back in the office. I can go get him for you, if you want," volunteered the young lad.

"You do that. Tell him Sam Dunlap would like a word."

"Yes sir."

Sam looked over some hardware and tools as he waited for the store owner. At the sound of footsteps, he turned and extended his hand in greeting.

"Nice to see you again, Mister Morgan," Sam said as he shook the older man's hand.

"Samuel, you're a sight for sore eyes. When did you get home? Sorry about losing Alex. Your ma took his death real hard. Never saw a woman grieve so."

"Appreciate your words of sympathy," Sam said as he cleared his throat and tried to express what he really needed. "I uh, um, need your help with something. I want to buy a wheelchair for my Pop."

"A wheelchair, huh. Think he'll use it? I heard tell, he was bedridden and hasn't been out of bed since the accident."

Anger flaring, Sam had to temper his remarks as he faced the shopkeeper. "Well, you heard wrong. First of all, it wasn't an accident.

Somebody shot my Pop, and I plan to find out who. He can get out of bed, and that's why I want the wheelchair so he can get around more."

"Humph, good to hear. I don't know nothing about a gunshot," Morgan told Sam.

"So, can you get me a wheelchair or what?" asked Sam, impatient with the man now.

"Yeah, hold on now. I can get one for you; special order it from up in Cheyenne. Let me check my catalog and look up the price," Morgan replied, recognizing Sam's ire and not wanting to offend a paying customer. *"The young whelp came back from the war a different man; not the skinny, scared kid he used to be," thought Morgan.*

Sam followed the merchant to his office at the rear of the store and studied the pictures of three different chairs illustrated in the large worn catalog.

He pointed to one of the chairs shown in the book, "This one. I like this style. How much for this?" Sam asked.

"Lemme give 'em a call and see what I can do for ya," Morgan said as he took a pencil and circled the picture and stock number.

"Yeah, okay. How long do you think it will take to get the chair from Cheyenne?" asked Sam.

"Dunno, I'll check on that when I call. If they have one in stock, maybe just a few days. 'Course, I need to add on some shipping costs, driving all the way up to Cheyenne is gonna use up my gas ration stamps."

"I'll pay it. You give me a call when you know for sure," Sam told him as he scribbled his phone number on a scrap of paper.

Sam left the man to do his calls and went in search of Mary. He found her practically drooling over some mason jars of canned beans and tomatoes.

"Can we purchase a few jars? Just look at these vegetables, aren't they beautiful? I can't wait to plant our own garden and grow delicious vegetables like these," Mary exclaimed as she lovingly fingered the pint jars.

"Let me get an empty box; we can put in a few jars of each. Okay?"

"Wonderful. I'd rather have those more than anything," Mary said as she gave Sam a quick peck on his cheek.

Mary carefully selected several jars of tomatoes, beans, beets, and pickles; she handled them as carefully as fragile eggs. She added a five-pound sack of potatoes and a head of lettuce to her treasures.

Sam looked over her choices and nodded approvingly. "Well, at least we'll eat good," he said.

They left the store and loaded the food items into the back of the truck. Sam held Mary's hand and led her down the street, pausing to window shop here or there. As they stopped in front of a woman's clothing shop, Sam recognized Mary's yearning to see more. She had been hesitant to do any more than just peeking through windows, but Sam placed a hand on the small of her back and propelled her into the frilly boutique.

"Go ahead. Spend as much time as you like. I've got to stop at the bank and check on our accounts and maybe have a word with the sheriff," Sam said.

"Shall I meet you back at the truck?" Mary asked.

166

"Yeah, sure you'll be okay? I promise I won't be very long."

"I'll be fine. You go ahead and take care of your business. I want to learn what the women of Wyoming wear." Mary smiled and kissed him softly before they parted, her hand already on the doorknob of the shop.

Sam strode purposefully into the Deer Springs Bank and Trust. Two women stood behind teller windows; they smiled in greeting as he entered the bank lobby. Sam nodded and tipped his hat to the ladies as he walked toward the manager's desk located along the far wall.

Earl Clemson resembled a typical banker with his starched white shirt and pin-striped suit, a pocket watch chain hung from a vest pocket. Despite the warmth of the day, every vest button was closed. His thinning black hair lay parted on the side and shone with Brylcreem pomade liberally applied. A pair of bifocal glasses perched on the end of his nose. He nervously watched Sam approach his desk.

"Good afternoon. Can I help you?" Clemson asked.

"Sam Dunlap, Mr. Clemson, I'd like to discuss the Circle-D accounts." Sam extended his hand to shake the banker's sweaty one.

"Ah, um, certainly," Earl Clemson said as he shuffled papers on his desk and pointed to an empty chair for Sam. "What do you need to see?"

"I've been away from home for a while, my brother and I both served in the Army. I'm back now and running the ranch. I need to see how much cash we have on hand, what kinds of debts might be open, and the status of the ranch's line of credit."

"If you can wait right here, I'll have one of the girls pull your file," the banker said.

Sam stretched his legs out before him and crossed his ankles, folded his arms across his chest, clearly not going anywhere until he had his information.

The banker scurried between his desk and the clerk's; sifting through records in tall metal file cabinets. Clutching several brown folders, he returned to where Sam waited.

Earl Clemson made a big production of placing the files on his desk, sorting through the documents until he was satisfied that he'd found the current records.

He coughed lightly as he glanced at Sam. "My condolences to you on the loss of your mother. Such a tragedy coming so close to your brother's death. Must be difficult."

"Yes, well, that's why I'm home now. I'm running the ranch; I need to know our financial position," Sam replied.

"Um, I see. Well now, this statement shows your correct balance on the account," Clemson said as he slid a ledger paper toward Sam.

Sam studied the figures in the columns; he raised an eyebrow as he noted the red numbers indicating withdrawals and the few small deposits.

"Who authorized these withdrawals?" Sam asked, pointing to three different amounts and dates.

"Um, ah, I would have to find the check copies or examine the teller records. I can't tell by looking at this ledger, but I assure you we protect all of our customer accounts."

"I don't see how my father took money out of the account with him being laid up and not leaving the house at all for the past six months. So, who did?"

"As I explained, I'll have to inspect our records."

"You do that," Sam said as he leaned across the desk toward the banker. "My Pop is careful with his money, especially after surviving the depression. He wouldn't be taking out big sums of money from his account; more likely, he'd be hoarding money under his mattress. So, I ask again, who did? It sure as hell wasn't my Pop."

"Are you accusing me or this institution of theft?" Clemson's voice rose in anger with each word spoken.

"Hey, if the shoe fits. Let's just say I'm going to be looking at these records very closely. I better not find any more discrepancies," Sam warned in a level, quiet voice; he stood and stared at the banker until the man squirmed in his chair. "I'll be back."

Sam nodded at the tellers again as he put on his Stetson and walked out of the bank. His jaw hurt from gritting his teeth, rage boiling under the surface. His long stride quickly took him down the block to the sheriff's office. He opened the door and stepped inside in one motion as he scanned the room until his eyes fell on the man he came to see.

Sheriff Gus Kingman dressed like a wild west lawman of the 1800s instead of a police officer in the modern twentieth century. He wore a plain, blue denim shirt tucked into a pair of faded jeans topped with a brown leather vest edged with fringe. The sheriff star pinned on his vest rested above his heart; a black leather holster strapped around his waist rode low on his hip, a pair of pearl-handled Colt's within easy reach.

Kingman had one hand on a tin pot of coffee, burnt coffee grounds filled the air, as he studied a corkboard on the wall with its collection of wanted posters; he turned to greet Sam as he entered the stark room.

"Howdy, Sam. Heard you were back. How's it going?"

"Good to see you, Gus. Got a minute?" asked Sam as he shook the sheriff's hand and settled himself into one of the two wooden chairs positioned in front of the lawman's desk.

"Sure. Coffee?" he asked as he settled the pot back on the stove. "I can see by your expression that something's eating you. Wanna tell me about it?"

"I've taken over running the ranch. Think you know my Pop is laid up. That's another whole matter that needs investigating, but I just came from the bank, and I need to report a theft, or whatever you want to call it. Somebody's been stealing money from the ranch account," Sam stated.

The sheriff leaned back in his chair, tipped the brim of his hat off his forehead as he studied Sam's face. "You have any proof of what you're saying? Bank fraud is a serious charge."

"Clemson just showed me the bank ledgers. There are several withdrawals made while my Pop lay crippled in his bed. You know the old man; he squeezes a nickel hard enough to make the buffalo cry. I don't see him spending his money like that."

"I understand. But I need hard evidence before I can act, not just your gut feeling."

"I want you to know I plan on investigating this, with or without your help," Sam said as he held the lawman's eyes with his own, not blinking or glancing away.

"All right, if that's how you feel. I'll look into the matter. Just don't go acting on something without checking with me first; I'm the one that wears the badge here. Do we understand each other?"

"Agreed," Sam said. "What can you tell me about the shooting that crippled my Pop?"

"Well, I can tell you the facts, that's about all. Don't know too much. He was working the northern part of the county, checking brands and watching for strays, that kind of thing," Sheriff Kingman stated.

"Yeah, I know all that. What I don't know is why he was shot; did he cross paths with someone? Had he been in any fights earlier? Was it personal or something to do with the Stock Association?" Sam asked as he shoved a lock of hair off his forehead and slapped his hat against his thigh impatiently.

"I'm working on it. Don't know yet for sure, but I'm thinking it may have been both. You know your Pop's temper; think he may have rubbed somebody the wrong way," Kingman said.

"We've lost some cattle on the Circle-D; he may have been tracking rustlers. Frank Costello has found fence wire cut along our borders. We're fixing it now; I'll be hiring some men to get it done, then I'll patrol my own fence line," said Sam.

"Before you get yourself in over your head, maybe you ought to keep it legal and resume your Pop's job as brand inspector. Job's still open; yours if you want it."

"Humph, maybe I will. I gotta get going; left my wife shopping down the street. She'll be wondering where I got to."

"Wife, huh? Congratulations, I hadn't heard that bit of news.
What's her name?"

"Mary, she's a Brit. Prettiest gal I ever did see, not sure what she
sees in me, but she said yes," Sam told the sheriff as he shook hands
again and laughed.

"I'll come out to the ranch in a day or so and make it official about
that brand inspector post. Got some papers you'll need to sign and
swearing-in. I'd like to pay my respects to your father too."

"Okay. See you in two days then," Sam said as he left the office
and hurried down the street to find Mary waiting on a bench near their
parked truck.

"I was beginning to fear you had forgotten me," she said as he
rushed to her side. Mary softened the reprimand with a smile, though,
so Sam knew he wasn't really in hot water.

"Sorry. Time got away from me. I went to the bank then saw the
sheriff. Don't know about you, but I've worked up a powerful thirst
and could use a bite of food. How about we try that new restaurant
everyone's been telling us about?"

"Yes, let's do. I'd love a cup of tea," Mary replied.

"Great. Let me duck into Morgan's for a minute, I want to buy a
newspaper and see about posting a notice for help wanted," Sam said
as he escorted Mary back into the store.

"Forget something?" asked the store clerk as they approached the
counter.

"Got a blank piece of paper? Need to post a notice on your
board," Sam said.

The clerk handed Sam a square of brown wrapping paper and a thick lead pencil. "Thanks," Sam mumbled as he quickly printed his help wanted notice for two day-laborers and added his telephone number and address.

He handed the pencil and paper back to the clerk, who promised to tack up the notice on the bulletin board near the door.

Sam picked up a copy of the Cheyenne News and scanned the headlines. He snorted as he slid a nickel across the counter for the paper, then shook his head as he read the glaring headline and lead paragraph of the story.

"'April 25th, *General George Patton insults Russian Allies in a speech given in Knutsford, England. Patton states United States and Britain were destined to rule the post-war world. Kremlin offended; Patton reprimanded by Eisenhower.*'"

"What a crock!" mumbled Sam. "Politics, that's all it is. Patton is right not to trust those Ruskies." He remembered all too well the stories the Polish mechanics told as they worked together at Duxford about the Russians and their cruelties.

"What's wrong?" asked Mary as she tried to read over his shoulder.

"Huh? Nothing, just war news. Things are getting crazy back there," he said as they walked the two blocks to the new diner.

Sam stared into the cloudless sky as his thoughts drifted back to the men in his squad and wondered how Pete was getting along. He still felt a sense of guilt over leaving them behind, quitting the war effort and his men to return home early while they had to remain in Europe apart from their own loved ones.

"Do you miss it? Your squadron, I mean?" Mary asked as she laid a hand on his arm.

Sam squeezed her hand tenderly and pressed a kiss on her cheek as he opened the door leading into *The Eatery*. "Sometimes I miss my men, but my place is here with you now and the ranch. What about you? Do you miss your job, driving for the general?"

"Occasionally. In England, I knew I was doing my bit for the war effort. Everything's so strange here; I don't feel like I fit in."

"You will. Don't worry. You are making the ranch into our home; I couldn't do it without you," Sam said as he hugged her once more.

They stepped inside and glanced about. A few men sat at a counter drinking coffee while two other couples chatted over luncheon plates.

Maybelle Parker poured coffee with one hand while she flipped burgers on the sizzling hot griddle with the other. She called out a greeting to the new customers as they entered, "Come on in! Take a seat wherever you like. I'll be right with you folks."

A trio of paddle fans hung from the ceiling, gyrating slowly, circulated the warm air through the narrow confines of the former railroad car turned restaurant. Cozy, red vinyl upholstered benches filled the dining booths arranged along the walls in an L-shape. The red color created a cheery contrast to the waxed black and white checkered linoleum that covered the floor and with the bright yellow painted walls that brought the sunshine in.

Sam and Mary slid into one of the comfortable booths. The aroma of beef sizzling on the grill and potatoes cooking in a deep fryer made their mouths water, and tummies grumble in anticipation.

"Howdy, folks. Don't believe I've seen you here before. My name's Maybelle; I own this place with my husband, Ralph. Special today is a burger and fries, but I can fix you anything on the menu hanging on that wall."

"A burger and fries sound great; make that two please," Sam said. "I'll have a Coca-Cola, and my wife would like a cup of tea."

"Coming right up," said Maybelle as she sauntered back behind the counter again. Her long brunette hair was held back under a checkered scarf with a matching red checked apron tied around her waist under an ample bosom. The young woman always had a friendly smile for her customers and maintained a steady chatter as she maneuvered between counter and cooktop, poured drinks, and plated food.

Within a few minutes, Maybelle served Sam and Mary their food and drinks. She wiped her hands on her apron as she told them, "You let me know if you need anything. Enjoy."

"Thank you; it looks delicious," Mary said. One bite into the juicy burger elicited a satisfied "Mmm."

They each savored the rare treat before Sam, swallowing a mouth full of crisp potatoes, spoke. "The sheriff wants me to take on the brand inspector job with the Stock Association that my Pop held. I told him I would."

"What does that mean, brand inspector? I understand about brands; we had them on sheep in England, not exactly like what you do to cattle, but the same idea, I guess. So, what would your duties be? Will you be gone from home very much?"

"I'd have to be gone some of the time, not every day. I still need to work the ranch. But it will give us a paycheck until I can get the ranch to start earning more money again. We need an income. Mostly I'll just have to patrol our county. Other inspectors work the surrounding areas," Sam explained.

"Oh, I guess that makes sense," said Mary.

"Sheriff Kingman is coming out to the house in a couple of days; he's got some paperwork for me to sign, and then I'll be official."

Chapter 20

Five men showed up at the Circle-D in answer to the posted want ad. Sam stood on the open porch as the men gathered in front of him to learn the details of the job.

"Thanks for coming out. I need two men to dig fence posts, string fence wire, and help move cattle. I can pay wages for two weeks. Sorry, it can't be any longer," Sam said.

A couple of the men looked disappointed and complained about making the trip out to the ranch for a small job. One guy stepped forward, glanced at the men standing to his side, then spoke up.

"I'm willing. Been out of work for nigh on three months now; two week's wage is better than none."

"What's your name?" Sam asked.

"Hank Butler. I can start today."

"Nice to meet you, Hank. Anyone else?" Sam asked as he scanned the faces of the men. An older Mexican man tucked his sombrero under his arm as he stepped forward.

"Miguel Lopez. I am strong and not afraid of hard work. I give you a good day's work for a day's pay."

"Okay, Miguel, you've got a job. You other men, thanks for your time. I might have more work in the future, depends on how well the ranch does this year," Sam said as he stepped off the porch and shook hands with both Miguel and Hank. The other three men shared a ride back into town.

Frank Costello walked out of the barn and shot Sam a sideways look with an inquiring nod toward Miguel.

"You guys wait right there," Sam directed as he strode toward Frank and then turned toward the barn to speak privately.

"You sure about that wet-back?" asked Frank.

"He's willing to do the work; I don't see why not. One thing I learned in the Army, don't judge a man by his name or the color of his skin."

"All right by me, if you say so," Frank replied as he crossed the yard to greet the new ranch hands.

"Do you men own a horse?" asked Sam. Both shook their heads. "No, all right then, come on over to the corral and let's pick out a mount for each of you."

"We'll be using the pickup for the fencing, but you'll need to mount up when we work cattle," Frank said.

"Can you ride?" Sam asked as he questioned each man.

"Sí señor. I be on horseback since a boy," Miguel said proudly.

"How about you, Hank? You ride?" asked Sam.

"Yeah, I can ride. Got thrown by a horse once, banged up pretty bad. Not my favorite thing to do, but I'll give it a go if I gotta," said Hank.

"Well, there's a little mare over there that's pretty gentle, Hank. She'll be yours to ride when we work the cattle. Just give her the lead; Daisy knows what to do. That pinto will be your ride, Miguel. He can be kinda spirited at times, but I think you'll be okay with him," Sam said as he pointed out each animal in the pen.

"Today, let's load up supplies and head out to the west pasture. Got some fencing to repair," Frank said as he tossed a post hole digger into the truck bed.

All four men tugged on heavy work gloves; finished loading bales of wire and hand tools into the truck. Miguel and Hank road the tailgate as Frank hopped into the passenger seat, and Sam slid in behind the wheel.

They drove the perimeter of the ranch until they arrived at the section of broken fence posts. New wire would have to be strung, and wooden posts reset. It was hot, tiring work and would take all four men working together to repair the miles of fencing before their day was done.

Mary conquered the wringer washing machine and now had a load a fresh laundry drying on the line while a pot roast simmered on the stove. Chores done, barn animals all fed and cared for, satisfied, she decided to survey the patch of ground that had been designated for the household garden. The hard ground required tilling to turn the fertile soil; more weeds than plants filled the space. Mary shook her head in dismay as she wondered if she could possibly prepare the land to grow a bountiful vegetable garden. She missed her compact victory garden back in England. She looked up as she heard Sam's truck enter the yard.

Sam waved to her as he pulled to a halt near the barn. Four very sweaty and dirty men hopped out of the truck; it looked like it took their last ounce of energy just to move. Frank filled a bucket of water from the hand pump by the barn, and each man gratefully splashed the cool water onto hot necks and faces. A second bucket of cold water was passed around, and a shared dipper quenched their thirsts.

Sam Joined Mary and gave her a quick kiss then turned to introduce her to the new men.

"This is Hank and Miguel; they're going to be helping out for a couple weeks or so. We got a good piece of fencing repaired today. Tomorrow, we'll inspect the rest of the ranch borders and check for more broken posts."

"Hello. Thank you for helping my husband," Mary said as she smiled at both men. "I have a big pot of food cooking in the house; you're both welcome to a bowl if you're hungry."

Surprised expressions flashed across the men's faces; the kind invitation to share their meal endeared the lady of the house in their hearts.

"Señora Dunlap, mucho gracias. You are very kind," Miguel told Mary.

"Appreciate the offer, ma'am, but I'm way too dirty to enter your home," Hank said.

"Nonsense! We'll set up a table in the shade, and we can all eat together outside, a picnic of sorts. Sam and Frank, you carry out some chairs from the kitchen," Mary commanded.

A makeshift table was erected under the giant elm, and seats were carried outside. Sam went inside to speak to his father as Frank helped Mary carry plates and flatware for use with their meal.

"Hey Pop," Sam greeted his father as he entered the bedroom. "How about I take you outside for some fresh air? Mary's got a delicious pot roast ready, and we're eating outside. I can set up a table and chair for you on the porch."

"Now, why the hell would I want to eat outside?"

"Let's just say it would be a change of scenery for you. You need some air. This room is getting stuffy. C'mon, what 'dya say?"

"Is that the only way I'm going to get some food to eat around here?" grumbled Alexander.

"Quit your complaining. I'm going to move this table and chair outside, then I'll come back to get you."

"Humph, doesn't look like I have any choice in the matter," Alexander mumbled as Sam went about preparing a place for him. Minutes later, he returned to lift his father and carry him onto the open porch.

Alexander settled himself into the comfortable chair as he took in the scene at the corner of the house. Frank carried a large cast-iron pot, two towels wrapped around the hot handle, as he set the heavy pot in the middle of the wooden table. Mary quickly began to ladle the rich beef stew onto plates. A pair of strange men eagerly waited for their serving.

"Who the hell are they?" Alexander demanded as he grabbed Sam's arm.

"I hired some laborers to string fence wire. That's Hank and Miguel; they're gonna be here for two weeks," Sam explained. "Want some coffee or something cold to drink?"

"Humph. Coffee." Alexander watched the men politely thank Mary as she filled their plates; one man crossed himself and said grace before he began to eat. He raised an eyebrow as he observed his son interact with the trio of men and his young wife.

Sam's attention was on Mary; he was so proud of her… her kindness and friendly acceptance of the strangers. He took a plate of food from her and filled a mug of coffee, then served his father before sitting down to start his own meal.

"Never had anything so tasty," Sam said as he took another forkful of beef and potatoes. Mary had cooked the potatoes and carrots in a rich broth with the tender beef and flavored it all with diced onions and just the right amount of seasoning.

"I'm so glad you all like it. This bread is what we call Yorkshire pudding; in England, we always served it with beef. It was one of my mother's recipes. Not a fancy meal, but it'll stick to your bones," Mary said.

"Much obliged, Missus Dunlap. Didn't expect to be fed such a fine supper," Hank said sincerely with a nod to Sam and Mary.

Miguel pointed to the patch of overgrown garden space after he finished his plate. "I see you want to grow a garden. I would like to help you as payment for this good meal. I can dig the dirt, make it ready for plants; maybe some carrots and onions or beans." He quickly looked over at Sam, "After I finish my work with you señor, I help the señora. Is okay?"

"Miguel, if you still have enough energy to till a vegetable patch after putting in a full day, I certainly won't turn down your offer. Mary has wanted to get some plants in the ground before the weather turns too warm. Mucho gracias, Miguel."

"Bueno," Miguel said, nodding to Mary.

Frank offered to drive Miguel and Hank back into town as soon as their meal ended; tomorrow, they could stay over in the bunkhouse. They all piled into the pickup as Sam carried the heavy iron pot back into the kitchen, and Mary collected the soiled dishes. It only took a few minutes to put the kitchen chairs back and dismantle their impromptu picnic ground.

As Mary began washing dishes, humming softly to herself, Sam carried another mug of coffee outside to join his father on the porch.

"Get enough to eat?" Sam asked as he took the rocker next to his father, rocking in a slow rhythm.

"Don't blame me if I get fat on her good cooking; you won't be able to carry me around this house anymore." Alexander laughed in the first show of humor in a very long time.

"Don't worry old man. I think I'm still strong enough to haul your ass around," Sam said with a chuckle. "Besides, in a few days, I'm gonna pick up a wheelchair that I ordered for you, and you can get around by yourself."

"I told you I don't want no damn wheelchair," Alexander shouted.

"Well, you're going to get one. I need you to be able to supervise what's happening around here, and you can't do that from your bed," Sam stated in a voice that brooked no argument from the older man.

"What do you mean, supervise? Just what will you be doing if you aren't here looking after the work?"

"Gus Kingman asked me to take over your brand inspector position. He's gonna be out here tomorrow to swear me in," Sam said.

"That something you want to do? You going to have time for that and the ranch, plus a new wife?" Alexander studied his son's face and read the determination in his eyes. He had never really paid much attention to Samuel; he had to admit that he had no time for the lad but confronting the man he had become oddly pleased him.

"Tell me about the day you got shot. Where were you? What were you doing?" Sam asked.

Alexander Dunlap closed his eyes, remembering the pain and the anguish. When he opened his eyes, he stared into the distance, reliving the flash of time that changed his life forever. "I was riding north in the free range, rounding up our stray cows and checking other brands as I went. It was late in the afternoon; you know how the sun sets behind Rattlesnake Ridge, blinds you with the glare of its red glow. I couldn't be sure, but for just a second, I thought I saw a flash of sun on metal, maybe a gun barrel. The next instant, I was lying on the ground bleeding. Couldn't feel my legs, just pain in my back like I never knew before."

"Who found you? Do you remember?"

"Don't know how many hours I laid there. Brody found me, tossed me across the back of my horse, and brought me home. I was unconscious by then, damn near bled to death. Dan Hartman gave me some of his own blood; doc hooked up one of them transfusion bottles and tubes right here in the house. Guess I wouldn't be alive without Dan; kind of makes us blood brothers."

"Where's Brody now? I was expecting to see him here," Sam said.

"Don't know. After your brother and Ma died, I didn't much care who was here."

"Okay. I can see you're getting tired; I'll take you back inside. Hey, one more question… have you withdrawn any money from the bank in the past three months? Ask anyone to do it for you?" Sam asked as he lifted his father and carried him into his bedroom.

"No. What would I need money for? Why are you asking?" Alexander asked, worry etching his face.

"I stopped by the bank yesterday, checked on the accounts, and had some questions, that's all. Don't worry, I'll take care of it," Sam said.

It was mid-morning when Gus Kingman pulled into the drive and parked near the house. Sam and Mary had just finished milking cows, gathering eggs, and feeding chickens and were walking toward the house. Frank had taken Hank and Miguel to continue their work on fence posts. All in all, it was a quiet routine day. Sam waited on the porch for the sheriff to join him.

"Morning, Gus," Sam greeted. "Coffee?"

"Sounds good, don't mind if I do."

"Have a seat, I'll go get us a couple mugs," Sam said. He went into the kitchen and poured two cups, nodding to Mary that he'd be outside with the sheriff.

"Thanks," Kingman said as he accepted the steaming mug of black coffee.

"I've been meaning to ask you if you've seen Jim Brody around town," Sam said as he sipped the hot brew.

"Nope, not for over two months. Didn't he work for your Pop?"

"Yeah, he did. Pop used to rely on him to run the ranch when he was away doing Stock Association business. I'm wondering if that's who stole the money out of our account. I asked Pop if he took out any cash recently or in the last few months; he said no."

"Sounds plausible. I suppose the bank might have allowed him to transact the ranch business, knowing your Pop was laid up and your mother was gone. He could have told them he had authority," the sheriff said.

"That's what I'm thinking too. So, where the hell is he? Did he skip town with our money? If that was his plan, why didn't he steal more? I'm not saying we can easily afford the loss of a few hundred dollars, but if I were going to rob somebody and disappear, I'd sure as hell make it worth my while. Know what I mean?" Sam speculated. He studied the sheriff's expression, trying to read his thoughts.

"I'd have to agree with you there. In for a penny, in for a pound. I'll ask one of my deputies to check on Brody's whereabouts. See what we turn up."

"Good. I talked to Pop about the day he got shot; he said he was out near Rattlesnake Ridge at sunset. He saw a muzzle flash right before he was hit; said Brody found him after a couple hours. That the same story you heard?"

"Your mother called our office when Brody carried him home. I hadn't heard exactly where the shooting took place; Brody never said, and your Pop didn't cooperate when he was questioned. Rattlesnake

Ridge… isn't that near the boundary of the Circle-D with the Diamond Bar ranch?" Gus asked.

"Yeah, that's right. Our disputed boundary that is. Pop told us when we were young that his father always talked about that land belonging to the Dunlap family and that Logan stole it, but we never had any proof of that. Just an old man's ramblings, I think. My gramps died in a gunfight when my own father was just a kid, so I don't put too much store in those old tales."

"Maybe I'll take a ride out that way, look around, although it's been a long while now since your dad got shot. I'm not likely to find any evidence still out there, but I'll go check it out," the sheriff said as he set his empty mug on the porch rail. "Want your wife to witness your swearing-in as brand inspector?"

"I'll go get her. Be right back," Sam said as he jumped up and rushed into the house.

Mary stepped out onto the porch and smiled warmly at the gruff-looking lawman.

"Hello, I'm Mary Dunlap," she said as she extended her hand in greeting.

"Nice to make your acquaintance, ma'am."

Sam brought his father into the living room where he could sit near the door and witness the ceremony without being embarrassed about his disability. Sam patted his father's shoulder affectionately then returned to the porch.

"Okay, I'm ready," he said to the sheriff.

"All right then, let's get this done."

Mary took a seat to watch as Sam stood before Gus Kingman. Her eyes shone with the love and pride she was feeling at that moment.

"Raise your right hand and swear after me that you will uphold the laws of the state of Wyoming and to the best of your ability, fulfill the duties as Brand Inspector of the Wyoming Stock Growers Association."

"I will," said Sam.

"Congratulations, you are now the duly appointed Brand Inspector of Platte County. Now so there is no misunderstanding, let me tell you your duties. As Brand Inspector, you've got to complete a physical inspection of all livestock for brands and ownership. Check the brand record, the actual brand, and any paper documentation, such as inspection certificates. That means any cattle, horses, mules, asses, even sheep gotta have proof of brands and ownership. Understand?" asked Kingman.

"Yeah, I get it," answered Sam.

The sheriff continued, "Brand Inspections are required for a change of ownership and to legally cross county or state lines. You'll have to issue title certificates during any change of ownership. As inspector, you're promising to protect the livestock interests of the State of Wyoming from all theft. You'll be acting as the investigative arm for Animal Health, Brand Recording, and Inspection Unit agencies."

"Guess I never realized it was so involved or important. I knew brands had to be inspected but thought that was just to catch rustlers," Sam admitted.

"Well, it is, but there's a whole lot more too. Still want to do the job? It'll keep you busy," Kingman said.

"Yeah, I'm sure. I gave my word; I won't let you down. I've got priorities to finish around here this week before I can start, though. That okay?" asked Sam.

"Yeah, that's okay. We've been without an inspector for over six months now, another week ain't going to matter none," said Kingman.

"How much does it pay? Do I get a badge or something?" asked Sam.

The sheriff pulled a circular badge out of his pocket and handed it to Sam. Large capital letters WY were in the center of a circle with the words Stock Grower's Association Inspector printed along the outer border.

"Job pays thirty-four dollars a week; you'll get your check twice a month," the sheriff explained.

"Not much; guess I won't get rich, but it will help put groceries on the table and pay some bills," Sam said as he winked at Mary.

"Right. I gotta be going," said the sheriff as he shook Sam's hand. "You take care now, Alexander," he called into the house, catching a glimpse of the old man near the open doorway.

Chapter 21

Mary fingered the new badge pinned to Sam's shirt. She studied his thoughtful expression and saw the way his eyes went to his father sitting paralyzed on a living room chair. Was he worried that the same fate might await him?

"I think I understood most of what the sheriff was saying but is it difficult to read these symbols? How can you tell one from another?" Mary asked.

They entered the cool interior of the house and gathered around the kitchen table as Mary poured tall glasses of iced lemonade and automatically started to fix sandwiches for lunch. Alexander was moved into the kitchen and listened to the conversation.

"Let me see if I can show you what brands I'll be reading. Correct me, Pop, if I draw these wrong," Sam said as he took out paper and pencil and scribbled three designs for Mary to see.

"Ours is simple to understand," Alexander pointed out. "Just a round circle with the letter D in the middle."

Sam pointed to each drawing and identified the ranch name that used the symbol. "The Diamond Bar is easy to read too; you can see the diamond shape with the horizontal bar. Now, Cedar Hill is a bit more unusual, Dan Hartman likes a triangle with initials CH inside it for Cedar Hill. See what I mean?"

"What about other ranches? Aren't there more?" asked Mary.

"I only have to patrol Platte County, and in this county, there are only three large ranches; we own most of the land. Some folks own an acre or so with a house, but they don't run cattle like the three of us do. Most folks live near town or just have a small farm, not a cattle ranch."

"Oh, I see. So, you only have to look for just those three marks. It seems straight forward enough," Mary said as she studied the pencil drawings again.

"You'd be surprised how those brands can be altered by serious rustlers. I've run across animals with part of their hide cut away just so a different brand can be burned," Alexander added.

"Burned? What do you mean?" asked Mary looking at each man.

"Brands are burned into the animal's hide. A branding iron is a tool created in a forge with its symbol or mark. Cowboys heat the iron in a fire until it turns red hot, then the cowhand presses the hot iron against the hide of the cow. Guess we do it different than in England, huh?" Sam said.

"Oh, my goodness, that sounds barbaric," Mary exclaimed.

"Well, it serves a purpose, like you heard the sheriff say, cattle can roam the range and graze with other cows and then be separated at roundup time and returned to each legal owner. My job will be to call the brands, check on the ownership," Sam explained.

"I see. How long does it take to ride around the county? It doesn't sound immense if it is only one county. We had counties with large estates in England, but you could drive from one end to the other in an hour or so."

Sam and Alexander both laughed, causing Mary's face to turn red. "What's so funny?" she asked indignantly.

Sam pressed a quick kiss onto her petulant lips, seeing her humor was not restored, he tried to explain, "Honey, our ranch is close to one hundred and fifty thousand acres of land. The county itself covers over a million acres. I guess Cedar Hill is probably about four hundred thousand acres, and Logan's Diamond Bar spreads out over the rest. Ain't that right, Pop? Think the Diamond Bar is still the biggest spread?" Sam asked.

His father nodded, yes. "Takes a man on horseback a full day to ride from the east to western boundary of the county, and that's the narrow part; maybe three days to ride north to south."

Mary's eyes were as round as saucers as she tried to visualize the expanse of land being described. She shook her head and swallowed; she was definitely not in England anymore and would have to become used to what America referred to as wide open spaces.

"I think maybe we should spend an afternoon riding, so you get a better idea of what I'm talking about. Will give me a chance to see to the cattle too. C'mon Missus Dunlap, about time I show you where you live," Sam said as he reached for her hand, approving of the trousers she wore. "Pop, where do you want to spend the afternoon – out here or back in your room? I'll see you settled before I leave."

"Reckon I'll spend time out here. Need to use the commode before you leave, then I'll be okay for a while," Alexander said.

A few minutes later, Sam had saddled the gentle mare, Daisy, for Mary to ride then lifted her to gain stirrup and saddle. She adjusted her seat before taking the reins in a firm grasp and nodded.

Sam stepped into his stirrup easily, throwing a leg over Blackie's back, his black Morgan, and took command of his stallion as he guided him out of the corral and toward the open pasture. He and Mary rode side by side in an easy trot as he pointed out landmarks to her, such as the Laramie mountain range and Rattlesnake Ridge in the distance. A gentle breeze caressed their skin and tickled tendrils of hair as they rode. Sam shared stories of his youth riding with Alex across these same meadows and of the Oregon Trail with his own grandparent's history of traveling that western trek to settle on the Wyoming plains.

They had ridden several miles, past the herd of cattle grazing contentedly, then into lush meadows filled with tall grasses and sweet-smelling wildflowers. A riot of color - yellows, lavender, white and red, dotted the rolling land; the floral heads gaily swayed in the soft breeze. Mary breathed in the fragrant scents.

"Beautiful! Flowers as far as the eye can see. I don't even recognize some of the varieties, but they're lovely," exclaimed Mary.

"I don't know the names of all of them, but those red things are called Indian paintbrush, and the lavender ones are lupines. My mom always picked the yellow daisies; they were her favorites."

They walked their horses toward a stand of Ponderosa pines bordering the meadow and sought their shade to rest a bit and allow the horses to drink from the shallow stream nearby. Sam dismounted and lifted Mary down then tied their reins onto some brush at the water's edge.

He removed a blanket rolled up behind his saddle and spread it among the sweet flowers and grasses, motioning for Mary to join him on the soft bed.

"Nice, isn't it? You know, we haven't had any privacy since we got home, always a cowhand or my father nearby. I think we should take advantage of it, hmm?" Sam said as he laughed and made a lecherous grin, wiggling his eyebrows.

"Why Samuel Dunlap, whatever do you mean?" Mary asked, pretending to be shocked as he pulled her down next to him and wrapped his arms around her.

"Has it been so long that you don't remember?" Sam asked as he spread butterfly kisses along her neck, across her cheek, and captured her lips in a passionate kiss.

"Mmm, remind me some more," whispered Mary as she clung to him and returned his kiss with her own passionate one.

Two hours later, the lovers lay quiet in the afterglow of their lovemaking. They listened to birds chirping in treetops and watched cottony-soft clouds float by overhead. The afternoon sun began its path across the sky, slipping lower behind the distant mountain range, reminding the couple of the late time. Air began to cool as Mary and Sam slowly dressed, hands still caressing bare skin as buttons and zippers closed. A final kiss and embrace were shared before the pair walked to their waiting horses and prepared to ride home after a thoroughly pleasant afternoon.

Miguel was true to his word. At the end of his day moving cattle from the north pasture into the newly fenced western land, he returned to the house and began working the soil in Mary's garden. Mary could hardly contain her excitement as the possibility of planting a vegetable garden became a reality.

Miguel weeded and hoed the rich earth and helped to create straight furrows for planting. Maureen Hartman had visited the day before and gifted Mary with a flat of young starter plants from her own garden: onion sets and carrots, even some small green bean plants that would transplant easily. Mary added some seeds for tomato plants and squash then faithfully watered her young garden, tending to it each day, anticipating all the wonderful produce the family would enjoy.

Mary wiped her hands on her apron as she entered the kitchen. Her father-in-law sat at the kitchen table, finishing his lunch. He was joining Sam and Mary more each day and spending less time isolated in his room. Mary smiled at him as she noted the empty plate; his appetite had undoubtedly improved.

"Feels like it's getting warmer. Is that normal for late May? I was wondering if my plants might suffer in the heat. What do you think?" Mary asked Alexander.

"Should be ok; you didn't plant any cold-weather vegetables like peas or lettuce. We'll begin to heat up from now on, but our nights are still cool. We're high enough elevation that it doesn't normally get too hot even at the peak of the summer. You got those plants in the ground just in time. May and June are usually our rainy months, although we've suffered droughts in the past."

"Sam told me about the lack of rain and how farmland turned into dust bowls. Was that during the Depression?"

"A couple bad years right before the crash. Probably what helped to cause the crash; folks lost their land and homes, but we hung on.

Yeah, it was tough, but we made it," Alexander said. He stared out the window, lost in thought.

Mary stood next to his chair and gently placed a hand upon his shoulder, patted it once then left him to his memories. She looked up as a sound outside caught her attention. Leaving Alexander at the table, she walked outside, quietly closing the screen door.

Sam had dropped the tailgate on the truck and tugged on a knotted rope to release a wheelchair that he had strapped into the truck bed. He rolled the chair toward the tailgate so he could grasp it and lower it to the ground.

"What do ya think?" Sam asked Mary as she walked toward the truck.

"Very nice. I think he'll like it," she said.

"Where's Pop now?" Sam asked.

"In the kitchen, just finished lunch."

"Okay, let's see if he'll use this."

Sam wheeled the chair over to the house, lifted it up the couple porch steps as Mary held open the door. He silently wheeled the chair into the living room then turned toward the kitchen.

"Hey, Pop. I've got something for you."

Alexander turned in his seat to study the new chair. "Humph, guess since you went to all the trouble of getting the damn thing, I should probably try it out. See if it fits."

"I'll lift you into the chair for now, until you get used to how it moves, then you can practice sliding off your bed onto the seat, or moving from a straight chair onto it," Sam said as he placed his arm under his father's shoulders and carefully lifted him.

196

The chair was a newer style, with hand brakes on the wheels and a slung leather seat and backrest. Sam raised his father's legs and placed a foot on each rest, then steadied the chair until his father felt comfortable. Alexander slowly gripped each rubber wheel cover, pulled to start the chair in motion, then glided across the wooden floor from kitchen to living room. He looked up at Sam, tears glistening in his eyes before he quickly wiped them away.

"I didn't think I'd ever be able to move or get around again. Once more, I've been proven wrong. Thank you," Alexander's voice was strained and low as he spoke.

"I need you, Pop. Besides, they can't keep a Dunlap down," Sam said as he pressed a hand against his father's shoulder in a small show of affection. "I'll get one of the boys to help me build a ramp off that porch so you can get up and down; we'll do it tomorrow."

"I think that's a good idea if you expect me to run things around here while you're gallivanting around the countryside," Alexander told Sam as he squeezed Sam's hand in a rare show of emotion.

Chapter 22

Sam took a sip from his canteen as he sat in the saddle and surveyed the herd of cattle stretched across the rolling hillside before him and to the north. He had stopped to speak with Dan Hartman yesterday to inform him that he'd be on his land, and after two days of riding, he had covered Cedar Hill's range and accounted for most of the Hartman herd. Now he slowly walked his horse among the cows, reading brands as he went, spotting a few Diamond Bar head grazing with Circle-D cows.

Tomorrow when he returned home, he would direct Frank and Miguel to round up those cows and push them toward their own pastures. If there were a drought again, Circle-D would need all the alfalfa and grasses it could get. Sam couldn't afford to share.

He followed the deep wagon ruts cut into the land from decades of heavy Conestoga wagons pushing westward on the Oregon Trail. Over fifty years later and a person could still find signs of pioneers who made that dangerous journey; broken pottery, a discarded cast-iron stove, or a broken wagon wheel left behind. Here and there, a pile of stones or wooden cross on a solitary grave marked their passage. Sam shaded his eyes as he stared across the vast land. *"What courage it must have taken to make such a journey,"* he thought.

Rattlesnake Ridge rose ahead of him as he urged his horse forward, climbing the rocky, uneven ground. His eyes scanned the area. A wariness, uneasy feeling came over him. The hairs on the back of his neck stood up. He couldn't explain it, but instinct told him he was being watched.

Sam knew to be aware of signs of trouble - wolves, mountain lions, or rattlesnakes that could spook a horse and throw a rider. Nature could be unforgiving; there was always danger riding the range. Somehow, this felt different. He decided to listen to his gut reaction and pulled back on his reins, turning the big stallion and coaxing him back down the trail. Another day, in more daylight, he'll come back and explore that ridge better.

When Sam entered the house, he heard the crackle of the radio and an announcer's excited voice. Mary and his father both huddled in front of the radio; Mary clasped the older man's hands as they tried to see the images being described over the wireless.

"It's started!" exclaimed Mary as she noticed Sam enter the room. "D-Day… the Allies have invaded France."

"Wow, this is it then. The big push that was building up. When did it start?" asked Sam as he pulled a chair over.

"Yesterday, I guess, June sixth. Details are just being released. Oh, to have been there and seen that force," Mary said as her voice dwindled to a whisper.

Sam placed his hand on her shoulder, "I know. I'm thinking of Pete and all the men in my squadron too. Sounds like the Mighty Eighth gave 'em hell. Can you just picture the channel filled with every type of ship imaginable? Where was the landing zone? Did the news report say?"

"Normandy. Along the coast of Normandy. Our troops are still fighting on those beaches, trying to gain a foothold," Mary said.

"The Germans won't give in without heavy losses; they'll fight even harder now that the Allies are in Europe and threatening their Fatherland," speculated Sam.

They left the radio turned on as they all went about their chores, listening for more details of the D-Day invasion called Operation Overlord. It was toward evening when news broke that the 101st Airborne had participated in D-Day with a daring drop of men behind enemy lines during the night before and early morning hours of June sixth.

Sam prayed for his friend. Chris Hartman would have been part of that airborne group parachuting into France, fighting the enemy hand to hand. Sam pictured his friend's easy smile and recalled their childhood years spent running and riding, teasing one another. God, he hoped he was safe.

The next morning Sam helped Mary feed the stock and milk the cows before he saddled up and prepared to ride out again. She handed him a wrapped parcel of food and a thermos of coffee.

"Thanks, Babe. I'm going back up to Rattlesnake Ridge to have a look around. I may camp out; be back tomorrow, so don't worry," Sam told Mary.

His father rolled down the new wooden ramp off the porch and slowly moved toward Sam. "Did I hear you say you're going up to the ridge? Watch yourself; something funny's going on up there. I don't know what it was, but I could feel it."

"Me too, Pop. I sensed the same thing, that's why I want to have a look around in broad daylight. I don't plan on being spooked by any ghosts creeping around in the dark or let my mind play tricks on me," Sam said as he tied a kerchief about his neck and adjusted his Stetson firmly on his head. He checked the number of rounds in his Colt, spun the cylinder, and holstered his gun. Sam gave Mary a thorough kiss before he mounted Blackie, waved farewell, and rode toward the northern lands.

"I hope that boy knows what he's doing," Alexander Dunlap said as he watched his son ride away.

"Why? What's wrong with that ridge?" asked Mary worriedly as she pushed the wheelchair back toward the shaded porch.

"Other than the fact that the ridge is where I got shot? Don't know, just something's not right. I never got close enough to investigate," Alexander said.

"Do you think Sam will be in danger?" asked Mary.

"Now don't you worry your pretty little head; he'll be okay. He's got a good head on his shoulders. He won't take any chances."

"I hope you're right," said Mary as she went back inside the house.

As Sam entered the Circle-D's northern pastures, he encountered Hank, Miguel, and Frank branding the young calves born on the ranch. Sam reined in to check on their progress and speak with Frank.

"How's it going? How many head branded?" asked Sam.

"Got twenty-three new calves. We're just finishing up," said Frank.

"Good. Hank and Miguel can finish up here and head those cows into the new western pastures. I need you to come with me," Sam told Frank.

"Okay, where we headed?"

"Up to Rattlesnake Ridge; want to look around, and I might need some backup," Sam said.

"You're the boss. Let me grab my gear and saddle up."

Ten minutes later, Sam and Frank directed their horses toward the distant mountain ridge; the big stallions easily ate up the miles in a steady canter. They followed the same path that Sam had climbed the day before, gained the summit then slowly started down a short ravine. Sam motioned Frank to stop; he dismounted to inspect footprints and hoof marks pressed into the earth. He followed the path on foot, leading his horse and studied the signs on the trail until they stopped abruptly in a wall of shrubs and underbrush against a cliff wall.

Frank tied his horse to a low branch, then poked and prodded the underbrush with his rifle barrel, exploring the wall of vegetation. He and Sam separated the bushes to expose a secret cave's entrance hidden in what had appeared to be a solid rock wall.

"Didn't know this cave was here. Did you?" whispered Sam.

"Nope," replied Frank in a low voice. "Somebody's gone to a lot of trouble to hide something or someone."

Both men drew their handguns as they quietly inched their way into the mouth of the cave. A narrow shaft of sunlight shone at the far end, making it appear more of a tunnel than an enclosed cavern. Sam nodded to Frank as they carefully followed the rocky path only to exit into a hidden corral filled with cattle.

Sam and Frank hid behind two large boulders at the edge of the tunnel and tried to listen for voices but could only hear the noise of cattle bawling. Finally, Sam decided to venture forth and slipped into the corral; he moved among the cows, reading brands and pushing cows out of the way as he tried to determine how many were there and whose brand they wore.

Frank kept watch as Sam made his inspection, then both men crept around the perimeter of the corral to investigate further. A cold campsite was concealed behind a short rock formation, the ashes several days old. Two different boot prints were found on the ground and signs of horse manure left in the copse of trees. It was evident that someone had used the campsite, and recently; the past sensation of being watched now made sense.

"Well, now I know what happened to our missing herd; must be at least thirty head. Most of those cows all have Circle-D brands, but a few others are Cedar Hill's. Looks like we've got some rustlers at work," Sam told Frank.

"Let's drive them back down. If they managed to get 'em up here, we ought to be able to drive those stupid cows back through that tunnel," Frank suggested.

"Agreed. Let's get back to our horses and round up that cattle before we get any visitors."

Suddenly, as they headed toward the tunnel entrance, shots rang out behind them, ricocheting off rock, narrowly missing them. Both men dove for the ground and sought cover behind the mammoth boulders. Sam and Frank each returned fire, aiming at the muzzle flashes coming from the wooded copse. A scream then silence, followed by the pounding of hoofbeats as their attackers fled.

Sam and Frank hurried into the cavern.

"You hit?" asked Sam.

"No, I'm okay. You?"

"No, but that was close. C'mon."

It was darker now within the tunnel's rocky confines as they carefully felt their way. Frank stumbled once; he peered into the shadowy space then jumped back, startled.

"What's the matter?" asked Sam as he turned back toward Frank.

"I stepped on something, and now from the smell, I'm pretty sure it's something dead."

Sam could also smell the decomposition as he got closer to the cave's hidden recess; he bent to examine the find further. Tattered clothing clung to bones and mangled flesh that had once been a man. Sam poked about the denim pants and found a gold pocket watch; he recognized the piece.

"Think we just found Jim Brody. Gotta get Gus Kingman out here, but first, we need to hurry and grab that cattle," Sam said. He left the watch where he had found it, not touching the body anymore, as they ran toward the cave's entrance and their waiting mounts.

Sam and Frank both leaped into their saddles and urged their horses into the dank cave tunnel toward the far entrance. Frank quickly unlatched the corral gate and entered the penned cattle. He rode to the far side of the crowded cows and coaxed them toward the opening. Sam sat atop his horse, controlling the cows along the path into the tunnel. Frank took up drag position with the last cow and herded the cattle through the tunnel as Sam guided the lead cow onto the steep path downward. The cattle bawled loudly and churned up dirt as they moved forward.

As soon as they gained level ground, the two cowboys took up their positions on each side of the herd to direct them toward the safety of Circle-D lands.

"I didn't see any Diamond Bar brands among this lot. Makes me wonder who our rustlers might be. What d'ya think?" Sam asked.

"Does look awfully suspicious. What about Brody? What happened to him?"

"Guess the Sheriff will have to figure that out. Meanwhile, I want two men staying with the herd tonight and tomorrow. Let's keep them bunched up and close to home."

"There's going to be hell to pay when those guys return to find all those cows gone," laughed Frank.

"Won't that be just too damn bad," Sam said. "These are my cows, and I'm taking them back."

No sooner had Sam spoken when another shot rang out behind him; the bullet whizzed past his head, too close for comfort. He turned in his saddle and spied two riders coming down the ridge slope. Sam drew his rifle and took aim at one of the men, fired a shot, then kicked Blackie into a gallop as frightened cattle stampeded. He and Frank had to work to keep them pointed in the correct direction toward safer pastures.

"Did you get him?" shouted Frank as they sought to distance themselves from the rustlers.

"Don't know, but I'm not going back to see. Gotta call Kingman as soon as we get back to the house."

Cattle and horses gradually slowed as men and beasts alike panted and sweated. It was in the wee hours of the morning when Sam and Frank rode into the ranch barnyard. They had moved the cattle into the newly fenced western pastures and rode all night, not bedding down, only stopping to rest for an hour before pushing on.

Alexander Dunlap wheeled into the kitchen, awakened by the sound of low voices. He had always been a light sleeper, and since his injury, found his rest to be fitful at best. His relief was evident when he recognized his son and Frank Costello in the dim light.

"Sorry Pop, did we wake you?" asked Sam, glancing at his father in nightshirt and bare feet.

"No, just heard a noise and came to see what it was. Thought you were going to camp out, what are you doing back in the middle of the night?"

"Frank and I found a bunch of cattle hidden behind Rattlesnake Ridge. You were right about that place. We also found a body; think it's Brody," Sam said.

Fatigue threatened to overcome him as he sipped a mug of hot coffee, dragged his kerchief across his face moist with sweat, and covered in grime. Sam stretched his legs out in front of him, relaxing on the wooden chair. He noted the time shown on the kitchen clock and slowly rose to walk over to the phone hanging on the wall.

"Reckon five o'clock is a decent enough time to wake the sheriff," Sam said as he dialed the number. The telephone rang four or five rings before a groggy voice answered on the other end of the line.

"Hello, Gus? This is Sam Dunlap. We've got trouble on the Circle-D and need you to come out here." Sam listened for a minute as the sheriff questioned him. "Yeah, that's right. Think I may have found Jim Brody, or at least what's left of him. Okay, see you later."

Sam hung up the phone and poured himself a second cup of coffee before he motioned Frank and his father to join him outside.

"Frank, I know you're beat too. Why don't you go grab some shuteye in the bunkhouse? Pop can tell Hank and Miguel what needs to be done today. I've got to wait on Kingman to get here then ride back up the ridge with him. I'm gonna try to get some sleep before he gets here."

Frank nodded as he dragged himself toward the small ranch bunkhouse.

"And Frank," Sam called after him, "thanks for having my back."

Frank raised a tired arm and waved as he stumbled toward his bed.

Sam sunk onto the living room sofa, propped his booted feet up on the arm, and closed his eyes; within minutes, he was sound asleep. He was still there when Mary came out of her bedroom two hours later to start her day.

"Why's Sam sleeping on the sofa?" she whispered to Alexander as he met her in the kitchen.

"Long story, I don't know all of it. Sam and Frank rounded up our stolen cattle and rode all night to get back to the ranch. The sheriff is supposed to be on his way out; Sam called him."

"Stolen cattle? Oh, my goodness, was there trouble?" Mary asked.

"From what I gather, there were some shots fired, but don't know any more than that." Alexander nodded toward Sam's prone figure, "He needs his rest now."

"All right. I'll wait until he awakens to learn more. I'll go collect some eggs and will start breakfast," Mary said as she tied an apron around her waist and hurried out to the barn.

Bacon sizzled and eggs fried in an iron skillet on the woodstove. A fresh pot of brewed coffee tantalized Sam's nose as he pried his eyes open and stumbled toward the delicious smells. He hadn't pulled an all-nighter like this since the time his squadron worked sixteen-hour days during the Bremen raid. He was bone-weary, but there'd be time to sleep later. He had too much to do right now.

Sheriff Kingman knocked on the screen door with one hand as he turned the doorknob with the other and entered the house.

"Is that coffee I smell?" Kingman called out as he walked into the Dunlap kitchen. He surveyed the breakfast scene as he took a place at the table. "Looks like I got here just in time," he said with a big grin.

"Hungry, sheriff?" asked Mary as she served him a mug of the strong brew.

"Got enough? Don't mind if I do since someone called me at an ungodly hour and woke me from a sound sleep."

"Stop your complaining; at least you got a good night's sleep. More than I can say," countered Sam.

"So, what's going on here? Fill me in on the trouble you're having," the sheriff asked as he started on a plate of eggs and toast.

"Frank and I rode up Rattlesnake Ridge yesterday and found a pen of stolen cattle, mostly ours and some of Hartman's. Then a pair of men shot at us, and while we were taking cover, we stumbled over the body of Jim Brody. By the looks of things, he's been there a while," Sam related his story in between bites of food.

"Hmm, got any ideas who shot at you? I need to see where you found the body."

"Figured you would. We can ride up to the ridge as soon as you're done eating. You can ride one of our mounts; I'll need a fresh horse myself, Sam said."

"Okay, let's go. Much obliged, Missus Dunlap."

"You're welcome, Sheriff. Take care of my husband, please," Mary said.

Chapter 23

Gus Kingman knelt beside the body as Sam shined his flashlight onto the remains. It was Brody all right, with a bullet hole in his head. A shell casing was lodged inside the skull. The sheriff carefully poked inside pockets and under pieces of clothing in hopes of uncovering more clues. A faded piece of paper was stuck inside a front jean pocket. The crumpled paper was barely legible; Kingman handed it to Sam. It appeared to be a bank receipt, like the type a teller would provide for making a deposit or withdrawal.

"Yep, appears my suspicions were right; Brody withdrew that money from our account. That's our account number printed there."

"Well, one mystery solved. Still would like to learn why he took that money; what he planned to do with it. Did he act on his own, or was he following orders?" the sheriff speculated as he collected evidence around the body and placed it in a large envelope.

"Yeah, well, I still want to know who shot my father or, for that matter, who took a shot at Frank and me yesterday. I think I may have winged one of them," Sam said.

"Show me the campsite."

Sam and Gus left the tunnel and walked past the empty corral. Sam pointed out the cold ashes and signs of the abandoned camp. Footprints were scattered about the scene, and near a stand of trees, they found fresh blood.

"We heard a yell after Frank and I shot back; thought I hit one. Obviously didn't kill him, 'cause they chased after us and attacked again."

"And you say the cattle stolen had Circle-D and Cedar Hill brands?" asked Kingman.

"Yeah, mostly mine. We counted about thirty head. Frank and I moved them down to my ranch; I'll call Hartman and let him know about his."

"Well, you're brand inspector; rustled cattle fall under your jurisdiction. Let me know what you find. Meanwhile, I'll be investigating this murder. I'll get the doc up here to retrieve the body; he's our acting coroner," Sheriff Kingman said.

"Yeah, okay. I'm thinking that Brody worked for someone other than the Circle-D," Sam said as they made their way back to the tethered horses and headed back down the ridge toward home.

It was Wednesday when Sam and Mary drove over to visit the Hartman's at Cedar Hill. Mary was excited to share the news of her garden's progress with Maureen and had baked a loaf of zucchini bread for her as a gift. Sam rapped on the front door as he noticed a strange car parked near the garage.

Daniel Hartman opened the door and ushered the couple inside. Maureen was in the kitchen with a young woman who hastily turned her back and wiped at reddened eyes as they entered the room.

"So good to see you both again," Maureen greeted Sam and gave Mary a quick hug. "I don't think you know our daughter-in-law Diane, Christopher's wife."

"Hi," Mary said as she extended her hand to Diane. She quickly took in the tear-streaked cheeks and red eyes. "I'm sorry, but is everything all right?"

Dan stepped forward and put a comforting arm around his wife's shoulder. He picked up a yellow piece of paper from the table.

Sam instantly recognized the Western Union telegram and braced himself for dreaded news of his best friend. He reached for Mary's hand as he waited.

"Christopher has been wounded in action; someplace called Carentan. He's coming home. He's lost his left arm," Dan spoke softly, the shock of their son's injury taking root.

"Thank God he's alive. Chris is a strong man. If anybody can learn to cope with a disability, he can. When I saw you pick up that telegram, I feared the worst," Sam said.

"Yes, you're right. We need to be thankful that he's alive and will be home soon," Maureen agreed.

"Do you live nearby, Diane? I didn't know Chris had married."

"Like so many soldiers, we wed right before he left for boot camp in 1941. I've been living with my parents in Laramie ever since," Diane explained.

"We're hoping that Diane and Chris will live with us on the ranch once he's home; help him recuperate," Dan Hartman spoke up.

"You'll let us know when you hear anything more?" Sam asked.

"Sure. I know you boys are close," Dan said.

212

"Dan, can we talk for a bit? I hate to bring this up while the family is dealing with news of Chris, but I gotta."

"Okay, Sam. Let's go out to the barn; we can talk while I tend to some chores."

The two men left the womenfolk to their coffee and chatter and strolled toward the stables and barn. Sam began to tell his story of cattle rustling and something more sinister.

"So, Dan, I've got about five head of your cattle grazing on my western pasture that we rounded up. Looks like the thieves took as many cows as they could; most were ours. You can have one of your hands move them whenever you want. They're safe for the time being. Frank is taking turns with a couple of men I hired keeping watch on the herd."

"You mentioned there was more; what was it?"

"Sheriff Kingman is investigating the murder of Jim Brody; we found his body hidden up on the ridge," Sam spoke quietly as he followed Dan Hartman into the shadows of the stable.

"Sure it's murder?" asked Dan.

"Yep, a bullet through the head doesn't leave any doubt. I think Brody has been stealing money from the Circle-D too. I don't mind telling you, from the loss of cattle and funds, if that had kept up, the ranch would be hard-pressed to pay our taxes when they come due. As it is, it's gonna be tight."

"Huh, I see what you mean. Almost like there's been a plot working against your Pa. I haven't wanted to say anything to you until I had some proof, but I've had my suspicions concerning your father's shooting."

"Can you share those suspicions with me now?"

"Just seems like we never had trouble around here until some of those sodbusters moved here right before the war. I know those folks had it tough during the Depression; a lot of them lost their farms and all, but they're just not our kind of people. They aren't cattlemen; they don't have any respect for boundaries. It wouldn't surprise me if you found some of our cows mixed in among their animals," Dan Hartman said as he fed the horses in the stable.

"Well, I don't like pointing the finger at anyone with false accusations. One of my best friends in the army was a sodbuster from Oklahoma. But I appreciate your insight. All I can do now is protect what's mine and keep an eye out," Sam said.

"I think that's a smart idea. I'll do the same. You know, I believe I may have to hire a new cowhand since Frank Costello seems to prefer working your ranch more than mine," Dan said with a laugh.

"Sorry, I know you were only loaning him to me. He's been my right-hand man; I'm afraid I've grown to count on him. If he wants to come back to Cedar Hill, I won't try to keep him," Sam said.

"Actually, Sam, Frank has already approached me about staying on permanent at your place and gave me notice. That is, if you want him and can afford to pay him full time."

"I'll speak to him when I get back. As I said, I don't know how I'd get along without him. If you do hire someone to replace him, I can recommend a fella. I hired a pair of men to work part-time, and I can't keep them both on. Hank Butler's been a good worker and would be grateful for a job. Can I tell him to come around and talk with you?"

"You do that. I trust your judgment in men; if you vouch for him, I'll be glad to take him on," said Dan.

"Thanks. Hank's got a family to support; this will mean a lot to him, and I feel better about letting him go since he'll have another job to go to."

"It's settled then. Come on back to the house and let's get something to eat," Dan invited.

"Great, meanwhile, I'll keep you posted on any progress with this rustling. You keep an eye out too on your property; will you?"

"Count on it."

Chapter 24

Rachel Yoder and Mary worked side by side harvesting vegetables in the warm autumn sunshine. Ripe squash, cucumbers, and succulent tomatoes would all be canned and added to the winter pantry. Mary smiled at her friend as they dug into the fertile soil, satisfied with the fruits of their labor.

Frank Costello hovered nearby, finding more than one excuse to come up to the house and speak with Rachel or Mary. His eyes betrayed him as they were wont to seek out Rachel and linger on her soft smile and pleasing features. Mary caught him staring more than once and quickly arrived at her own decision about the pair.

"Hey Frank, did you ask Miguel about repairing that window in the bunkhouse?" Sam asked as he walked toward the back of the house.

"Yep, sure did. I was just seeing if the ladies needed my help carrying some of these baskets," Frank replied.

"Uh-huh. So I see," Sam said, not fooled for a minute. "Well, when you finish with those heavy burdens, do you think you can spare me a moment?"

Alexander Dunlap sat on the porch relaxing in the pleasant afternoon sun and temperatures. He listened to the conversation between Frank and Sam and chuckled to himself.

"You know, a blind man could see how smitten Frank is with that lass," he told Sam as Sam stepped up onto the porch.

"He sure is; trips over his own feet and gets all tongue-tied when he's around her then goes back for more," laughed Sam. "Actually, that's what I wanted to speak with you about."

"What? How Frank better ask that pretty thing to marry him before some other man beats him to it?"

"Not exactly. I was thinking of deeding two acres of land to Frank and Rachel when they marry as a small homestead. Frank has become part of the Circle-D, and I haven't always been able to pay him much. I'd like to gift him with some land of his own; help him build a home. Any objections?" Sam asked his father.

"I think that's a fine idea. The ranch isn't going to miss a couple acres of land with all that we've got. Where did you have in mind?" Alexander asked.

"Thought about surveying a parcel along the northwest boundary with some road frontage on Aspen Drive; he'd be adjacent to our own entrance but separate. Close enough for Frank to get back and forth; be here when I need him."

"Have you told him yet?" asked Alexander.

"No. I wanted your permission first; it's your land, not mine."

"Appreciate that, but you're wrong."

"Wrong? What do you mean?" asked Sam.

His father rolled his wheelchair closer to Sam's seat and reached out to touch his son's arm. "I had a lawyer out here last week while you were riding the range; made some changes in my will and put your name on the deed of this spread."

Surprise showed on Sam's face as he dragged his fingers through his hair then hastily wiped a moist eye before turning to study his father's features, once stern and now softened with pride and love.

"You've done this for me?" asked Sam.

"Reckon it's more your place than mine now. You're the one working the ranch and keeping our heads above water. High time, don't you think?"

"Thanks, Pop. I don't know what to say. All I've ever wanted is for you to be proud of me," Sam said as he hugged his father and cherished the moment.

Embarrassed by the show of affection, Alexander broke the contact and gruffly cleared his throat, "Well, enough of that. It's done. Just wanted you to know."

Frank Costello hesitated as he walked near the front stoop; he had witnessed the rare father and son occurrence and was reluctant to intrude. Now he was the one pretending to clear his throat to announce his presence.

"You wanted to see me?" asked Frank.

"Yeah, Frank. Pop and I both agree that it's high time you propose to Rachel before she decides you're not worth waiting for."

If a man could blush redder than a tomato, Frank Costello's scarlet neck and face were a good example. He started to speak, stuttered, and tried again, "Propose to Rachel? Marry?"

"Yes, marry her. Think we all can't see how much in love you are? Where's your courage? Ask her, for Pete's sake," Sam said as he laughed at the stricken expression on Frank's face.

"Do you think she'd say yes?"

"Only one way to find out," Sam said. "No time like the present. Hey Mary, can you and Rachel come around front?" Sam shouted.

Mary and Rachel both dropped their gardening trowels and wiped soiled hands on their aprons then hurried around to the porch to see what the emergency was. Rachel stopped and approached shyly as she studied the group of men; Mary nodded her head in agreement as she quickly reached an accurate conclusion. She nudged her friend forward as she joined Sam and her father-in-law on the porch, leaving Rachel to stand near Frank.

Frank glanced at his friend. Sam nodded and threw him a look of encouragement. Both men looked nervous as Frank turned to Rachel and gently reached for her hands in both of his.

"Rachel, I um, that is, I wanted to say that I, um, I love you. Will you be my wife?"

Rachel stood quietly, with lowered head, as Frank spoke; his sudden words of affection were both a surprise and prayer come true. She blushed a pretty pink as she raised her eyes and studied his face, his expression eager and intent. She glanced at her friend Mary, seeking her guidance. Mary and Sam both nodded in unison. Rachel looked back at Frank as he waited on her answer.

"I love thee too. I would be honored to be thy wife, Frank Costello," answered Rachel as she smiled happily.

Tears clung to Mary's eyes as she smiled and clasped her husband's hand, witnessing their friend's happiness and declaration of love.

"Hurrah!" exclaimed Sam as he clapped his hands while Alexander joined in with the applause.

"Perfect time of the year for a wedding, young man," Alexander said. "We'll have a house raising party to get you under roof before the winter sets in."

Frank was still in shock; his confusion evident as he stammered, "House raising? What do you mean?"

"You need a place to live, don't you think?" asked Sam. "Pop forgot to tell you, he and I are giving you two acres of land to build a house on. A wedding gift to you and Rachel."

"Really? My own land?" Frank asked.

"It's not much, only couple acres, but it should be big enough for a nice house and space for a garden, room for a man to make it his own," Sam said.

Sam and Frank shook hands. Mary and Rachel embraced, both excited to begin wedding plans. Rachel insisted on the ceremony being held at the Quaker's meeting house in Deer Springs. She would need to speak with her minister.

Three weeks later, Samuel Dunlap escorted a radiant Rachel Yoder up the aisle to stand next to her nervous bridegroom, Frank Costello. Rachel was lovely in her pale blue gown and wore a crown of flowers on her head. The solemn Quaker meeting house was filled with several Quaker members, the Dunlap family, Miguel Lopez, cowhands from both Cedar Hill and the Circle-D, and all of the Hartman family to witness the couple's marriage.

The newlyweds were greeted with hugs, kisses, best wishes, and more than one raised stein of beer following the ceremony at a wedding reception buffet hosted by Sam and Mary. Miguel strummed a guitar and sang a plaintive Mexican love song, serenading the couple. Large pieces of plywood rested on carpenter horses to create makeshift dining tables outdoors. Sam joked that the plywood would later be used for walls in the newlywed's house. It was a day of happiness, of celebration and relaxation, a break from the routine chores of running a cattle ranch.

"Good to see you up and about," remarked Sam to Chris Hartman. "How goes it, friend?"

"Slow, but I'm learning to make do with the one arm. I find my balance is off at times, or I want to lift something, and it's too heavy for one hand. Sometimes I swear I feel pain in my left arm and it's not even there. The doctor calls it phantom pain; guess it's common," Chris told Sam as they sat together away from parents and worried wives looking on.

"Do you need anything? Can I do something to help?" Sam asked his friend, concerned but careful to not show signs of pity.

"Thanks, Sam. Nothing anyone can do; I just have to learn to live my life with only one arm. Don't know how I'll ever rope a calf again or ride a horse easily. I don't want anyone feeling sorrow for me; that's one thing I can't take."

"Know what you mean. We're all here for you; you understand that, right? We all love you. It's not pity... just caring," Sam said.

"Sometimes I see Diane watching me, and I wonder if she's sorry she's married to a cripple. Do you think she can still love half a man?"

"Now listen, I'll tell you the same thing I told my old man; you are only as much a cripple as you want to be. I told your folks when they read the telegram about your injury, that you are one man who could overcome any disability. I believe that with all my heart," Sam said sincerely, placing an arm around his friend's shoulder.

"I don't know, Sam. I just don't know."

"Give it some time. Let yourself heal. You are still the same man I knew and the same man that woman over there fell in love with. I'd bet the ranch on it," Sam said as he raised his glass in toast.

"What are you two cooking up over here; I've been watching you with your heads together," Diane asked as she strolled over to sit next to her husband.

"Oh, just two old veterans sharing war stories," Sam said with a wink to Chris as he got up in search of his own wife and a refill of beer.

Alexander Dunlap raised his mug to salute the happy couple, then while he had everyone's attention, he announced, "Drink up folks because tomorrow we've got a house to build. We're going to have a good old-fashioned house raising like they haven't seen around here in years. Counting on everyone here to lend a hand and grab a hammer."

Rachel and Frank embraced to the cheers of their friends and thanked everyone for their support and love; tomorrow promised to be a new beginning for the young couple.

Chapter 25

Snow fell steadily on the Wyoming plains as winter tightened its icy grip on the land. Sam stamped his feet to knock off the wet snow clinging to his boots and pants clear to his knees. He was chilled to the bone and sought the warmth of the blazing logs piled in the stone fireplace. With fingers that trembled from the cold, he pried off wet gloves and laid them on the hearth to dry.

Mary hurried to wrap a quilt about his shoulders and thrust a cup of steaming coffee into his hands to help warm him.

"Thanks, Babe. It's brutal out there. Got all the animals bedded down in the barn. Miguel and Frank herded the cattle close by in the meadow; should be more protected with that line of trees, and we can keep a better watch on them."

"Sit down and thaw out. You've done all you can for the time being," Mary said.

"Where's Pop?" asked Sam.

"He was cold and not feeling well, so he's bundled up in his bed to take a nap. I'll check on him later."

"Miguel is hunkered down in the bunkhouse, and Frank rode back home before the snowstorm worsens. I keep thinking I've missed something or should have done something, but my brain is so frozen I can't think what."

"I can't imagine what. Does it usually storm like this in winter? There must be at least four feet of snow out there. I tried to gather eggs earlier and could barely walk to the barn," Mary said.

"I want you to stay in the house for the next several days until this lets up some. People have been known to freeze to death in mere minutes or get lost. You can easily lose sight of the house. I'm gonna tie a rope between the porch railing and the barn to act as a guide. I'll take care of it next time I go out," Sam said.

"You aren't going out again today, are you?" Mary asked, worriedly.

"Not unless I have to," answered Sam.

"Good." Mary kissed his cold cheek and laughed at the appearance of him.

"What's so funny?" Sam asked.

"You are. With that cherry red nose and frosted cheeks, you are the image of Saint Nick. All you need is a red suit, just in time for the Yule time."

"Think I look like Santa, hmm? I'll get you for that later, Mrs. Claus. Turn on the radio, will you? Maybe we can listen to some holiday music since your thoughts have turned to Christmas."

"I can't believe it's been a year since we were sitting in my flat in Peterborough with a lit yule log and worried about the blackout. Our first Christmas."

"I remember that night well; first time I made love to you," Sam said as he kissed his wife and drew her to him.

Mary returned his kiss with a sigh then wiggled out of his grasp to walk over to the radio and turn on the switch. The radio crackled and came to life. The announcer's voice provided the latest war news as she and Sam snuggled close on the sofa to listen.

"German forces have begun a counter-offensive attack in the heavily forested Ardennes region. American units near the Belgium town of Bastogne are surrounded and continue to fight despite heavy losses and wintry conditions. General Anthony McAuliffe sent a message to German commanders at Bastogne demanding his surrender; it read 'Nuts!'"

"Sounds like Hitler is getting desperate and throwing everything he can at our troops," Sam said as he listened to the news and tried to picture the battle being waged halfway around the world.

"Do you think so? God, I pray this war will end soon. I don't know how much more the Allies can take, or for that matter, how long can the German people continue to hold on?" Mary wondered. Her thoughts turned to her friends and countrymen left behind in England. She worried about their welfare and felt like she betrayed them by escaping to the bounty she enjoyed in America.

Sam guessed her silent thoughts as he turned to her, "Thinking of your friend Miriam and the drivers in your unit?"

"Yes, I was. How'd you know? They're likely still rationing, and here I sit with my abundant food and safe home while they continue battling on and risk danger of daily bombing. I feel like a traitor."

"How do you think I feel with my buddies and my squadron still over there, and here I sit worrying about a bunch of cows? I know I'm needed here, but there are days when I feel like I should be back in England doing my duty," Sam admitted.

"Do you? I was afraid that I was the only one feeling that way," Mary said.

"Well, doesn't do either one of us any good playing what if. I'm here now and have to concentrate on catching those cattle rustlers before they become a danger to more than just cows. They're getting bolder and more daring with every raid. I tracked them as far as I could before this snow started, then I lost them, but I'm getting closer. It's just a matter of time, and they'll be mine."

The young couple snuggled before the blazing fire, each lost in their own thoughts as they listened to the holiday music being broadcast. Sam's attention was drawn by the noise of his father's wheelchair squeaking as he slowly made his way down the hall and into the warm living room. Sam studied his father's appearance; he had gained weight during the past eight months and appeared healthier and more robust. He had mellowed and wasn't as quick to criticize as before, although he hadn't given up all of his cantankerous ways. Still, Sam felt like their relationship had come a long way.

"Pop, I'm gonna need to oil those wheels. You're never going to sneak up on somebody with that loud squeak," Sam joked.

"And just who would I be sneaking up on anyway?"

Sam laughed, "Nobody, Pop. I'm just kidding."

"I thought I heard voices. You listening to the radio?"

"Yeah, war news; a big battle is going on somewhere called Bastogne. I think they said the 101st Airborne is involved. Wonder what Chris Hartman might think if he hears," Sam said.

"How is that boy? He getting used to the loss of his arm?" Alexander asked.

"Guess he's managing about as well as he can right now. He'll be okay; he just needs some time."

"Hmm, maybe so."

"Come over closer to the fire," Mary said as she fuzzed over him and placed a lap robe across his legs. "Can I get you something? Maybe a coffee or cup of hot soup?"

"You're spoiling me. A cup of coffee sounds good, though," Alexander said as he patted Mary's arm to soften his retort.

"Be right back," said Mary.

Sam and Alexander both watched her leave before Sam approached his father and asked for advice.

"I've tracked the rustlers onto Diamond Bar land, Pop. What do you think I should do? Should I confront Logan and accuse his men or just let the sheriff take it from here? I don't have any hard evidence."

"Think it's the same men who shot at you up on the ridge? Any chance different thieves are working the area, and just hiding out on the Diamond Bar?" asked Alexander quietly.

"I dunno, think it's the same men; they look to be the same build and height. I've only seen them from a distance."

"Hmm, Kingman will expect you to handle the cattle business yourself. Has he turned up any more clues on who murdered Brody?" asked Alexander.

"Haven't talked to him in a while. If he has, he's keeping it close to the vest."

"Watch your back when you're riding alone, especially in the north. You know where I mean," Alexander cautioned.

"I will, but I'm counting on you to keep an eye on things around here."

"I'll do the best I can."

"Thanks, Pop."

Chapter 26

Pungent evergreen scents from the freshly cut Christmas tree blended with the spicy gingerbread cookies baking in the kitchen. Holiday music played softly in the background while Sam and Mary decorated the tree with handmade ornaments and tinsel. Alexander directed the project, pointing out a bare spot here or there and helped to hang Christmas balls on the lower branches where he could reach.

It was a time of harmony and family togetherness. Sam couldn't remember when he had enjoyed a holiday celebration more than this one. As a child, he and Alex savored the holiday food and typically fought over who received what presents, but his parents were usually solemn or argumentative. He never saw his father decorate the tree; he would grudgingly cut down a pine and bring it home, but that was the end of his participation. To witness his father actually smile or laugh as he admired the holiday decorations, was indeed a miracle and almost too good to be true.

Mary stepped back from the finished tree to admire their masterpiece as Sam plugged in the lights. She clapped her hands in glee as she hugged her father-in-law and then embraced Sam.

"Isn't it beautiful?" she asked. Her eyes sparkled as much as the baubles on the tree.

"You did a fine job. With my help, of course," Alexander said with a chuckle.

"Tomorrow we'll feast on venison; I bagged a six-point buck last week. Frank and I got all the meat dressed and cut for the freezer; we each took half. I've invited everyone to dinner; Miguel, Frank, and Rachel will be here to celebrate the day," Sam said.

"I better get busy in the kitchen if we're having company. I've still got bread to bake for tomorrow and dinner to finish for us now. I'm afraid Henrietta is gracing our table tonight; that old hen might be a bit tough," Mary said as she set dishes on the table.

"Roast chicken, my favorite," said Alexander as he wheeled himself closer to the warm fireplace. "We still have enough birds to produce eggs, don't we?"

"Oh, yes. What with some of the younger chicks grown now, we've got eight good hens laying. I don't think poor Henrietta will be missed except maybe by that cantankerous old rooster," Mary said. "He chases me every time I enter the chicken coop."

"Hah, can you blame him? He knows a pretty chick when he sees one!" joked Sam. "Come here and let me take a peck at you." Sam made a grab for Mary as she ducked to avoid his hands, giggled, and hurried back into the kitchen away from his playful antics.

"I'm going out to check on the animals; it's getting dark, and temperatures will be below freezing tonight," Sam said as he bundled up in hat and gloves then zipped his coat up. He opened the door just wide enough to step out as a gust of cold air blew into the room, making both Alexander and Mary shiver.

Sam hunched his shoulders as he fought the blowing wind and gusts of snow; the distance between the house and the barn doubled with each step he took as he was blown backward. He finally progressed to the solid barn and managed to slide open the door.

The dairy cows huddled together inside as cold air seeped through the cracks in the barn siding. Sam grabbed a pitchfork and scooped more sweet hay into their pen then turned the fork around to use the handle to break up pieces of ice in their frozen water trough.

Two chickens squawked and ran under his feet as he turned and saw the coop door had been left ajar. *"That's funny,"* he thought, *"it wasn't like Mary not to secure the door to the hen house."* He waved his arms and shooed the hens back into their roost then shut the door firmly.

A movement caught his eye, a dark shape flitted by in the shadows of the barn. The horses whinnied, and his stallion Blackie snorted and stomped his forelegs. Sam peered into the darkness as he approached the stabled horses.

"What is it, boy?" he asked as he rubbed the stallion's nose and tried to quiet him.

Suddenly, a heavy timber thudded against the back of his head; he saw stars just before he fell to the ground. Sam moaned in agony as his body was dragged outside. He felt cold and wet as heavy snow covered his body, and his world blurred to blackness.

"That'll teach you to snoop where you're not wanted," a gruff voice mumbled.

Alexander wheeled into the kitchen as Mary carved the roasted chicken to serve for dinner. He glanced at the wall clock then looked about the kitchen empty except for Mary.

"How long has Sam been gone?" he asked.

"I don't know. Why?"

"He said he was just going to check on the animals for the night. Shouldn't have taken that long. I don't like it. Something's wrong. I can feel it in my bones."

Mary put down the carving knife and wiped her hands as she read the concern on her father-in-law's face. "You're scaring me. What are you saying?"

"A man can get frostbite in just a few minutes; he can freeze to death in this kind of weather. Our winters are not forgiving. He should have been back by now."

Mary knew that she would have to be the one to search for her husband. "I'll get my coat and boots on. Sam told me to follow the guide rope when it storms; I'll use it to get to the barn. I'll find him."

"Maybe we better telephone Frank," Alexander said.

"It would take too long for him to get here; no, I'll have to go. I'll be careful. I promise."

Mary quickly dragged on a pair of her wool uniform trousers under her skirt, wrapped a wool scarf about her neck, and tugged on a knit stocking cap to cover her head and ears. She buttoned up her woolen coat and shoved hands into thick gloves before she ventured out into the cold night.

She gasped as a gust of icy wind took her breath away as soon as she stepped out onto the porch. Mary grabbed onto the guide rope and held on as she made her way along the line, hand over hand, toward the bulky barn structure just visible in the blinding snow. She was exhausted by the time she reached the panel door that still stood ajar. Angry bellows came from the animals as they voiced their objections to the cold air chilling their surroundings.

"Sam! Are you in here?" Mary shouted above the whistling wind. She lit a lantern hanging from a peg, then searched the stables and cow-pen, cautiously moved among the animals than stopped abruptly as she spied a splatter of blood on the ground and nearby hay.

"Oh my God," Mary said out loud as she raised the lantern higher to follow the trail of blood drops outside. She braced herself as she stepped back outside into the howling wind, shielding the meager lantern flame, and prayed she could find Sam. She couldn't do it alone.

The bunkhouse was a small building adjacent to the barn and stable; Mary struggled to find her way to it. She pounded on the door as a startled Miguel opened the portal.

"Señora, what are you doing here? Come in quickly."

"Miguel, I need you. Sam is hurt. Can you come?" Mary gasped as she tried to regain her calm.

"Sí, señora. Uno momento. I come." Miguel wrapped himself in his warm clothes, and the two ventured into the stormy night.

They called Sam's name and searched the area near the bunkhouse as they crawled their way toward the barn and corrals. Mary held the lantern as she peered into its shallow glow of light. She grabbed Miguel's arm excitedly when she spotted a blotch of red staining the white snow. They tried to hurry now as they hunted for more signs of him.

Miguel was the first to identify the oddly shaped pile of snow as he and Mary crouched down to dig and claw their way through the icy mass to the body covered beneath.

"Get him out, Miguel. Oh, hurry!" Mary cried.

Miguel lifted the unconscious man and slung him across his back and shoulders like a prized deer carried home. It felt like hours with every step as they struggled to follow the guide rope back to the safety of the study log cabin.

Miguel carefully laid Sam on the braided rug in front of the fireplace as Alexander looked on, pale and worried. Mary shrugged out of her heavy outer garments and knelt next to her husband, her fingers pressed against his cold skin, feeling for a pulse. It was there, but very faint.

"Get him out of those wet things," directed Alexander. "You've got to warm him up slowly if he has frostbite."

"We'll make a pallet for him right here. I'll get some blankets. Miguel, can you please try to remove his coat and boots?" Mary asked.

The cowhand nodded yes as his cold fingers worked the buttons of the snow-encrusted coat of his employer and friend. He had to roll Sam from side to side and yank his arms from the sodden garment, but still, no movement came from the injured man. A worried frown appeared on Miguel's face as he continued to undress his friend.

Mary rushed to spread a thick quilt on the floor then they rolled Sam onto it. She ran her hands along his arms and legs, checking for signs of injury; aghast when her fingers touched a bloody wound at the back of his head. Mary quickly reached for the first aid kit and bandaged his head. At least the cold snow had helped to stop the bleeding.

"Thank goodness we were given first aid training with my ATS unit in England. The cut doesn't look deep, but I'm afraid he might have a concussion. I don't know what to do about that. For now, we just need to warm him up."

They draped Sam in another quilt and warm blanket then wrapped him like a cocoon. He remained motionless. Now their vigil began.

"Better telephone Doc Stevenson. See if he can come out here tomorrow. Don't reckon there's anything more he could do tonight," Alexander said.

"Do you have his number?" Mary asked as she lifted the receiver.

"Should be on the wall next to the phone. There's a couple of numbers penciled there; top one is the doctor. Gotta call the sheriff too."

Mary paused in her dialing as she looked at Alexander, and her eyes flew back to the still body on the floor. The phone rang a few times before a man's voice answered.

"Hello, this is Doctor Stevenson."

"Hello doctor, this is Mary Dunlap at the Circle-D. My husband Sam has been injured, a head wound, and I think he may have a concussion. Can you come out?"

"Describe the head wound."

"Um, small two-inch cut on the crown of his head, bleeding has stopped. I've applied a bandage. He was out in the snow unconscious for maybe an hour, I'm not sure how long. We've got him bundled in front of the fireplace to try and warm him."

"Hmm, sounds like you've done all the right things. How'd he hit his head?"

"We don't know. I found him buried in the snow."

"All right. Just keep an eye on him throughout the night and I'll try to get out there tomorrow morning. Let's hope this damn snow stops, and oh yes, Merry Christmas." the doctor said.

Chapter 27

That Christmas Eve was the longest night Mary had ever spent. She had insisted that Miguel stay in the warm cabin in case she might need him with Sam. They took turns keeping watch, even Alexander sat with him for a few hours while Mary tried to sleep. Still no change.

Mary rubbed reddened eyes as she put a pot of coffee on to brew and went to check on her patient. Sam's skin was warmer to the touch and no longer wore a bluish color like it did the night before. His pulse beat stronger as Mary pressed her fingers against the side of his neck. If only he would wake.

She saw that Alexander had fallen asleep in his wheelchair. *"That couldn't be good for his back. He'll be the one with aches and pains when he awakes,"* Mary thought to herself. She tucked a blanket around his sleeping form before returning to the kitchen.

Miguel had arisen early and trudged his way through the deep snow back to his own quarters to change clothes and see to the animals. He promised Mary he would be back for the breakfast that she had offered.

It was mid-morning when the doctor arrived, bag in hand, and climbed down from a horse-drawn carriage. He knocked on the door of the Dunlap home and was immediately admitted.

"Good morning, doctor, I'm Mary Dunlap. Thank you so much for coming out."

Doctor Stevenson studied Alexander sitting in his wheelchair. "You're looking better than I've seen you in months. Having young Samuel home seems to agree with you, but please tell me you did not sleep in that chair."

"I'll sleep anywhere I damn well please, if you don't mind. You didn't come out here for me; just see to my son."

"Hmm, see you still have the same sweet temper," the doctor chided as he knelt next to Sam and inspected his injury, shoved a thermometer into his mouth and shone a tiny flashlight into his pupils. "Definite sign of a concussion. How long has he been out cold?"

"Maybe fifteen hours now," Alexander said.

"He went out to the barn right before supper last night, and when he didn't come back right away, I went searching for him," Mary explained.

"Good thing you found him when you did or he'd be frozen like a slab of meat," the doctor said as he placed his stethoscope on Sam's heart and then took his pulse and blood pressure. "BP is low, but his heart sounds strong, and the pulse rate is good. Temperature isn't quite up to normal but not too low, considering. I think he'll come around soon. We just have to wait."

Mary and Alexander both breathed a sigh of relief at the doctor's words. Mary smiled tentatively and patted Alexander on the shoulder as she waited on the doctor to stand.

"Can I get you a hot cup of coffee, Doctor Stevenson?" Mary offered.

"Thanks. It's still plenty cold out there. Had to hitch up old Bessie to make the drive out here, damn car gets stuck in deep snow, but Bessie gets through."

"I was going to ask you about the carriage, but I can understand how a horse might be a better mode of transportation," Mary said.

"I can tell by your speech, madam, that you're not from around here. England perhaps?"

"Yes, near York. I met Sam when he was serving on one of the airbases nearby."

"Well, welcome to America. You just be careful, young lady, to respect our Wyoming winters; they're much harsher than England. Not to be taken lightly," warned the doctor.

"Yes, I learned that quickly last night. It was a miracle that we found Sam in that snowstorm when we did."

"You tell Sam when he wakes up, that I think he has a very brave wife and a pretty one too."

"Thank you, I will," said Mary, blushing.

Three hours later, Sam's eyes slowly fluttered open. He squinted against the bright light of the fireplace flames and tried to move his arms tucked securely into his blankets as if he wore a straitjacket.

Mary sat nearby, a book in her lap fell to the floor as she jumped up and rushed to his side. She smiled with misty eyes as she kissed him on the cheek, his stubble of beard tickling her.

"Welcome back," she whispered. She couldn't stop touching him as her hand caressed his brow.

Sam returned her smile and turned his head to take in the scene around him. "What am I wrapped in? I can't move."

Mary laughed as she tugged on the pile of blankets and loosened his bonds. "We wanted to keep you warm; you almost froze to death."

He pulled his arms free then pushed the covers down below his waist in an attempt to sit up. Sam stopped his actions as the roomy suddenly spun crazily, and he pressed a palm across his brow to stop the sensation.

Mary recognized the problem immediately and quickly grabbed several pillows to prop behind him, allowing him to recline but slightly elevated. "Better? Dizzy huh? You need to move slowly; you've had a concussion. Do you remember what happened?"

Alexander came into the living room and moved closer to Sam, anxious to hear his answer to Mary's question. He studied his son's face, watching for signs of pain or relapse.

Sam ran his fingers through his hair as he glanced between his wife and father. He struggled to dress in a warm flannel shirt and dry pants as he related, "I was in the barn; the animals were restless. I remember standing by Blackie's stall when somebody hit me over the head. After that, everything went blank."

"You're sure you were hit from behind? You couldn't have bumped your head on something?" Alexander asked, worried over the growing suspicions in his mind.

"No, I was definitely hit. It was cold and wet, dark; I couldn't move. Beyond that, I don't know anything or how I even got back to the house."

Mary and Alexander exchanged looks before Mary confided that she had gone searching for Sam.

"Miguel and I found you; he carried you back to the house."

"You went out in that storm? Don't you know how dangerous or stupid that was?" Sam demanded, his face flushing angrily as he imagined Mary lying hurt or lost in the blizzard.

"Of all the ungrateful... don't you lecture me mister; bloody fool, wouldn't be alive if it wasn't for me. I'm not helpless just because I'm a woman," Mary said, gritting her teeth with hours of pent up worry and emotion. She flounced out of the room and ran upstairs. She threw herself across their bed and cried her eyes out - releasing both waves of relief that he was awake and frustration with her husband's chauvinistic views.

"That wasn't the smartest thing you ever said," remarked Alexander as he shook his head at his son and spun his wheelchair away to roll into the kitchen, leaving Sam alone to reflect on his words and the sounds of Mary crying upstairs.

A loud knocking on the front door interrupted Sam's reverie as he shouted from his pallet for the visitors to come in. A gust of cold air announced the arrival of Frank and Rachel with Miguel close behind. They all entered and stomped the snow from their feet before leaving the front entry.

Frank spied Sam lying on a pallet of quilts and rushed over to him. He turned to Miguel with an inquiring look as he took in the scene.

"What happened? You okay?" Frank asked.

"Thanks to Miguel and my courageous wife, I'm okay. Got knocked on the head yesterday and buried in the snow," Sam explained.

"Sí señor, we find you and get you back home. La señora es muy valiente," Miguel said, smiling from ear to ear.

Mary heard the sound of voices below and hastily wiped her face and hurried down the stairs to join her friends. She entered the room as all eyes turned to her, surprising her with their attention.

"What?" she asked as Frank and Rachel both enveloped her in a group hug.

"That's just our way of saying thank you," said Frank.

"Um, Merry Christmas everyone. I'm sorry, I sort of neglected Christmas dinner, it's going to be a bit late. If you don't mind waiting, I'll get things cooking," Mary said, embarrassed that she had forgotten their invitation in all the turmoil.

"Let me help thee," Rachel volunteered. "Thou hath had much to do and on thou mind. We intrude by being here."

"Don't be silly; Sam and I wouldn't want to spend the holiday without all of you. I appreciate your help; I'm sure we can get this meal on the table soon."

Both women dashed to the kitchen, grabbed utensils and pots as they set about peeling potatoes and basting the roast venison that Alexander had started in the oven hours earlier.

"God bless, Alexander. At least he remembered to start the meat cooking. This Christmas couldn't be any crazier than if we were in London during the Blitz."

Uneven footsteps stopped in the kitchen doorway; Mary turned from the sink to see Sam quietly watching her. She nudged Rachel and nodded toward Sam as the other woman understood they needed a moment of privacy.

"I'll be right back. I must speak with Frank."

Mary smiled her gratitude to Rachel as Sam stepped closer and reached for her hands. She nervously waited for him to speak.

Sam pulled Mary toward him, and tenderly kissed the palms of each hand. His eyes searched hers, imploring her forgiveness. He stood before her, caressed her cheek and tucked loose strands of her lovely auburn hair behind her ear.

"I'm sorry," he whispered as he softly kissed her lips.

A tear slid down Mary's cheek, Sam gently wiped it away with the back of his work-roughened hand.

"Me too," Mary said. "You scared me out of my wits."

"I don't know what I would do if something happened to you; I can't stand the idea of putting you in danger. You're a brave woman, Mary Dunlap. I sometimes forget that my little English soldier is made of stern stuff. Forgive me?"

"I love you," Mary whispered as she returned his kiss with enough heat to defrost any lingering cold.

"Unless you're of a mind to follow me to our bedroom, I guess I better leave you alone."

Mary blushed at his words as she said, "I promise we'll celebrate the holiday later." She grinned wickedly that left no doubt as Sam patted her fanny fondly when she turned back to her chores.

Mary was still smiling to herself when Rachel returned to assist with the cooking.

Later, friends joined hands and gave thanks for the bountiful feast spread before them and the miracle of Christmas. Sam lifted his glass in toast, "Thank you, dear friends, for your support. May we all have a year ahead filled with love, happiness, prosperity, and peace."

"I'll drink to that," agreed Frank.

Chapter 28

Sheriff Kingman was at an impasse with the investigation of Jim Brody's murder. The clues couldn't be any colder. Even the incident with Sam Dunlap being attacked led nowhere with any footprints erased by blowing snow and no witnesses or evidence left behind. Another dead end. The sheriff reviewed the photos of Brody's body and read through the autopsy details again, then shook his head disgusted as he shoved the paperwork back into its manila folder. He stuffed the papers into a file cabinet drawer and slammed it shut.

Sam walked into the county sheriff's office and paused until he spotted Gus leaving the jail cell area from the rear of the building and approached his desk.

"Hey Gus, how's it going?"

"I could ask the same of you," Kingman said as he reached for his cold cup of coffee, tasted it then tossed the bitter contents into a potted plant. "It's been really quiet, almost too quiet."

"Fortunately, my hard head proved difficult to crack, so whoever wanted me out of the way has been thwarted. Been two months and I haven't seen any more signs of trouble on the Circle-D and no missing cows that I know of. Our bank account hasn't had any more money stolen either, so I think that's proof that the culprit was Brody. Records show the withdraws stopped at about the same time that he went missing. I just wish I knew why Brody stole that money."

"You been out on patrol this week?" asked Kingman.

"Not yet; I was planning on heading up to the northern county boundaries tomorrow. We've got our cattle close to home in our western pastures; I think Dan Hartman has his herd where he can keep an eye on them too. I'll be heading into the Diamond Bar lands this week," Sam said.

"Watch your back; let me know if anything looks suspicious to you or just feels hinky. You were lucky at Christmas, but don't press your luck."

"You got it. Gotta run. I promised Mary I'd pick up some stuff from Morgan's before I head home."

Sam walked down the block to where he had left his truck parked near the front of Morgan's. The bell jingled as he opened the door and stepped into the warmth of the general store. A pair of ladies sorted through bolts of fabric; two little kids stared in wonder at the display of candy in a case, their noses pressed against the glass; an old codger picked up a can of chewing tobacco and headed to the cashier. A couple of strangers browsed through racks of clothing. Business as usual in a small-town shop.

Chris Hartman stood near the far counter as he weighed a sack of red beans, added another couple of scoops, then rechecked the weight on the hanging scale. He looked up as Sam waylaid him with an extended hand.

"Hey, good to see you, Chris," Sam said as he shook his friend's hand. "Beans, huh? Does that mean your Ma's making her famous chili?"

"Yeah, she sent me to town to get the fixin's. I think she just wanted me out of the house and out from under her feet," laughed Chris.

"You and Diane all settled now at Cedar Hill?"

"You know the old man; he insists that come spring we'll build a separate house for Diane and me. Someplace we can call our own and have some privacy."

"I think that's a good idea. Your dad's a smart man."

"Hey, I heard about your close call at Christmas. You okay?" asked Chris.

"Thanks for asking. Yeah, I'm fine. Lucky for me that Mary decided to ignore my command to stay indoors and came looking for me. One of my hands, Miguel, carried me back to the house to thaw out."

"Ever find out who thumped you?"

"Not yet, but I'm working on it. How are things over at Cedar Hill? Any trouble with cattle going astray? I haven't seen any signs, but you'd know best."

"We're good. Pop has four of our cowboys watching the herd, splitting twelve-hour shifts. That new guy, Hank Butler, is a good hand. He does what he's asked and doesn't complain about the long hours or conditions. We're glad to have him," said Chris as he removed the burlap sack from the scale, tied it off, and closed the lid on the wooden barrel of dried beans.

"Yeah, I liked him too; glad you found a spot for him. Tell your dad to let me know if he sees or hears of any trouble; I'll be up in north country for a few days, leave tomorrow."

"Okay, take care," said Chris.

Both men walked over toward the cash register, where Abe Morgan was ringing up a penny bag of licorice pieces for a very wide-eyed little boy. He glanced up as Sam and Chris walked up; for a split-second, a startled look flickered across his face before he quickly hid his expression and assumed a blank mien.

Sam witnessed his odd behavior and wondered what caused it. Was it seeing him alive and walking around? What had Morgan heard and from whom? He decided to needle the man.

"Hey Abe, what's the matter? You look like you've seen a ghost."

"What? No um, ah, I don't know what you mean," the merchant stuttered, flustered and hurried to turn his attention to Chris Hartman's purchase.

Sam studied the nervous man and saw him glance toward the rear of the store and the two strangers. Sam turned his attention to the men, noting their height and weight; he tried to visualize them on horseback and wondered if they were the same men he had seen from a distance. No, probably not. Could have been anyone. He shook his head to clear his thoughts as he faced the merchant again.

"Mary told me to pick up some catalog order; said you called her that it was ready," Sam said.

"Oh, yeah, sure thing. Got it right in the back. Gimme a minute," said Abe Morgan as he dried his sweaty palms on a towel and hurried into the stock room. He returned with a parcel wrapped in brown paper and string. "That'll be ten-fifty. Should I put it on the account?"

"No, Dunlap's pay our bills. Don't need any handouts," Sam said as he counted out fifty cents in change and the ten dollars. He glared at the man then tucked the parcel under his arm as he left the store.

Sam took a deep breath to calm his annoyance as he stood outside, then glanced toward his friend struggling to open his truck door while holding the heavy sack of beans with one hand. Sam casually walked over to Chris, grabbed the door handle nonchalantly, and tugged it open as he turned to speak to his friend, not offering pity, but empathizing with his wounded friend.

"Hey, meant to ask you if you had read the latest war news. I grabbed a newspaper back at Morgan's, looks like the Allies just captured two important targets in Germany – the Remagen bridge over the Rhine, and the city of Cologne. What do you think? Germany going to surrender soon?" asked Sam.

"Remagen bridge... bet the 101st was part of that deal. Yeah, I'd have made that jump," Chris said with a far-away look in his eyes. Sam knew that look. Chris was back with his buddies and fighting the war.

"Glad we served in Europe. Those boys in the Pacific are really going through hell. I read where over twenty thousand troops were killed on some damn island called Iwo Jima – that's a heavy loss for a scrap of land in the middle of the ocean. Sometimes I wonder if the war will ever end or if all this will ever make any sense," Sam said quietly.

"It's gotta matter. Why did your brother die, or why did I lose an arm, if it doesn't matter? I fought for a better world for my kids and theirs to come, a future with promise. I've gotta believe that."

Sam placed his hand on Chris's shoulder and squeezed lightly, conveying their brotherhood of arms, expressing their unspoken friendship.

"You're right. Let's pray this thing ends soon, and the rest of our boys can get home."

Chapter 29

For five days, Sam rode the northern country, crossed streams still frozen with a layer of thin ice as winter kept its frosty grip on the land. The tug of war between winter and spring had begun as trees defiantly showed buds of new leaves and tufts of grass poked their heads through the melting snow cover. Sam was always thrilled to witness the miracle of nature's seasonal change.

He searched for cattle straying from their herds, examined brands of ownership, and inspected the land. No matter where he would ever travel, this glorious land – this Wyoming, with its prairies and mountains, would always be home to him. Sam rode across the prairie toward the low hills, intending to spend one more night under the stars before heading home.

His thoughts turned toward his wife Mary; he missed her so much when he was gone like this. Hard to believe a year had passed since they'd taken their vows. In some ways, it felt like a lifetime ago and a different world. He needed to do something special for her when he got back to mark the occasion, even though he knew he'd missed their actual anniversary date. She'd forgive him; she was like that.

Spring meant calving on the ranch; births of new animals plus the chore of branding. Life sprung anew everywhere you looked; even the nanny goat showed signs of expecting kids, and Blackie had covered one of the mares who would soon foal.

Last week Rachel had shyly informed Sam and Mary that she was in the family way; Frank strutted around as proud as a peacock with the news. Sam's thoughts returned to when Mary had wistfully looked toward him; a silent communication passed between them that she still showed no signs of being pregnant. He knew she worried about her lack of motherhood status. They would just have to bide their time for nature to take its course.

Sam stoked his campfire and poured himself some coffee from the scarred tin pot nestled among the fire coals. He finished eating the trout that he had caught earlier, broke off a piece of his last corn muffin that Mary had packed for him, and dunked it into the hot coffee. The stars above him broke through the overcast sky, shining their meager light in the murky black night. Sam lay stretched out within his heavy quilted sleeping bag and listened to the sounds of the forest around him — an owl hooted, a rabbit scurried for safety, tree branches rustled in the strong breeze to disturb the night's stillness. As Sam began to close his eyes and surrender to sleep, he heard another rustling noise nearby; his senses became instantly awake and alert.

He waited, motionless, pretending to be asleep while he strained to hear more as snatches of muffled voices and footsteps reached him. He carefully reached for the rifle laying on the ground next to him; his finger touched the trigger, ready to fight the danger he perceived. To his left, a twig snapped, and footsteps halted; Sam rolled from his bed, crouched in readiness, and aimed the rifle.

"Who's there?" he shouted into the dark forest.

Shadows moved, the noise of running feet echoed in the night. Sam pointed the gun upward and fired a warning shot then listened to sounds of horses' hoofbeats as the miscreants fled.

He lay and waited, vigilant until he finally allowed himself to relax and succumb to a few hours of slumber. He'd break camp early and head home, aware that this time he had won, but what of the next attempt?

On April twelfth, Sam, Mary, and Alexander all sat stunned listening to the radio as the nation mourned the death of President Franklin D. Roosevelt from a cerebral hemorrhage. His Vice-President, Harry Truman, was sworn in as president of the United States.

"He was a good man," said Alexander. "He got this country through the Depression."

"He was my Commander in Chief," remarked Sam. "It's going to feel odd not having him in the White House; he served so many years."

Mary nodded solemnly, tears in her eyes as she thought of the American president and how she would feel if Churchill had suddenly died.

It didn't seem fair that the president that had fought so long and determinedly never got to see the end of the war when less than a month later on May seventh, Germany finally surrendered unconditionally. All across the country, people celebrated victory in Europe, or VE Day, as the date of May eighth would be remembered.

Deer Springs was no exception as horns tooted, and more than one firearm was shot into the air as people cheered and whooped.

Sam and Mary finished their delicious dinner at the *Eatery*, an unusual treat for them – a night out on the town. Sam had promised Mary an evening at the picture show and dinner as a much belated anniversary celebration. They sat holding hands, enjoying the delicious dessert that Maybelle had just served and listened to the commotion outside.

"Do you think people will ever stop celebrating the end of the war?" Sam asked with a chuckle and shake of his head. "Kingman must be going out of his mind with all the shooting going on in town."

"It's crazy, isn't it? By the way, I want to thank you again for my lovely surprise. The porch swing is just perfect. I can't imagine how many hours it must have taken you and Frank to build such a beautiful piece. How did you ever find the time?" Mary asked as she kissed Sam on the cheek.

"I'm just sorry I wasn't with you on our real anniversary, and you've had to wait almost two months to celebrate. But you know I love you, don't you?"

"Of course, I do. I love you too. Now that the weather has started to turn warm again, we'll be able to use that swing even more. I can just picture us with a nice cup of tea, enjoying the early evening air," Mary said.

"Can I get you two love birds anything else?" asked Maybelle as she refreshed their cups of tea and coffee.

"Thanks, this is fine," Sam said.

As Mary chatted gaily explaining her plans for the garden this year, Sam half listened as he glanced about the diner; his eyes fell on a pair of men seated in a corner booth. Sam studied other various patrons, each time, his eyes returned to rest on the pair of unknown men. Their eyes locked with Sam's as each dared the other to look away. Sam narrowed his stare as he tried to recall where he had seen the men before.

"So, do you think that will work?" Mary asked, gaining Sam's attention.

"What? Um, yeah, I suppose so."

"Samuel Dunlap, I don't think you heard a word I said," Mary pouted.

"Sure I did; you were discussing the garden." Sam rose and tossed a couple of dollars on the table as a tip as he helped Mary slide out of the booth. "Better get going if you want to see that movie."

"I'm really looking forward to seeing *Laura*; I like Dana Andrews, and I've read this is supposed to be an exciting mystery," Mary said as they drove through town to the theater located past the bank.

"Yeah, that's what I read in the write-up too. Deer Springs doesn't exactly get the first run movies when they're released, but this one is only a few months old."

Sam parked and as he helped Mary out of their truck cab, he noticed the two men from the diner slowly drive by. Were they following him? Who were those guys?

Summer months flew by in days filled with frantic activity. The garden produced a wide variety of vegetables that required constant weeding and picking. Bushel baskets of tomatoes waited in the kitchen for canning and the makings of catsup. Alexander had volunteered to pick some of the ripe peppers and beans that grew along the outer rows of the garden where he could roll his chair. Mary harvested the inner garden rows where the space between plants was narrower.

The ranch saw the birth of three new kids and a gangling young colt sired by Blackie. Mary counted a dozen young chicks that kept her busy between feeding them and collecting eggs every day from the laying hens. She encouraged Rachel to take three or four of the young chickens to build their own coop as Frank and Miguel finished the construction of a barn on the Costello land.

Rachel's belly grew in pace with the summer crops; Mary wondered which would come first – the fall harvest or the birth of the new baby. Rachel limited her visits to the ranch now that her time was growing near, so Mary mounted the mare Daisy and tried to ride the short distance to Rachel's house at least once a week. Today she planned a visit there to join Rachel for a day of canning.

"Pop, can you check on the baby goats for me? They're roaming the corral area harassing that bull; I worry he'll charge the fence or gate if they get him stirred up. Those kids' antics are cute to watch but can be trouble at times. I promised Rachel I'd help her with the canning. She can't lift those heavy steam baths."

"Will you be back for supper, or should I fix something for myself?" asked Alexander.

"Um, I should be back. Sam said he might be home by nightfall, so I want to get home as soon as I can."

"Okay. You riding Daisy?"

"Yes, thought I would," said Mary.

"See you later then."

Mary pressed a kiss to his bearded cheek before she walked down to the barn. She picked up bridle and reins and moved to Daisy's stall.

"Hey girl, want to go for a ride?" Mary spoke quietly to the horse as she rubbed the mare's nose and fed her pieces of apple. She saddled Daisy and mounted quickly, then led the mare out of the barn and down the dirt road leading to the ranch entrance and the Costello home on Aspen.

The horse snorted and flicked her tail, savoring the hint of crispness in the fall air as they trotted down the lane. Mary admired the changing colors on the trees and thought of all she had to do yet before another cold winter season took hold. *"This land that Sam was so proud of is beautiful, but summers were far too short, and Wyoming winters could be brutal,"* thought Mary as she rode along.

She stopped to watch a hawk soar high overhead; his wings spread wide, reminded her of the Yank's flying fortresses that had rumbled across the English skies. Another time, another world ago. All those courageous men, so many lost in the war, as she thought of Timmy and Alex. The lucky ones were home now.

Steam escaped through the open kitchen windows as Rachel and Mary labored over boiling pots of canning jars. A dozen jars each of green beans, tomatoes, carrots, and beets cooled on the table as Rachel listened for their lids to pop and seal, indicating the jars were ready for rings to be tightened. Mary rinsed a colander of berries while Rachel methodically peeled and pitted a basket of peaches. The fruit was added to saucepans to cook down into pie fillings or jam. The two women worked side by side for several hours until the shelves of the pantry bowed under the weight of the many canned jars.

"You need to take a break. Sit down and rest," Mary told Rachel.

"I am a bit tired. I've had an ache in the small of my back all day," Rachel confided. She eased herself into a chair and wiped perspiration off her brow with a napkin.

Mary watched in amazement as Rachel's pregnant belly rippled like waves on the shore. Her eyes grew wide as she observed the phenomenon again.

"Does that hurt?" Mary asked.

"Want to feel? Place thy hand here," directed Rachel as she held her friend's hand on her taut belly. The baby kicked and moved as if it resented the intrusion, and Mary lifted her hand in wonder.

"Oh my! I could feel him. That's marvelous."

Rachel fondly patted her friend's arm, "God's miracle. Thou will know the same soon. I am certain."

"I pray every night for a baby. Sometimes I think maybe I am expecting, but I'm not sure. Maybe I just want it so bad that I'm kidding myself."

"I will pray for thou too. In God's good time, you will be blessed."

"Thank you, Rachel. Are you okay if I leave now? I want to get home before it gets too dark; the sun is already starting to set," Mary said.

"Of course. I can clean up here; our work is done."

"Now you telephone me if that baby starts to make itself known, and your labor begins," Mary said as she hugged her friend and left the house.

Daisy trotted into the yard as Mary headed toward the barn. She hopped down and held the mare's reins as she walked her into the stable then stopped short.

"Who the bloody hell are you? What are you doing? I know that smell; that's petrol."

Mary cried out as she swatted at the man's arm with the dangling leather reins. Daisy whinnied and stomped her feet, pulling the reins from Mary's hand as it dashed into the open yard.

Mary took a step backward, intent on escaping, but he moved too fast for her. His hand tangled in her long hair and jerked her back into the barn as she twisted and fought his grip.

She kicked his shins, eliciting a howl of pain from him, then tried to aim higher with another blow as she raised her foot again only to be knocked off balance by the furious man. She rolled away and tried to gain her feet, but once again, he halted her attempt.

A second man laughed as he entered the open stall and observed the fight. "She's a real hellcat, ain't she? Can't you handle the bitch?"

Mary struck the new ruffian's face with her riding quirt, leaving an oozing welt across his left cheek from brow to chin.

The vandal cursed and grabbed for the whip before she could lash out again. "You bitch! You'll pay for that. Toss her ass into the back of the truck."

Mary screamed at the top of her lungs, "Help, help!"

She watched in horror as the other man lit a match and suddenly knew his intent. She pushed and kicked, broke loose for just a second, then tackled the man, knocking him into the horse water trough and distinguished the flame. He spluttered and came up drenched, quickly looked around, and made his decision.

"C'mon. Let's get the hell out of here. There are other ways to get to Dunlap," he said as he cuffed Mary on the side of her head.

He tossed the unconscious woman into the bed of the truck and jumped into the driver's seat. The truck bounced and rattled as the tires dug into the soft earth of the open pasture as they made their getaway unseen.

Chapter 30

Sam waited in William Logan's office at the Diamond Bar as the rancher slowly sorted through a pile of papers on his cluttered desk. A portly man with puffy jowls that wore gray mutton chop sideburns that stretched from a pate of scraggly gray hair, Logan didn't move very quickly. His ill-fitting clothing and hair gave him the appearance of a character right out of a Dicken's novel.

Sam watched as Logan seemed to take a perverse pleasure in making him wait, but he wasn't fooled and stood patiently, determined to obtain the necessary paperwork.

"I know I have that certificate here, Inspector. I'm sure I can satisfy your questions," Logan said as he shuffled papers around.

"You understand, I need to verify your ownership before you sell the cattle that I saw in the Deer Springs' stockyards. I can't issue a title certificate without proof of inspections and ownership. It's the law."

"Of course, of course. I've got it right here."

"There seems to have been some trouble with different cows going astray and their brands missing over the last year. I plan on putting a stop to that problem. You wouldn't know anything about that, would you?" Sam asked.

"Why are you asking me? I run a legitimate ranching business here."

"I'm sure you do, but if I ever see otherwise, I'll be back, and the sheriff will be with me."

Logan tired playing the cat and mouse game and pulled a stapled set of papers from a tray on his desk and handed the forms to Sam.

Sam read through the cattle description, dates of past inspections, and ownership title. Everything appeared to be in order. As he was handing the papers back to the arrogant rancher, a side door opened, and a young man slipped into the room. He stopped short when he spied Sam and realized Logan wasn't alone.

Sam's attention was drawn to the appearance of the man; an average build with dark brown hair cut in the military-style, he knew he'd seen him before and recently, but then he definitely hadn't sported that bloody welt.

"What do you want? Can't you see I'm busy?" William Logan asked testily before he also spied the cut. Realizing he was making a scene and increasing Dunlap's curiosity, he tried to diffuse the situation. "Ahh, you remember my son Avery? He just got back from the war."

"Avery... when did you get home? See much action?" Sam asked, studying him again as his memory clicked in.

"Some. Mostly I was stationed in England, like you," Avery snorted as if he knew a private joke and didn't plan to share.

"There were a lot of us in England," Sam said quietly as he thought of his brother then banished the sad memory as he glanced at the father and son before him. "Well, I've got to be going. That title of certificate will be posted at the stockyard, Mister Logan."

"Fine. You do that."

Sam pivoted, walked across the room, and moved to close the office door behind him, but not before he overheard the father slap his son and growl, "You fool. Why did you bring her here?"

Alexander rolled his wheelchair out the door onto the open porch, drawn by the racket being made by the mare Daisy. The horse stood in the open yard, snorting and stomping angrily, shaking its head and rearing up on its hind legs. The reins hung to the ground; Mary's saddle was still on its back.

He rolled down the ramp, approached the distraught animal, waving his arms in front of its head, and tried to calm her.

"Easy girl. Easy now. Where's Mary?"

Alexander spied the flecks of blood on the leather reins and feared it was Mary's. He searched the immediate area for signs of her and saw none.

He worked to navigate his wheelchair across the rough ground and to the barn. He coughed as he immediately smelled the gasoline fumes and saw the saturated bales of hay. The horses stomped skittishly, and the dairy cows bellowed in their stalls. The animals sensed danger.

Where was everyone? Then he recalled Miguel saying he would be rounding up strays in the east meadow, and Sam had gone to town. Frank... maybe he was near.

Alexander struggled to turn his wheelchair and travel back to the house; he held onto the side railing to pull himself up the sloped ramp and into the house. If only he weren't stuck in this damn chair, he could be doing more to help. Frustrated, Alexander flung his arm across the side table, sending newspaper, a half-eaten sandwich, and coffee mug to the floor in a crash.

Mary was in trouble; he knew it in his heart and couldn't do anything but wait. He'd be damned if he'd sit on the sidelines again when his family was in danger. He rolled into his bedroom and pulled open the bottom dresser drawer and removed his Colt '45, loaded the chambers then tucked the pistol into his waistband. He was ready.

Night had settled onto the land as Sam pulled into his driveway. He shut down the engine, breathed a sigh of relief at finally being home and climbed out of the cab. He raked his fingers through his hair and stretched tired muscles as he glanced over toward the house and registered for the first time that no lights shone through the windows. Why was the house dark?

He rushed into the house, calling out as he did, "Mary! Pop! Anybody home?"

He spied the debris on the floor as he searched from room to room, swallowing the fear and panic that rose like bile in his throat. A squeak made him turn suddenly to find his father moving in the dark hallway.

"What's happened?" demanded Sam.

Alexander agonized over that same question as he crept forward in his wheelchair. "I don't know. Mary's gone. Her horse was loose in the yard; I went to the barn and found gasoline splashed all over. I saw some blood. I don't know what that means."

Sam turned on a lamp and surveyed the room, seeing the debris he first stepped on was only his father's luncheon tray. He paced back and forth as he tried to digest his father's words.

"What time was this? When did you find Daisy?"

"I dunno exactly; it was just getting dark, maybe five-thirty or six?" Alexander said as he stared out the open door.

"That was three hours ago. Show me what you found," Sam said as he grasped the handles of his father's chair and pushed him down the ramp and toward the barn.

They entered the pitch back structure, and Sam stopped inside the wide doors as he also recognized the telltale gasoline smell. He reached for the lantern then thought better of it as he carried it outside before striking a match to its wick. He held the protected flame in its glass globe before walking back into the barn to investigate further. Daisy stood near her stall, her reins still hung loose, but she remained calm. Sam opened the gate and she placidly entered. He rubbed the mare's nose as he lifted the reins and studied the dried drops of blood dotting the leather. He shot a questioning look to his father.

"That's what I found. Didn't see any more. Might not be Mary's blood. If she were hurt, wouldn't we see more?"

"Probably. But whose is it then? Did Mary catch someone trying to torch the barn? Is that what happened?" Sam searched the remainder of the stable and barn and found nothing else out of order, just the soaked bales of hay. A quick search outside around the perimeter of the barn, he spotted deep gouges in the open meadow; tire tracks headed north.

"I couldn't find anyone. You and Miguel were both gone; I tried calling Frank, but there was no answer. Thought Rachel would be there; she and Mary were supposed to be canning all day. So, I waited."

"Sorry, Pop. I know you did all you could," Sam said. "Appears they went cross-country and avoided the roads."

He dragged the ruined bales of hay out of the barn, away from danger, when he spied something in the straw. He lifted the lantern to illuminate the object and recognized Mary's riding quirt. He had gifted her the thin braided rawhide when she began to ride on a regular basis. They had joked about it being more proper for the English lady of the manor to use a quirt. Now he picked up the leather whip and examined it, finding blood on the length of the braid.

"Looks like Mary put up a fight. I saw someone earlier who had a cut across his face like the kind made by a tiny whip." Sam's expression turned deadly as he realized who had taken his wife.

"What are you going to do? I'm going with you wherever it is. I'm not going to sit on the sidelines while that girl and my grandchild are in danger," Alexander stated emphatically.

"Grandchild? What do you mean?" Sam asked.

"She's pregnant; she may not even know it herself yet, but I've been a rancher all my life, and I know the signs."

"Okay then; we need to get some help. I'm not sure, but I think Mary is on the Diamond Bar."

Sam quickly pushed his father back toward the house; he ran inside and grabbed the phone off the wall as he rapidly dialed Gus Kingman's number. He barely gave the lawman time to answer before he started shouting into the line.

"Logan's kidnapped my wife." He paused to listen to the sheriff, "Yeah, that's what I said. Looks like he tried to torch my barn, and Mary found him or stopped him."

"Are you sure he's got her at his ranch?"

"No, I'm not positive, but I saw Avery Logan, and he's sporting a red welt across his face, and my wife's quirt is covered in blood. That can't be a coincidence. I'm driving out there. You coming or not? That's all I need to know," Sam growled.

"I'll meet you out there. Don't do anything dumb; wait for me," ordered the sheriff.

Sam smashed the receiver down and ran upstairs, taking the steps two at a time. He tore open his gun cabinet and pulled out a rifle with a box of shells then strapped on his holster with a pair of handguns. He flew downstairs and out the front, slamming the door behind him as he tossed the rifle onto the truck bench seat then turned to his father.

"I'm coming. You get me into that damn truck cab."

"All right." Sam lifted his father and placed him in the passenger side then hopped in behind the wheel. Gravel spewed under the spinning truck tires as he rammed the Chevy into gear and floored the accelerator. "Hang on. I'll kill that bastard if he's harmed a hair on her head," snarled Sam.

"It's past time the Dunlap family had a reckoning with those Logan's. This is my fault. I should have confronted Bill Logan years ago," seethed Alexander.

The pair barreled down the county road, their thoughts as black as the angry night. Sam steered around the bend in the street then stood on his brakes; narrowly missed broadsiding a vehicle stopped across the roadway.

"What the hell...?" He jumped out of his truck, the engine still idling, and ran to the vehicle emblazoned with the Cedar Hill emblem on its door. "Are you crazy? I almost hit you."

Dan Hartman sat behind the wheel; Chris beside him in the passenger seat holding a pair of shotguns and his service automatic.

"Kingman called me. Figured you could use some backup," said Dan Hartman. "I've never trusted William Logan as far as I could throw him. He's dishonest but smart, always kept just this side of the law, but this time he's crossed the line."

"Thanks. Appreciate your help, but this is my wife and my fight. I don't want anyone getting hurt," Sam stated.

"I don't plan on getting shot; just show those guys that you aren't alone," Chris asserted.

"All right then. Let's get going," Sam yelled as he ran back to his truck and waited for Hartman to spin about. In an instant, the pair of vehicles sped toward the Diamond Bar and whatever awaited them.

Chapter 31

Mary lay on an earthen floor, dampness seeped into her clothes; she could detect the sweet scent of apples mixed with the smell of potatoes or other vegetables. *"A root cellar?"* she pondered.

She struggled to sit up; her head spun, and her jaw ached. Mary cautiously reached out in the pitch-black room to touch dirt walls, blindly feeling her way along the wall, fingers finding burlap bags and baskets. One whiff confirmed her apple conjecture. Mary crawled on hands and knees; stumbled over a cluster of pungent onions and the reek of a rotten turnip.

She stopped her exploration and sat back on her haunches, trying to collect her wits. *"Okay, definitely a root cellar. There must be some kind of door. If I keep moving left to right around the space, I should find it. Nothing to be afraid of; I've been in worse places during the Blitz. I can get through this,"* Mary assured herself.

She wondered if Alexander knew she was missing; was Sam home? Was anyone looking for her? How would they know where to look when she had no idea herself?

Her fingers traced a crack, an edge in the wall, then felt hinges and a handle, and she almost cried in relief. She tugged on the handle and the portal inched open a crack allowing a sliver of dim light and fresh air to filter into the dank space. She stopped and listened for sounds of her captors, deciding whether to push the door wider. Did she dare?

Sam and the Hartman truck crept toward the entry drive of the Diamond Bar ranch. Sheriff Kingman's cruiser was parked near a stand of trees. Dan Hartman pulled in next to him, headlights doused. The men discussed their plan of action; Sam insisted he would drive up to the ranch house and announce himself while the others took positions undercover. The sheriff nixed that idea and demanded that he would accompany Sam to the Logan home; they agreed only after a few minutes of a heated argument.

"Hey, I'm airborne, not infantry, but I'll do my best," joked Chris Hartman. "Go on, we've got your back."

With assurances that no one would risk injury, Sam boldly drove his truck right up to the front of the sprawling adobe ranch house.

"I've got to do this, Pop. You understand, right?" Sam said as he squeezed his father's hand and approached the shut portal.

Gus Kingman joined him as the two pounded loudly on the door while Alexander Dunlap watched from the front seat of the pickup. They waited - hesitant, expecting resistance, unsure of their reception.

Kathleen Logan opened the door slightly and peered at the two, armed men. Her shocked expression was enough to give both men pause and make them realize how wild their actions and accusations seemed. Sam had a moment of doubt, then remembered Avery's cut face and knew he had to confront him.

The sheriff spoke first, "Evening Missus Logan. We need to speak to your husband and son. We'll wait here." He stepped down from the top of the wide stoop.

Clearly confused, the woman stepped back from the open doorway. "William!" she called out. "There are some men here to see you."

William Logan left his office and plodded toward the foyer, perplexed by his wife's frightened expression and nervous behavior. He brushed past her, then spied the reason for her concern.

"Well, if it isn't the little inspector, and he's brought the sheriff. A bit late for a social call, don't you think?" sneered Logan.

"Where's my wife?" blurted Sam.

"Don't know what you're talking about."

"You want to step outside with us, Mr. Logan? Your wife doesn't need to hear this. I want to speak with your son, Avery. Where is he?" demanded Kingman.

Logan turned to Kathleen, "Go find Avery. Move woman!" he bellowed as his wife skittered away and dashed upstairs.

The three men stared at each other as they stood in the narrow shaft of light spilling from the open doorway. An ominous silence built.

Sam's hand hovered just above the grip of his Colt as he waited; Kingman's eyes continuously scanned the house and doorways, alert for trouble. Logan puffed on his cigar, annoyed with his son for putting him in this position. The sound of a closing door from above drew their attention as Avery sauntered down the staircase and joined them outside.

"Wanted to see me?" Avery sneered.

"Interesting wound you've got there.   How'd you get it?" questioned Sam as he pointed to his cheek.

"Must have cut myself shaving," mocked Avery.

"Where were you about six o'clock today?" asked Kingman.

"Home, I think." Avery's eyes darted to his father then back to the sheriff. "Isn't that right, father?"

Bill Logan hesitated as he answered, "Yeah, that's right. He was home."

"Are you certain?" asked the Sheriff.

"What did you do with my wife?" demanded Sam, losing his patience with this polite questioning. "What's the matter, let a woman get the better of you? That cut's gonna leave a scar; you won't be such a pretty boy now," taunted Sam.

Anger flared as Avery shouted, "You shut your mouth. If you want to see her again, you'll do what I say. Hear me? I'm the one calling the shots now!"

Sam knew he had goaded the young man into spilling his hand. He had to get him talking more.

"You're in charge? Sure about that? You're not very successful, Avery. You act more like a dumb kid. Let a woman foil your arson plan. By the way, was it you who hit me over the head at Christmas?" Sam asked.

"Yeah, that was me. You're hard to kill. I even dropped a damn car on you in England, and you managed to crawl out - like you got nine lives or something," Avery sneered. "Your brother was easier; I missed with the train platform, but the Germans helped. I got lucky when his plane crashed."

"Shut up, Avery," his father warned.

"But I did it for you; to make you proud of me if I took out the Dunlap boys. I did it for you, Pop," Avery insisted.

The sight of his smirking face made Sam sick to his stomach, but he knew he had to provoke him to learn more. Sheriff Kingman nodded slightly to Sam, keep him talking.

"I have to say, Avery, I don't know how you managed to control Jim Brody to do your dirty work for you while you were all the way around the world. I have to give you credit for that," Sam said as he watched the gloating self-satisfaction wash over the man's demeanor.

"That wasn't me; that was Pop," bragged Avery.

"You close your mouth. You don't know what you're talking about," glowered his father. He moved toward his son as if he would throttle him, and Kingman stepped between them and the open threshold. They shifted their positions, as father and son glared at each other, like boxers in a ring.

Shifting light from the house created dancing silhouettes of the men as they shuffled about, voices raged, threatened. Alexander watched the group and caught snatches of their conversation.

"Why did Brody withdrawal such small amounts of money from the Circle-D accounts?" asked Sam. "What was that supposed to accomplish?"

"We know he was working for you, Logan. I've got plenty of evidence. It'll be easier on you if you come clean now," suggested the sheriff. "I can cut a deal for you if you come forward."

William Logan suddenly felt defeated. He thought he had covered his tracks, but Kingman must be smarter than he gave him credit. Frantically, he turned to look at his comfortable home and thought of all he had accumulated and stood to lose; his wife stood on the stair, a witness to his confession.

"Brody withdrew small amounts from the bank as a test. He was supposed to see if that frightened rabbit of a bank manager would catch it, then he was going to empty the account. I wanted to destroy the Dunlap ranch," William explained.

"What happened? I only found three drafts," Sam said.

"Stupid fool got a case of conscience. Brody refused to do it after Katie Dunlap died, then he had the audacity to hide the money that he did take. I had to make an example of him."

"That's all I wanted to hear. William Logan, I'm arresting you for the murder of James Brody. Turn around and put your hands behind your back," stated Sheriff Kingman, preparing to reach for his handcuffs.

Bedlam erupted as a loud scream and shouts averted their attention. Kingman paused as he looked to Sam, then peered into the inky shadows. A scuffle and commotion could be heard from around the corner of the house.

"Let go of me!" shrieked Mary as she tried to pull her arm out of her captor's grip. "Let go, I say."

"Shut up lady, or I'll toss you down that cellar again. We'll just see what Avery says," growled the ruffian as he yanked on her arm and half dragged her from the rear gardens and toward the front of the house. He was so intent on managing his prisoner that he didn't see the two men until they sprang up in front of him like ghosts in the night.

"Going someplace?" asked Chris Hartman menacingly as he pointed his revolver at the man.

"Release that woman, now!" Dan Hartman commanded, his rifle cocked and ready.

The man gulped and made the choice of self-preservation over honor among thieves; he immediately let go of Mary, shoving her forward. Dan Hartman caught her before she fell.

"I know someone who's going to be very happy to see you, young woman," Dan beamed.

Sam had moved forward to grab Avery by the front of his shirt and demand he release Mary when he heard her voice. He turned in surprise to see her being led to safety by Dan while Chris prodded a dirty scoundrel in the back with his automatic.

His relief that she was alive and unharmed made him careless as he let go of Avery and ignored the man.

All of a sudden, confusion and all hell broke out as house lights were turned off, plunging all into pitch blackness. Kathleen Logan screamed from inside the house to create a distraction. Logan knocked the sheriff off his feet in an attempt to run, and Sam got pushed to the side.

Avery pulled a handgun from under his shirt and shot at the sheriff, wounding him in the arm. William Logan tried to grab the gun away from his son, but Avery managed to break free and took a second aim at Sam.

Alexander Dunlap shouted, "Look out!"

Alexander opened the truck door and tumbled to the ground. His body rolled once before he could stop himself as he pulled his Colt from his waistband.

"Logan!" shouted Alexander, drawing his fire.

Avery, startled by the appearance of the elder Dunlap, spun as he shot, missing Sam but finding its mark in the crippled man.

Alexander simultaneously fired his own revolver as he reacted to the muzzle flash from Avery's gun. He had the satisfaction of seeing a splotch of red spread across the young man's chest like a sunburst as Avery fell forward.

"Pop!" yelled Sam as he raced to his father's side and cradled his head in his lap.

"You're safe, and Mary ... that's all that matters," coughed Alexander as red-tinged spittle dripped from the corner of his mouth. "... love you, son."

"I love you, Pop."

Alexander never felt the pain of the deadly bullet that ended his life.

Tears streamed down Sam's face as he stared in agony at his lost father. Dan and Chris Hartman had run forward to lend assistance, handcuffed William Logan, and wrapped the sheriff's arm in a quick makeshift bandage. Mary clung to Sam's arm, relieved the nightmare was over. Sam got to his feet to confront William Logan before he was placed in the back of the police cruiser.

"Why? With all that you own, I don't understand why you're interested in our scrap of land. Why couldn't you just let us live in peace?" Sam agonized. "How much more money does it take to satisfy your greed? I would gladly deed our ranch over to you if it brought back the life of my father. Appears the only ranch you destroyed might be your own. Someday, you'll regret this feud between our families," Sam lamented.

Sam stared at the broken man as Logan hung his head low, refusing to talk.

"Was it worth the loss of your own son's life? Do you hold life so cheaply?" Sam raged. "I pray to God that someday Avery's son will grow into a better man. I'm truly sorry he'll be raised without his father."

Sam turned his back on the man and returned to gather Mary into his arms as they stood in a dim halo of moonlight, grateful for each other and life.

"I'm so sorry," Mary wept, "Pop will never get to see his grandchild."

"I think it was enough that he knew the Dunlap name would be carried on. He told me earlier tonight that you were expecting. So, it's true?" Sam asked as he kissed her bruised face and held her tight.

"Yes, I was afraid to say something and give us false hope, but yes, I am. By summer, you'll be a father."

"Let's go home. I need to take Pop home," said Sam.

Epilogue

It was a somber household the next day. Miguel offered to dig the grave in the family plot as funeral arrangements were made for Alexander John Dunlap, Senior. Sam and Mary went about their daily chores by rote. Their eyes frequently drifted to the sight of the empty wheelchair. Sam decided to fold the chair and store it away in a spare closet; the sight too painful.

Miguel ran to the house, banging on the kitchen door as he called out excitedly, "Señor, señora come quickly. I find mucho dineros. Come, come!"

Sam and Mary followed him to the cemetery and watched as he pointed to the fresh earth and a buried metal box. Sam dropped to his knees and dug the dirt away from the rusted metal container until it was free. He peeked at the contents, then lifted the box from its hidden grave and handed it to Mary.

"Brody must have hidden the money he stole in someplace that no one would have thought to look; I think he knew the family would find it," Sam mused. "This will come in handy with a new baby coming and taxes due. In a way, Pop provided for his family again."

The telephone rang, its shrill ring calling them back to the house. Mary hurried to pick up the receiver and listened; a wide smile spread across her face with the news. She hung up and called to Sam as he entered the kitchen.

"That was Frank. Rachel had the baby last night! A boy, big and healthy," Mary shared the exciting news.

"Guess that's where he was when Pop had tried to call him. He must have gone to pick up the mid-wife. I'm glad for them. Tomorrow, we'll tell them about Pop."

"Okay. Can we share our good news tomorrow too?" asked Mary.

"Absolutely. What did they name the baby?"

"Frank Costello, Junior, of course," laughed Mary.

Several townspeople, including Maybelle and her husband, Earl Clemson and Abe Morgan, attended the memorial service for Alexander Dunlap. Sheriff Gus Kingman attended with a black armband covering his bandaged arm. He spoke a few words after the clergyman's service and praised Alexander for being a man of principle and a fellow lawman. The rustlers had clearly been tied to a gang led by Avery Logan and had now been disbanded.

Rachel and Frank came with the new baby. After the service, everyone was able to coo and ahh over the newborn and vied for a chance to cuddle the infant. Rachel and Frank were thrilled when Mary whispered her good news to them.

Maureen and Diane Hartman had thoughtfully prepared a luncheon that they served following the funeral. The house overflowed with friends and neighbors. Sam stood on the porch on that clear October day, breathed the pleasant crisp fall air; the sky above painted a deep blue. He greeted folks and accepted their words of sympathy as he stared into the horizon, his line of vision taking in the expanse of his land. As his father had done before him, he held the ownership of this land dear, a sacred trust.

A lone figure, a duffel back slung over his shoulder, walked up the lane from the road. He looked familiar to Sam, and as he shaded his eyes to see better, he whooped in happiness. He jumped down from the porch and hurried to welcome his best buddy. Peter Shultz had found his way to the Circle-D.

The two men clasped hands in friendship then hugged each other tightly, so thrilled to see one another again.

"That job still open?" asked Pete.

"Absolutely. God, you're a sight for sore eyes. I'm so glad you're here. We've got a lot to catch up on, but plenty of time for that. Come on up to the house."

"Looks like you've got some kind of party going on," said Pete as he mingled with the houseful of people.

"Hey Mary, look who's here!" exclaimed Sam as he dragged Pete into the kitchen.

"Welcome home, Pete," said Mary as she hugged him hello.

"We buried my father today," Sam informed his friend. "It's a long story. Grab some food, and I'll get you settled in later."

Dan and Chris Hartman joined Sam as they stepped back outside onto the porch. Both men showed their respect with black armbands around their sleeves.

"Thanks for backing us up last night. I've got to tell you that for a moment there, I couldn't tell what was going on," Sam confided.

"Got pretty crazy there. We're really sorry about your father," Dan said.

"He saved my life. I guess I never believed the Logans hated us so much. It's no secret that there's been bad blood between the Dunlap's and the Logan family ever since my grandparents started our ranch. My Pop used to say that Logan was probably responsible for killing his own father, but then again, he used to suspect some gunslinger named Cody Jarvis," Sam said.

"Ahem, I can tell you for certain, it wasn't Cody Jarvis that shot your grandfather. But that's ancient history," said Dan Hartman. "What you need to concentrate on now is the future."

"Sound advice; I plan on doing just that. Mary and I will be welcoming a new baby into our family next summer. My good Army buddy just showed up, and with his help and Frank's, I plan to make the Circle-D a profitable beef cattle operation."

"Congratulations on the baby; Diane and I have our own baby news too. Next summer will be a new beginning for everyone," Chris announced.

"Life begins anew," said Dan.

Sam raised his cup and called for everyone's attention as he proposed a salute, "To family and good friends, worth more than gold, and to a new generation with a future filled with peace and promise for all. Our moment in time has come."

APPENDIX A
DUNLAP FAMILY TREE
Circle-D Ranch

JAMES JOHN DUNLAP –
Born 1861, Died Jan.10,1887
Married – Nov. 2, 1883
MARGARET DOHERTY -
Born 1863, Died Mar. 9,1896
Son: Alexander John Dunlap - B. 1886
   Daughter: Anna M. - B. 4/12/1885; D. 4/13/1885

ALEXANDER JOHN DUNLAP
Born June 18,1886, Died Oct.6,1945
Married - 1903
KATIE ANN CANAVAN
Born Aug. 2, 1886, Died Jan.8,1944
   Daughter: Peggy Ann, B. 1906, Died 1913
   Son: Alexander J. Dunlap, Jr., B. 1916, Died Oct. 1943
   Son: Samuel J. Dunlap, B. 1920

SAMUEL JAMES DUNLAP
Born Oct. 17, 1920, still living
Married – Mar. 1944
MARY K. BARNES
Born Apr. 4,1922, Died 1989
Son: Alex J. III, B. 1946, D 1946
Son: Brian James Dunlap, B. 1947

BRIAN JAMES DUNLAP
Born Aug. 5, 1947, Died 7/21/1997
Married - 1973
SARAH CUMMINGS DUNLAP
Born Feb. 1, 1949, Died 7/21/1997
Daughter: Andrea Brianna Dunlap, B. 1977

APPENDIX B

HARTMAN FAMILY TREE

Cedar Hill Ranch

CODY JARVIS
Born 1859, Died Aug. 8,1898
Married - 1896
ROSALYN O'HARA
Born 1862, Died 1908
  Daughter: Maureen Anne Jarvis - B. 1896

MAUREEN ANNE JARVIS
Born Dec. 29,1896, Died 1971
Married - 1912
DANIEL JARROD HARTMAN
Born 1886, Died 1968
  Daughters:
  Deborah A. Hartman- B. 1915, Died 1996
  Patricia Sue Hartman – B.1913, still living
  Son: Christopher Cody Hartman - B. 1919

CHRISTOPHER CODY HARTMAN
Born May 3,1919, Died 1990
Married - 1941
DIANE M. BECKETT
Born 1926, still living
  Son: Jarrod C. Hartman – B. 1946
  Daughter: Ruth D. Hartman – B. 1949, still living

JARROD CHRISTOPHER HARTMAN
Born Aug. 5,1946, still living
Married - 1969
INGRID SCHMIDT HARTMAN
Born Nov. 9,1950, still living
  Daughter: Jessica Hartman, B. 1975
  Son: Jason Cody (J.C.) Hartman - Born 1972

APPENDIX C
LOGAN FAMILY TREE
Diamond Bar Ranch

ZACHARY LOGAN -
Born 1859, Died Oct.10,1898
  Married - 1878
SARAH MURPHY
Born 1861, Died 1890
  Son: William Henry Logan, B. 1880

WILLIAM HENRY LOGAN
Born Jan 2,1880, Died 1948
  Married - 1905
KATHLEEN MORGAN
Born 1884, Died 1935
  Son: Avery Harold Logan, B. 1915

AVERY HAROLD LOGAN
Born July 3,1915, Died Oct 6,1945
  Married - 1939
CLARA LEE
Born 1923, Died 1983
  Daughter: Annabelle Logan, B. 1940
  Son: Brent Logan, B. 1941

BRENT LOGAN
Born June 2,1941
  Married – 1965
IRIS PARKER
Born Sept. 18,1946
  Daughter: Veronica Lynn Logan - Born 1976

About the Author

Combining a love for travel with the joy of reading romance and mystery novels since childhood, Nancy M. Wade fills her writing with warm characters set in exciting locales.

She and her husband resided in central Ohio for over forty years; now retired, they claim the hills of Tennessee as home. An honors graduate of East Tennessee State University, Nancy studied film and criminology.

Nancy M. Wade's works include western romantic suspense novels: _Endless Circle: A Circle-D Saga_ and book two of _Circle-D Saga, Moment in Time_. A rich family drama, _Reflections: A Sentimental Journey_; a historical romance novel, _Frontier Heart_; plus, a contemporary short story called _Courtship of Laura._ Watch for _Gun For Hire_, the final book in the _Circle-D Saga_ trilogy, coming in 2023.

Nancy also pens an exciting cozy mystery series _A Meadowood Mystery_ with four books _Scarecrows and Corpses, Reunion with Death, Deadly Bones, and Berry Little Murder._

All of her works are available for order in both paperback or E-book formats on Amazon.com, or online in Barnes & Noble Books, Books-A-Million and IngramSparks.

Follow the author on her Facebook page: https://www.facebook.com/authorNancyMWade/ and on her web site https://nancymwade.com .

Endless Circle
Circle-D Saga, Book One

Do the ghosts from our past speak to us? Can we right the wrongs committed a hundred years ago?

Andrea (Andy) Dunlap is determined to save her family's financially struggling Wyoming cattle ranch. She'll need to summon all her strength as she copes with the loss of her parents in a suspicious plane crash. Was it an accident? Andrea is helped by her childhood friend, Sheriff Jason C. Hartman, as together they become embroiled in murder and treachery while following the clues to solve her parent's death and uncover secrets from three generations ago.

Jason and Andrea discover the path to justice may be found within the writings of Maggie Dunlap, Andy's great-great grandmother, as they read her remarkable diary and story of survival in this rugged land; the betrayal, heartache and loss she suffered of her own true love. Maggie's resilient pioneer spirit guides them as they unravel the mystery of an 1887 land swindle and murder.

The young lovers are caught in a mystery of deception and family legend as past meets present in this romantic suspense set in the rugged west. Jason must prove to Andy that his love is strong enough to bridge the gulf between family feuds and suspicions. Andrea and Jason draw their strength and determination from their pioneer stock, but little do they know that their lives were destined to be intertwined, proving that the **Endless Circle** of love remains unbroken.

A Meadowood Mystery

Meadowood is a small rural community with historic old buildings and folks who enjoy the quiet life – that is until murder comes to town. Follow Meredith Gardner, Aunt Fran, and all of Meredith's gal pals: Anna, Colleen, Barbara, Martha, and Carol as they investigate, snoop, and meddle in the affairs of their small rural hometown, Meadowood. If there is a crime a foot, you can be sure that Merry and her friends will be hard at work solving the mystery.

Merry is a busy housewife, Avon cosmetic saleswoman, mother, and cub scout den leader who manages to insert herself in her husband Doug's sheriff department investigations. Nothing stops Merry - a body found in a Halloween corn maze only presents a challenge when Merry has to prove a friend innocent while also uncovering a financial swindle in town *Scarecrows & Corpses*. A high school class reunion turns into an investigation of a murdered woman with Doug the prime suspect until Merry puts the pieces of the puzzle together in *Reunion with Death*. Murder runs in the family when Merry's mother becomes a person of interest in the death of a famous paleontologist with *Deadly Bones* during a disastrous cub scout field trip. And Christmas will never be the same in a *Berry Little Murder*. This cozy mystery series contains plot twists and turns with fun characters you'll admire, laugh with, and root for in a small town setting.